ENSNARED
KNIGHTS OF 3 BRETHREN

I0694471

Books by Jody Hedlund

Knights of Brethren Series
Enamored
Entwined
Ensnared
Enriched

The Fairest Maidens Series
Beholden
Beguiled
Besotted

The Lost Princesses Series
Always: Prequel Novella
Evermore
Foremost
Hereafter

Noble Knights Series
The Vow: Prequel Novella
An Uncertain Choice
A Daring Sacrifice
For Love & Honor
A Loyal Heart
A Worthy Rebel

Waters of Time Series
Come Back to Me
Never Leave Me

The Colorado Cowboys
A Cowboy for Keeps
The Heart of a Cowboy
To Tame a Cowboy

ENSNARED

KNIGHTS OF BRETHREN 3

JODY HEDLUND

NORTHERN LIGHTS PRESS

TUNDRA SEA
N
W
E
S
St. Olaf's
Abbey
Frozen
Wilds
The Hundreds
Finnmark
Golden
Plateau
SNOWDEN
MOUNTAIN
RANGE
SWAINE
NORVEGIA
DARK SEA
HARDANGER FOREST
Romsdal
ATLAS RIVER
BLOOD RIVER
Moors of
Many Lakes
Wahlburg
Castle
Valley of
Red Dragons
Richlande
Lowlands
Vordinberg
Bay of Fire
Ostby
Sound
Cimbrian
Strait
WHITE SEA
UTHELANDE
Cimbrian Peninsula
THE WEND

Chapter 1

Mikaela

"This woman is hereby sentenced to death by drowning." The bailiff's pronouncement rang out over the silent crowd gathered on the high rocky plateau above the fjord.

Chills slithered up my spine.

Lola was innocent. The earl was a murderer. And everyone knew it.

But poor Lola stood near the edge of Trollveggen Cliff anyway, her long hair swirling in the wind. I didn't know her well since she'd only recently started working as a laundress. From what I guessed, she was a scant few years older than my twenty-one years—too young and full of life to die. Although she lifted her chin and glared at the earl defiantly, she couldn't hide the trembling in her hands as the bailiff grabbed them and wound a cord around her wrists.

Only Frans's presence beside me and his grip upon my arm kept me from rushing at Bernhard, the Earl of Romsdal. The earl held himself rigidly, his angular shoulders straight, his thin face severe. Attired in a black fur cloak over a surcoat and leggings, he was well protected from the biting April wind gusting off the waterway below.

Lola, on the other hand, had no cloak, and the woolen cloth of her undyed tunic was threadbare and frayed. Like all the earl's other bondservants, she had no choice but to endure the long Norvegian winter and cold spring without proper garments.

The bitter breeze slapped at my cheeks and my own thin smock and tunic, stinging my exposed flesh. At least I had a cloak and hat along with sturdy leather boots to protect me—though I would have given them to my sister Kirstin if I could have done so without bringing repercussions on both of us.

Instead, I was stuck. Stuck watching Kirstin—and the rest of my family—wear rags. Stuck watching them go hungry. Stuck watching them suffer.

Just as I was stuck now, unable to do or say anything for Lola unjustly charged with stealing. No, her only crime was being a pretty woman who refused the earl's advances. And because of her insolence, the cruel lord was sending a message to the rest of his subjects not to defy him, or we would meet the same fate.

Familiar helplessness ate away at my insides, making my stomach burn.

I loathed myself for my inability to change the circumstances almost as much as I loathed the earl for his unwillingness to see us as more than property to do with as he pleased.

The bailiff finished cinching Lola's wrists, then knelt and began fastening a stone wheel to her ankles so that it would function as a weight.

I couldn't bear to look a second longer.

Frans's muscular arm tensed against mine, and his fingers tightened. No doubt he was holding himself back from attacking the earl as much as he was restraining me. He despised the earl too. Especially after the earl had stolen the extra coins Frans earned from the hand-carved furniture he made during the little free time he had.

Of course, the earl didn't think he was stealing Frans's savings. Rather, he blamed Frans and his father, the estate blacksmiths, for causing the fire last month that had resulted in damage to the forge as well as the brewing house and stables.

Thankfully, Frans had spotted the flames early and sounded the alarm so that everyone working together had doused them before they spread even further. Alas, the roofs of all three buildings and the support beams had needed replacing. Bernhard had administered a steep fine for recklessness, threatening to throw Frans and his father in the dungeons if the fee wasn't paid in full. Somehow the fine had been for the exact amount Frans had saved, almost as if the earl had known of the earnings.

Frans had emptied the crock where he'd hidden the meager stash. His burly face red with rage, he'd handed it over to the bailiff . . . and in so doing, he'd also handed over the chance of paying the bride price in order to marry me.

After a year of saving, Frans had been but weeks away from requesting a marriage certificate. Would he have to wait another year?

I'd wanted to be more upset about having to

postpone our union. But I hadn't been. Maybe I just wasn't ready. Maybe I would be more so next year. I wasn't sure. Whatever the case, I still resented that the earl had so much power.

The Earl of Romsdal was one of many among the nobility who clung to the ancient tradition of overseeing the marriages of his subjects. He arranged them without allowing any input... unless the bondservant paid a bride price. Only then could a man choose his own spouse.

"Eyes up, Mikaela," Frans whispered urgently.

I snapped my gaze forward to find the bailiff standing and brushing off his hands, as though absolving himself of his dirty deed. I didn't want to witness any more of Lola's fate. But as with every public punishment, the earl required all his hired domestics as well as his bondservants to attend. He also demanded our fullest attention. Anyone caught looking away was subject to a whipping upon return to the castle grounds.

The Sagacite, Pontus, stood beside the earl with parchment and quill pen, taking notes on the doings and likely recording any behavior that could be construed as insolent. Middle-aged with a well-rounded stomach, Pontus wore the black robe of a wiseman. He'd been the advisor to the earl as long as I could remember. But it had only been over the past year that I'd noticed him watching me with overmuch interest, the kind of interest that made my skin crawl. It was all the more reason not to draw any attention to myself.

The bailiff glanced at the earl, who gave a curt nod.

It was time.

I had to say something. Even if it jeopardized my position as nursemaid to the earl's children. Even if I could no longer provide the little I did for my family.

The bailiff shifted Lola, but the heavy weight upon her ankles made moving her cumbersome. He paused, and I prayed he would put an end to this scene and suggest locking Lola in prison instead. Though he seemed hesitant, he lifted Lola another inch.

Quiet anger pierced me. The bailiff was a coward and would have to live with the guilt of his deed for years to come. Then again, we all would have to live with guilt for not speaking up while we still could, for not trying to come to this woman's defense, for not demanding the truth.

"I can't do this," I whispered, tugging to free myself from Frans.

He didn't let go. Instead, his hold turned into a manacle. A thick-boned and brawny man, Frans was twice my girth and at least a head taller. Strands of his curly blond hair hung out from his woolen cap, only a few shades lighter than his scruffy beard.

I jerked my arm harder. I had no idea what I could accomplish, only that I couldn't stand back and do nothing.

Frans nodded at his father on my opposite side. Just as big as Frans, Valter clamped my other arm. His hold was gentler but no less confining.

A scream of rage pulsed inside, one I'd tried to suffocate, but one that kept building with each punishment I was forced to watch. Would the guilt and remorse eventually burst inside me and leave me a madwoman?

"Please, Mikaela." Frans spoke more firmly.

I could sense we were drawing attention, and sure enough, the earl was watching us. His brows came together in a scowl, and his lips pinched.

I quickly bowed my head, letting my hood shield my face as Nanna had taught me to do whenever I was in the presence of the earl, warning me that the more invisible I remained, the safer I'd be. She'd also done her best to keep me in the nursery and away from his roving eyes. Since the earl never came to visit his children, I hadn't needed to concern myself with his unwanted advances.

Stop. Gather your wits. Stay calm. I silently chanted a litany of self-rebukes. I'd had to do it more and more oft of late.

At the prevailing tense silence, I peeked up to see Bernhard open his mouth as though to demand to know why we were causing a disturbance. Before he could speak, the wind brought us the heavy thud of horses riding toward us.

The earl's sights shot to the newcomers—two knights and their squires. Their emblem, dragon heads on a background of red, belonged to the king's knights. It was draped over their steeds as well as upon the cloaks they wore over their chain mail.

What were the king's knights doing in Romsdal? And could I petition them for Lola's life? If they knew she was innocent, they would save her from the earl's death sentence, wouldn't they?

I rose on my toes, needing to see above the other servants. The larger of the knights rode stiffly with a façade of stone. Even from a distance, 'twas easy to identify the golden clasp at his throat, one crafted in the likeness of the Sword of the Magi. Though I hadn't seen the ancient sword, I'd heard enough to recognize the special emblem belonged to only one group of knights, the Knights of Brethren, given to them by King Ansgar after he'd freed the sword from the case last autumn.

If these two were Knights of Brethren, then perhaps . . .

My heartbeat gave a traitorous extra beat even as I took in the second knight riding toward us.

Yes, it was Gunnar, the earl's younger brother. He held himself more casually than the other knight, as if he didn't have a care in the world—or had tossed them all upon the shoulders of his companion.

Underneath his hood, Gunnar's dark-brown hair was loose and wavy, framing his face, which was just as beautiful as always. I didn't usually resort to calling men beautiful. Handsome, good-looking, attractive. But *beautiful* was a term I reserved for glorious sunsets and majestic mountains.

In Gunnar's case, however, *beautiful* was completely appropriate. His features were perfect. Full lips, slender nose, high cheekbones. And his eyes . . . were wide and framed by the longest lashes ever known to mankind. The dark blue of his eyes was oft like a summer night, sometimes playful and full of twinkling stars, but at other times sizzling and sultry with heat.

It was as if a great sculptor had chiseled Gunnar into the ultimate representation of what all men should aspire to look like. If only he had a flaw—even a tiny one, like a wart on his nose or bump on his forehead. But he'd always been too handsome for his own good. And he'd known it.

The closer he rode, the clearer it became that time

had given him even more to boast about. His jaw and the set of his mouth contained a maturity and leanness that hadn't been there in the past. His body, too, seemed more defined and muscular, as though he'd honed his strength and purpose.

I bunched my fists at my sides in a silent protest of my easy admiration. I needed to control my reaction to this man—couldn't allow myself any longing or an inkling of attraction. I was past that.

In fact, he was my sworn enemy every bit as much as the earl, and I wouldn't forget the way we'd parted five years ago when he'd been home for a few short weeks after completing his knight's training.

Regardless of my personal issues with Gunnar, he'd become an important knight—one of the closest to the king. Surely, he could but say a word and stop his brother. He would take one look at the woman condemned to death by drowning and would demand to know her crime.

At the cliff's edge, the bailiff, however, hadn't paused to watch the newcomers the way the rest of us had. Instead, he'd been too focused on moving Lola one tiny increment at a time. Before I could shout out at him to wait, he released his hold of her arms. She was already too close to the edge of the precipice and started to tip backward. Without her hands to flail and find her balance, she fell backward.

I gasped, my horror cutting off my cry.

In the next instant, she was gone.

Desperate to rush to her aid, I jerked free of Frans and Valter, who were distracted by the knights. I bolted to the edge of the plateau. But I was too late.

Chapter 2

Mikaela

A scream lodged in my throat.

As I peered into the deep blue-green waters of the fjord a hundred feet below, all I could do was watch Lola hit the surface with a splash and disappear underneath, leaving only a ripple to mark the place.

Bile rose swiftly.

How could he? How dare he? What right did the earl have to destroy a life so callously? Just because he was wealthy and powerful and born of nobility didn't make him more worthwhile than those of us born into servitude.

Frans's fingers caught mine. His solid presence grounded me, held me in place, kept me from tossing myself off the cliff after the woman in a vain endeavor to rescue her. Ami, one of my friends and a kitchen maid, sidled next to me on the other side, likely an effort to keep the earl from noticing my distress again.

Behind us, voices carried in the wind, the greetings of the earl and the knights, Lola's fate now forgotten.

I stared out over the waterway that cut its way into the heart of Norvegia. Rugged cliffs lined the fjord for many winding leagues until opening into the Dark Sea in the west. The calm waters made the fjord a major water highway to the port city of Romsdal, which sat along the shore to the east of where we stood. Typical of most coastal cities, the terraced buildings were constructed of strong Norvegian timber and painted in colorful hues. The harbor was lined with traditional longboats and other sailing vessels, attesting to the thriving fishing industry of the area.

Beyond the city limits, the land flattened into a patchwork of farm fields that were being plowed and planted for the short growing season. In the far east, the fertile soil gave way to the hilly moors. Beyond the Moors of Many Lakes, the white peaks of the Snowden Mountain Range filled the interior and eastern border of Norvegia.

Behind us, Likness Castle, with thick walls and tall turrets, towered above Romsdal like a proud lord overseeing all that belonged to him. With three of the castle's sides positioned atop cliffs, an enemy had only one way to attack—uphill and exposed in the open rocky hillside that led down to the city and waterfront.

While much of the land adjoining the castle and Romsdal had been cleared of its timber, Hardanger Forest covered a hundred leagues, a dark and overgrown woodland that had never been tamed, that no one dared to enter for fear of the jotunn.

It was on days like today that I wondered if the jotunn would be a better ruler over our lands than the earl. If I could trade one monster for the other, who would I choose? Why must I choose at all? The questions that had plagued me for years clamored for answers: Why must we subject ourselves to such heartless leaders? Why couldn't we select someone who would rule justly and fairly?

The breeze again struck my cheeks, and I didn't realize I was weeping until the air nearly froze the trail of my tears.

"Come," Frans said gently. "It's time to go."

Huddled in her cloak, Ami squeezed my arm and then joined the others who were dispersing, most heading up the trail to the fortress, their heads hung low, their shoulders bent, the weight of the drowning heavy upon them too.

I breathed in deeply, letting the cold air settle painfully in my lungs. With my stiff fingers, I swiped at my cheeks. "You go without me. I need to hike off my frustration."

Trails wound all along the fjord, some descending to the water, others leading to more secluded precipices with stunning vistas. Birch woods and all manner of dwarf willow and juniper grew on the rocky terrain. Waterfalls and even a few hot springs added to the beauty.

Since my childhood when I'd started working in the nursery, I'd spent many hours exploring the cliffs around Likness Castle. I knew them better than anyone. Not that I had much free time anymore. Only one afternoon a week on Sunday after mass.

Since today was Sunday, I'd already gone home to visit my family. As I'd been walking back, I'd had no choice but to join the rest of the castle staff at the cliff's edge to watch the punishment. And now, with but an hour until dusk, I needed time to myself more than ever.

"I can't go back yet, Frans." I pulled free from him and offered an apologetic nod.

Gunnar's voice drifted my way as he spoke with his brother, but I refused to look at him again. When he'd left the last time, I'd vowed to put him from my mind once and for all. I'd done well keeping my vow, and I aimed to continue no matter how long he was home this time.

If he followed the same protocol as previous visits, he wouldn't stay overlong. Gunnar was a wandering soul, never making promises, never getting serious, never thinking beyond tomorrow. Surely I could avoid him until he left.

He wouldn't seek me out anyway. I was simply one more conquest in a long string of women he'd charmed. I was a poor bondservant—earning nothing but food and clothing for my labor. To make matters worse, I was the daughter of a villein—a tenant farmer, the lowest of all bondservants, no better than a slave.

Nobody called us slaves. That was too harsh. But we weren't free. I most certainly wasn't now—never had been—free to consider a relationship with Gunnar. If I'd ever entertained the prospect, I'd buried it that day after our tryst.

Frans's bushy brows folded together, and his forehead creased. "Sit and talk with me while I finish the roof repairs."

I couldn't keep from glancing down at the waters below again, and I could only pray Lola had gone peacefully, that her suffering hadn't lasted long.

"We haven't talked much all week." Although Frans was never demanding of me, I could sense the growing frustration that warred within him. After years of being my friend, he wanted more from our relationship. He deserved more. But somehow, I always seemed to be falling short of giving him what he needed.

I'd told myself that once we were married, I'd be able to satisfy him better, that we'd have more time to talk and be together. But sometimes I wasn't sure if I'd ever be enough for him.

"I'm sorry." My apology came out a strangled whisper, an apology not just for now but for all the times I'd failed him. I would try to do better in the future. But today, at this moment, I wanted to be alone.

He reached up as if he intended to brush a strand of my loose hair out of my face but then dropped both hands to his sides. Valter waited several paces away, his eyes downcast, attempting to give us some privacy. But there was never privacy anywhere, which was all the more reason I needed the hike.

Frans took a step back. "Please be careful, Mikaela. Don't let anyone follow you."

"Don't fret. I know where to hide." I started away from the fjord with the others, keeping my head down and steering well away from Gunnar and the earl. As I rounded a bend and moved out of their sight, I ducked past a shrub and started down another path that led west along the fjord.

Though the trail was narrow and rocky, I picked up my pace. Only a moment later, I heard the slap of footsteps behind me.

Had I been too hasty in sneaking off on my own and seeking time by myself? Most knew and loved Nanna, as she'd been with the Likness family since both Bernhard and Gunnar were infants. Because of their love for Nanna, the rest of the staff accepted and protected me. Most also knew Frans wanted to marry me. With as big and muscular as he was, no one dared to offend him.

Even so, Frans's concern echoed in my mind. As did the fact that I'd garnered the earl's attention during the gathering. I'd be wise to hide until whoever was following me gave up the hunt.

Without a second thought, I scrambled up a low incline, peeled back the branches of a juniper, and ducked into a hidden alcove.

A moment later, the footsteps passed. From my secluded spot, I couldn't see who it was, but my nerves tightened anyway.

I held myself motionless. After a few minutes passed, the same footsteps returned the way they'd come. Only when they were gone did I allow myself to breathe normally. I climbed down and hurried along the trail, treading as silently as I could. I wanted to deny someone had purposefully followed me, but I couldn't be too careful as a maiden alone.

It wasn't as if I was the comeliest maiden in Romsdal. There were others prettier than I was. My copper-brown hair wasn't anything special, nor were my amber eyes. I was small of stature, although not overly so. And I was too thin. Especially now that I was giving as much of my daily rations to my family as I could.

As I reached a fork in the path, I took neither of the trails, but set out through the shrubs farther inland. I knew exactly where I needed to go, passing each familiar landmark. Before long, I descended into a basin with steam rising from a small clear pool. The surrounding cliff walls acted as a shield, keeping out the wind as well as prying eyes.

I breathed out my relief. The hot spring was as deserted as always.

In spite of the frigid temperature, I shed my cloak, tunic, stockings, and boots, stripping away everything down to my shift. As I unplaited the single thick braid that fell over my shoulder and halfway to my waist, I waded in, the water bathing first my toes, then ankles. I lowered myself to my knees, letting the warmth embrace me. Maybe I wouldn't be able to forget what I'd witnessed on the cliffs or shed the guilt. But for a few moments I could allow the beauty of this secret place to soothe me.

With a groan of pleasure, I lay back and submerged myself up to my neck. Then I sank down, floating underneath, pressing against the smooth stones at the bottom of the pool.

While I couldn't sneak away to this hot spring every week on my afternoon off—especially during the harshest parts of winter—I came as oft as I could. I tried not to think about why I'd never invited Frans to come with me, why I'd never even told him about the spot.

It wasn't because I feared he might take advantage of our being alone. Frans was a man of honor, and he respected me so much that he'd never once attempted to kiss me . . . unlike another man who'd had no hesitation in claiming a kiss.

I broke through the surface, my face suddenly hot. And not because of the water. Even after these many years, the memory of the kiss I'd shared with Gunnar still evoked the same heated reaction within me.

Of course, I'd known him as a child since Nanna had taken care of him. With only two years in age difference, I'd been well aware of who he was and his importance. But since I'd been but a girl of five when I'd come to the castle to work and he only seven, we'd become playmates and friends, having many childhood adventures for the few years we were together in the nursery.

When Gunnar turned ten, he was fostered out to begin his knight's training. It was also the year Bernhard married Sofia. Although Nanna was no longer needed to care for Gunnar, she'd still had Viola, until Bernhard decided to send his youngest sister to a convent to avoid someday having to pay a dowry for her. By then, Sofia had started having children.

During the eight years Gunnar was away, I tried to forget about him. It almost worked, since I was busy helping with Sofia's babies. But the summer I turned sixteen, Gunnar finally came home for a visit. When he'd ridden through the gatehouse, hopped down from his horse, and swaggered into the castle, I'd been smitten like every other woman for miles around.

Not only was he beautiful—yes, even at sixteen I'd considered him beautiful—but he oozed charm and wit and life. He was like nectar, and the women around him were like dancing, buzzing insects needing a tiny taste of his sweetness.

I hadn't expected him to seek out Nanna, but he'd been eager to see the woman who'd raised him and came searching for her the first night he was back. He found me instead.

I resisted him as long as possible, ignoring and rebuffing his flirtatious remarks and regard. But over the next couple of weeks, he made a point of talking to me, paying me compliments, and showing me more interest than any man ever had.

Foolishly I was flattered, even as I continued to keep him at arm's length. Nanna noticed Gunnar's attention upon me and cautioned against spending time with him, reminding me that we were no longer children.

However, the more I resisted, the more Gunnar sought me out, clearly seeing me as a challenge he needed to win. The day before he was scheduled to leave to meet up with the king's forces and fight against the invading Ice Men, he followed me out to the hot spring and surprised me by jumping into the pool fully clothed.

I joined him—also fully clothed—and we splashed and played until we crawled out and lay on the basin beside the pool, letting the afternoon sunshine dry us. We talked for several hours about everything and anything. When dusk began to approach, I pushed up and began to re-braid my hair.

From where he was still sprawled out on the warm stone, he grabbed my hand and drew it away from the half-finished braid. "Leave your hair down."

I swatted him and resumed my plaiting. "I can't leave it down. 'Twouldn't be proper."

"Fie on all things proper."

I paused and lifted a brow at him. "On all things?"

"Yes, proper is overrated."

"Then you would have me run around like a loose woman?"

"No, not loose. Just beautiful."

My fingers tangled in my hair came to a standstill.

Had he just called me beautiful?

He reached up again, and this time when he grasped my hand, he laced our fingers. The touch of his skin against mine sent my insides into an eddy, twirling fast and leaving me breathless, speechless, unable to formulate a response.

His bottomless blue eyes locked with mine, and they were aglow with a burning I didn't understand. All I knew was that he sent shooting stars across the distance, transferring a heat to my skin, setting me aflush.

"You always have been the most fascinating and beautiful maiden I've ever known." His words, his eyes, his body radiated with sincerity. Then he lifted our intertwined hands to his lips.

If I'd thought I was hot already, it hadn't compared to the explosion of heat inside when his lips pressed against my hand—soft, full lips that had smiled at me countless times and easily chased away my cares.

I was so mesmerized by the new sensations that I wasn't aware he was tugging me down until our faces were mere inches apart. All I noticed was the length and lushness of his lashes. Then he raised himself up and caressed my lips with his.

The contact was sweet and warm and tender. But it scared me. Before I could rationalize my action or let him explain what he was doing, I jumped up and scrambled over the basin wall. I didn't wait to see if he followed me. Instead, I ran the whole way back to the castle until I was in the nursery. Even there, I closed myself in the garderobe until my heartbeat returned to normal and my skin stopped burning.

All through the night, I tossed and turned on my

pallet among the rushes, trying not to awaken the infants with my sleeplessness. My mind couldn't stop reviewing Gunnar's kisses to both my hand and mouth. Even though the kisses had been as soft and brief as the touch of a butterfly wing, they'd left me shaken and wanting more.

By morn, I'd decided I needed to see and talk to him again before he left. I tiptoed out of the nursery and made my way through the castle toward his chambers, certain the sound of my wildly thumping heart would wake everyone.

As I entered the hallway leading to his room, hazy dawn light spilled from his open doorway, enough light to outline him half-clad and kissing another woman. Passionately.

I halted abruptly and wasn't able to contain my gasp. It echoed against the stone walls and must have been loud enough that he heard it. Though he didn't release his hold of the woman, he broke the kiss and swiveled his head, enough that he could see me standing there two dozen paces away.

I was too shocked to say anything and could only stare.

For long seconds I waited. I wasn't sure what I expected—that maybe he'd thrust the woman away in disgust, admit he was making a mistake, and beg me for forgiveness.

But he did none of those things. Instead, he bent in and captured the woman's mouth in another kiss. Another ardent kiss. One so ardent he forgot—or didn't care—I was there.

Still too stunned to move, I gaped several moments more before reality grabbed and shook me awake. If he expected me to run away sobbing and heartbroken, he didn't know me well enough. I marched toward him and stopped when I was directly in front of him.

The woman, a noblewoman I'd seen around the castle from time to time, was the first to pull away, scowling at me. I used the interlude to slap Gunnar on the cheek. Then without a word, I spun and stalked away without looking back.

I hadn't seen him since.

While I'd learned the kiss at the hot spring hadn't meant anything to him, it had been my first and only. And I despised myself for thinking about it, thinking about him.

"'Tis fresh on my mind because he's here," I murmured. I just needed to endure the next few days or weeks. Then once Gunnar was gone, I wouldn't have to see him for another five years, ten if I was lucky.

I pushed back under the water, giving myself over to the comforting heat, trying to reassure my soul that all would be well. As I came up for another breath of air, the cold temperature greeted me. Wafts of steam rose all over the pond, keeping my skin and hair from freezing.

"And the reason I haven't invited Frans here is because he wouldn't consider it chaste." My whispered statement sounded false the moment I spoke it aloud. "I love spending time with him. I really do."

"You love spending time with Frans?" The question came from behind me. Gunnar. And his tone was laced with humor. "I find that difficult to imagine."

I stiffened but didn't turn. Had he noticed me in the gathering at the cliff when he'd ridden up? And had he sent one of his squires to follow me? Were those the footsteps I'd heard a short while ago?

Whatever the case, I'd ignore Gunnar. He didn't deserve an answer from me. In fact, he didn't deserve to even talk to me. I needed to simply get up and walk away.

I started to rise, glanced down at my shift, then sank lower into the water to cover myself. No. I wouldn't be able to get up and walk away with any dignity in a wet shift. I was stuck waiting until he left.

"Frans isn't the man you need." Gunnar spoke with a confidence that only made my muscles tense.

"Why are you here?" I let my irritation edge each word. "Go away."

Chapter 3

GUNNAR

Mikaela had every right to hate me.

I was a scoundrel, blackguard, knave, ruffian, weasel, glutton, idiot, fool . . . if there was any other derogatory term I'd missed, I was that as well.

Sitting in the hot spring, her spine was as rigid as a brick wall. "I have no wish to speak with a miscreant."

Miscreant. Of course. One more name to add to my lengthy list of faults—a list I took responsibility for in the fullest.

I sat back on my boot heels, unable to tear my gaze from her.

Her hair was loose and longer than I remembered, hanging almost to her waist. Even wet, it was a luxurious brown the color of the fox fur that trimmed my cloak. And though I couldn't see her eyes, they rivaled her hair in richness, except the brown was an ever-changing hue, sometimes light and playful and at others deep and dark.

I imagined right now the color resembled a dangerous rocky valley—one I had no right to cross, but one I wanted to bridge, nonetheless.

"Frans will never make you happy." The words were out before I could stop them. And why should I stop them? All it had taken was a few discreet inquiries by my squire, and I'd learned Mikaela wasn't yet married, not even betrothed, but that she and Frans had been making plans for a future together.

"Frans already makes me happy." Her tone was as sassy as always, one of the many qualities that had drawn me to her the last summer I'd been home.

"Frans is much too serious and steady for you."

"And who crowned you the expert matchmaker?"

"I did."

"You need to lose your crown. Better yet, lose your head."

I laughed. I couldn't help it. This was what I'd missed. Her sharp wit, her unbridled tongue, her ability to speak her mind. Even when we were playmates as children, she'd regarded me as an ordinary and normal friend, never deferring to me or bowing to my wishes.

I'd grown too accustomed to women telling me what they thought I wanted to hear. And Mikaela's refusal to impress me was like a refreshing spring breeze blowing through the clutter in my heart and mind.

She'd always drawn me like no other. Even though I'd tried to resist for her sake.

If only Torvald and I had discovered the sacred chalice by now, then I wouldn't be here putting her at risk.

But no amount of searching for the relic last autumn and winter throughout the abbeys and Stavekirches of the Richlande Lowlands had produced any leads. This spring we'd broadened our investigation to the Moors of Many Lakes, working our way steadily north.

Even though I'd vowed I would never return, I'd had no choice but to direct my steed toward home when Maxim and Princess Elinor, the wisest advisors in the land, uncovered clues that pointed to the chalice's location in the vicinity of Romsdal.

Not only had I made the vow in order to keep Mikaela safe, but I'd made it because I despised being around my brother and didn't want to see him ever again.

Almost ten years my senior, Bernhard had taken over the earldom after our parents died when their ship sank. I'd been a lad of six at the time, old enough to understand how much Father bullied, mocked, belittled, and shamed Bernhard. Old enough to avoid Father and his cruelty. Old enough to feel relief instead of remorse at his passing.

The problem was, Bernhard had turned into our father. Before he sent me away for my knight's training, he'd become quite adept at bullying, mocking, belittling, and shaming me. I, in turn, had become proficient at deflecting him and masking my truest feelings, hiding them where he wouldn't be able to see and use them against me.

Now here I was, back in Romsdal. And here Torvald and I would stay until we discovered if the rumors of the chalice being in the area were true or false.

During the past day of riding, not only had I steeled myself for seeing Bernhard, but I'd also fortified my heart against Mikaela. I reminded myself of the grave trouble I'd nearly brought upon her during my last visit home. I told myself this time I would stay as far away from her as the eastern horizon was from the western. I even promised myself I wouldn't look at her or speak to her.

For part of the journey, I'd prayed she was happily married to save me from any temptation. But then the rest of the time, I'd stewed with resentment at the prospect of her being with any other man.

Not that I could ever have her for myself. The idea was as unfathomable now as it had been five years ago. Nevertheless, as we drew closer to Romsdal, my longing for her crested the barriers I'd erected.

As I'd ridden with Torvald across the open expanse of the high plateau, I'd easily spotted her in the crowd beside Frans. Even in her cloak and with hood drawn, she stood out to me. It was as if she was the shore and I the wave, drawn to her regardless of how much I tried to stay out to sea.

Of course, the moment I'd noticed a bound woman tottering on the edge of the cliff, all other thoughts had fled except that of saving her. I'd rapidly formulated an excuse for Bernhard, a request for the woman to become my servant for the duration of my stay in Romsdal. But before I could offer greetings and make my suggestion, the woman had slipped to her death.

So much for fortifying my heart against Mikaela. All it had taken was one look at the despair on her face as she'd turned away from looking down into the fjord for my walls to crumble completely and my vows about staying away from her to turn to dust.

"Begone, Gunnar." This time Mikaela's tone contained a bitter edge, one I'd put there. "You'll find I'm not so gullible anymore."

Gullible? Is that what she thought? Of course, she wouldn't know the truth. I'd never made an effort to share it with her, and I never would. "Methinks you came here to the spring hoping I'd follow you."

Before I could prepare myself, she spun and sent a spray of water my way. It splashed against my face with such force, I could only splutter.

In the same instant, she stood and grabbed her cloak from the stack of her garments on the edge of the pool. Even with the water dribbling in my eyes and blinding me, I pivoted so that my back was facing her, giving her the privacy that she needed to get dressed. I may have gained a reputation as a ladies' man, but I still retained a shred of decency. Nanna's influence over the first ten years of my life hadn't been for naught.

"The truth is," she said through chattering teeth, "I wouldn't come here with you, not even if someone bound and forced me to comply."

"And I am the opposite. No one could keep me away from meeting here with you, even if they bound me and forced me to stay away." Though I spoke flippantly, trying to keep the moment from weighing too deeply, my declaration held more truth than she'd ever know.

For several long seconds, she didn't respond, and the air around us was quiet save for her labored efforts to don her garments over her wet shift.

Did I dare put aside my glibness and speak forthrightly with her? This might be my only chance to repair what I'd purposefully broken. But what good could come of it? She would remain safer during my time in Romsdal if I kept far from her, where I wouldn't draw undue attention or rumors her way.

"Listen, Mikaela." I let the pretense fall away. "The truth is, I came after you because I want to apologize for hurting you."

"You didn't hurt me." Again, her tone was sharp.

I hadn't hurt her? Maybe I was being proud to assume that I had. "I regret I led you on—"

"You didn't lead me on."

Then why had she said she wasn't gullible anymore? "Regardless, things ended badly between us, and I apologize."

"It doesn't matter. It was long ago. And we've both moved on with our lives."

Had I moved on? Or had I merely moved around? "Oh yes. How could I forget. You're waiting to marry your soul mate, Frans."

She huffed and then scrambled past me as she wound up her hair and tucked it under her hood.

I rose and started after her. This time, I didn't plan to let her get away without talking. I wanted her to understand she'd never been to blame for anything. And I wanted resolution for myself. Perhaps if I finally put to rest my feelings for her, I'd eventually be able to develop fondness for someone else.

She was as nimble now as in the past and darted out of the basin and down into the shrubs, practically running away from me. But I was quick too. In fact, I'd sharpened my muscles and speed over the years that I'd served as one of the king's knights. She made it only to the trail fork before I snagged her arm and drew her to a halt.

She strained and struggled against me for several seconds before holding herself motionless and stiff, apparently concluding she was no match for my strength.

"You are clearly determined to say your piece. So, say it." She stared straight ahead, her dainty chin lifted, her pert nose turned up, her exquisite lips pursed into a line.

I wanted her to turn and look at me so I could stare into her eyes and watch the brown take on speckles of gold or green. But she kept her focus on the trail ahead, to the rugged outcroppings of rocks.

What should I say first? How could I convey my

sincerity? "Do you love him?" The moment the question slipped out, I wished I could summon it back. Why was I making such an issue of Frans? I ought to be encouraging her union with him, not undermining it.

She snapped her eyes to me, and the brown churned, dark and stormy. "My feelings for Frans are none of your concern."

"If you loved him, you would have wedded him by now."

"If Frans hadn't been forced to hand over every last coin of his savings to pay for fire damages, we would be able to get married this spring. But now he cannot afford the bride price."

I had never agreed with Bernhard's methods of governing his subjects, especially his policy about requiring his bondservants to gain his permission and pay a fee in order to marry someone of their choosing. Already, life was difficult for so many of them, never having enough to feed and care for their families. If they happened to find love, that shouldn't be denied them.

"Then you would marry him if he could pay for you?" I persisted.

"Yes. Of course I would."

"If you tell me that you love him and mean it, then I shall give him the money he needs."

Her lashes swept up, and for the first time since I'd returned, she seemed to truly look at me. She made a trail around my face, starting at my forehead, then stopping at my cheek, chin, and nose, before turning her attention to my lips and lingering there.

Was she thinking about the kiss we'd shared last time we were out here together? Though the connection had lasted but a few seconds and had been the softest, gentlest of touches, it had knocked into me with the power of a siege engine boulder. I had never experienced a kiss either before or after that had affected me so powerfully.

Even now, my gaze dropped to her mouth, drawn there against my best judgment. I couldn't—absolutely wouldn't—think of kissing her again. Doing so would only cause more hurt and confusion instead of clearing it up.

"Tell me you love him," I whispered.

She captured her bottom lip between her teeth.

The very motion captured me, drew me up like prey caught in a snare. There I hung, breathless with anticipation, not wanting her to release me, but also knowing she had to set me free. Or I would be forced to do it myself.

Except I didn't want to be free from her. From the moment I met her, even as a child, I'd only and ever wanted to be hers. Clearly, neither time nor distance had changed any of my feelings, except perhaps made them stronger.

"I don't know." Her whisper was barely audible in return.

"What don't you know?" I had no idea what we were talking about anymore. And somehow, I found myself standing mere inches from her. Had I closed the gap between us, or had she?

At the crackling of brush down the trail, my hand slipped to my belt and to my knife, my weapon of choice. I had it unsheathed and ready to throw before I could make myself look away from her.

A bear-sized man halted in the middle of the path. His concerned gaze bounced back and forth between us as his thick eyebrows rose.

"Frans." I gave him a curt nod. "Good to see you again."

Chapter
4

Mikaela

"Frans. What are you doing here?" I hopped away from Gunnar as though we'd been caught doing something unseemly. We hadn't even been touching, and I had no reason to feel guilty, so why did I?

"I was worried and came to check on you." Frans stood with his feet apart and his shoulders angled like a buck about to charge and clash antlers with his competitor.

I put another arm-length of distance between myself and Gunnar, not daring to look at him, too afraid of revealing how Gunnar affected me.

What was wrong with me? Gunnar was my mortal enemy. But here I was, talking to him rationally and considering his offer.

How could I not? He'd proposed a generous solution to our dilemma. All I had to do was tell Gunnar I loved Frans, and he would pay the bride price. Frans wouldn't have to labor hard for another year to save. I wouldn't have to worry about the earl making advances toward me or choosing someone else for me to marry—someone I might not know or like.

At least with Frans, even though I might not feel sizzling sparks the way I did with Gunnar, I would be safe and content. My amiable feelings would likely someday develop into more. Even if they didn't, I could ask for no better man.

Frans's brows dipped into a deeper scowl. With his face covered in a scruffy beard, I couldn't see his mouth well, but he seemed to be pinching it closed, as though he was keeping himself from saying something he might regret.

"No need to worry, Frans." Gunnar closed the gap between us and peeled a wet strand of my hair away from my cheek, his fingers brushing against my cold skin and sending warmth tingling across every nerve ending. "I was with Mikaela and taking care of her just fine."

Like always, Gunnar's voice held the hint of innuendo and teasing. From the sidelong look he slanted at Frans, I got the distinct impression he was baiting the burly man, as though he was just as eager as Frans for an opportunity to spar and prove his dominance.

"I can take care of Mikaela and don't need your help." Frans took several menacing steps forward. Gunnar stiffened, but thankfully his knife, which had made a brief appearance, was already well out of sight and back in its sheath.

I stepped into the middle of the path and held out a hand as if that would stop Frans if he decided to barrel ahead. "I don't need either one of you watching over me."

Frans jerked his head at Gunnar. "Knew from the minute he left the others that he'd decided to come out here hunting after what doesn't belong to him."

"From what I understand, she doesn't belong to you yet either."

"She's mine." Frans's tone dropped. "And I want you to stay away from her this time."

This time? Had Frans noticed Gunnar paying me attention during his visit home five years ago? Back then, Frans and I had been nothing more than friends—at least, that's what I'd assumed. Was it possible Frans had aspired after me, and I hadn't known it? Perhaps he'd been jealous of Gunnar coming home and so effortlessly winning my heart. After all, shortly after Gunnar left, Frans had expressed his feelings for me. I'd been angry and hurt at the time and had relished knowing someone wanted me.

Gunnar and Frans locked eyes. As Frans's fists balled, Gunnar visibly tensed, the muscles in his jaw flexing.

I had to put an end to whatever this was. Surely Frans knew he had nothing to worry about. I'd only ever spoken negatively about Gunnar. And while I hadn't shared the details of Gunnar's rejection, I'd told Frans enough for him to know my friendship with Gunnar had ended badly.

Besides, Gunnar's reputation as a womanizer had grown over recent years along with his fame as a Knight of Brethren. Rumors abounded about his wooing and winning women only to break their hearts. Why would Frans think I wanted anything to do with a man like that?

Maybe I'd once been naïve and easily charmed by a

handsome face and winning smile. But I'd learned my lesson and had turned into a strong, independent woman. Couldn't Frans see that? He ought to know Gunnar was the last man I'd want to be with. If I hadn't made that apparent, I needed to.

I started toward Frans. "The good news is that we'll be able to get married very soon."

My declaration worked like magic. Frans halted, and his attention jumped from Gunnar to me. "How?"

I gave him what I hoped was my most comely smile. "Gunnar has offered to pay the bride price for us so that we might wed."

I'd assumed the news would continue the magic and make everything better. But I was wrong. Frans's thick brows only dropped into another deep scowl that he tossed at Gunnar. "I'm not taking money from him."

"It doesn't matter where the money comes from, so long as we can be married."

"It matters to me." The frustration radiating from Frans's muscular frame rolled in waves down the path. "I refuse to be beholden to a man like him."

Gunnar didn't respond except to narrow his eyes.

I understood Frans needed to retain a measure of his pride and earn his own way. He didn't want charity and didn't want to be indebted in any way to Gunnar. But he had to see that this was different. "Gunnar realizes you were cheated out of your money, and this is his way of trying to right a wrong."

Though Gunnar hadn't said so, I'd sensed it. Underneath all the layers of defense Gunnar had erected over the years, I still saw the kind-hearted, giving, and sensitive person he was at his core. No, he wasn't a perfect man, had been influenced by

Bernhard, and had hurt me. But ultimately, he was a good man, good enough that King Ansgar had wanted him to be part of his closest group of knights. Surely that testified to his character.

"If Gunnar wants to right the wrong," Frans tossed the words like a gauntlet, "then have him go to his brother and get my money back."

Gunnar remained where he was, all arrogance now gone. "Doing so would only draw Bernhard's attention upon your situation and upon Mikaela. I would do anything—anything at all—to keep that from happening. Would you not agree?"

I needed only to think of Lola toppling from the cliff to know what happened when Bernhard set his attention upon someone. From the loosening of Frans's fists, I could tell he was remembering the same.

Silence hung heavy in the air, giving way to the rushing of a waterfall on the cliffs below as well as the distant call of a hawk. The cloudy sky above was beginning to turn a shade darker, and Frans and I would soon need to be within the castle gates for curfew or face punishment.

Frans eyed Gunnar as if searching for an answer to a riddle. "What do you stand to gain from making such an offer?"

"Mikaela's happiness." Gunnar's response was quiet and sincere.

It caught me off guard, and I couldn't keep from studying him the way Frans was, noting again the golden sword pin at his clasp signifying him as one of ten elite Knights of Brethren. I could only imagine the adventures he'd experienced, the battles he'd fought, the justice he'd brought to many.

If only I had the means to fight against the evil here in Romsdal. But I felt as if I were the one with my hands and feet bound with a stone weighing me down.

"If marrying you will bring Mikaela happiness," Gunnar continued, "then I would gladly pay the fee to see it happen. . . ."

Standing but a dozen paces away, Gunnar had the bearing of a man who'd been shaped and changed by all he'd gone through, and I had the sudden, strange longing to sit down with him and hear every detail of his time serving beside the king. Even if I didn't like Gunnar anymore, I couldn't deny that we'd always been able to converse with each other about everything.

Not that I couldn't talk with Frans. I could. But most of the time our conversations centered around simple everyday things and rarely delved into the deeper aspects of living.

Only when Gunnar's brow inched higher on one side and a smirk began to tug at the corners of his mouth did I realize I was staring at him.

Gunnar stared right back, unabashedly. "There is one condition to the offer."

"Should have known," Frans muttered.

"It's easy enough," Gunnar added. "All Mikaela has to do is tell me that she loves you and mean it."

All I had to do. I hadn't yet told Frans I loved him. He'd whispered the words to me on a couple occasions. But he'd never asked or pushed me to do likewise.

As both men turned their attention upon me, I had the sudden urge to flee, to run somewhere and hide from their probing eyes.

I cared about Frans and could tell him I loved him and mean it, couldn't I?

Drawing in a breath of cold air, I spun to face Frans. His eyes were filled with hope. The tenderness that softened his features told me he loved me. I needed only whisper it to him. Three little words. That was all.

I opened my mouth.

Gunnar's gaze bore into my back. I could feel him watching my every move, daring me to speak the words. And oh, how I wanted to say them, wanted to mean them. But in the deepest places of my being, I knew I didn't love Frans. At least not yet. Not the way he loved me and deserved to be loved in return.

Frans waited, his eyes getting bigger, something within them begging me to say the words, and not for the money we would gain but because he wanted the assurance that I felt about him the same way he did about me.

My mouth fell closed, and my shoulders deflated. Before I could decide how to proceed, Frans was already shaking his head and glaring again at Gunnar. "I don't want your lousy payment!"

I pinched my eyes shut, disappointed in myself for hurting Frans.

"I don't need anyone to help me." Frans heaved a deep breath, one shuddering with emotion.

"I'm sorry, Frans," I whispered, opening my eyes only to find him looking off into the distance. "I do care about you—"

"Don't," he whispered harshly.

I swallowed the rest of my words of admiration. They were flimsy and couldn't take the place of what he'd wanted to hear.

What was wrong with me that I was so callous? Why couldn't I conjure up love for this dear man?

"I know what I need to do to get the money." He backed up several paces. His attention shifted to the north, and a strange determination settled into the crevices of his face.

My heart stuttered its protest at what I guessed he was about to tell me. "No."

He nodded. "I'm taking up the earl's challenge."

The protest took on a life of its own, hacking like an axe at my chest. "You can't."

Without replying, he spun and stalked down the trail in the direction of the castle. He wouldn't dare accept the earl's challenge, would he?

Each of his steps echoed with resolve.

"No, Frans."

His stride didn't falter, but my heartbeat did.

I raced after him, not caring that I was leaving Gunnar behind. Suddenly all that mattered was stopping Frans. I grabbed his arm. "Please stop."

In spite of my efforts to bring him to a halt, he kept going, dragging me along.

"Let's forget all about Gunnar's offer." My panic was mounting. "What's important is that we get to have a future together at some point, and that won't be possible if you go into the forest."

Everyone knew the earl's challenge was a death sentence. The three men who'd already gone in had died—or at least that's what we believed, because none of them had come out of Hardanger Forest.

"What makes you think you can succeed when the others have failed?" I didn't care that my tone had grown sharp.

We broke into the clearing on the open plateau. The castle stood a short distance away with Hardanger Forest not far beyond, a mass of tangled limbs and thorny shrubs. The new foliage on the hardwoods should have made the forest greener and brighter, but the growth only seemed to add to the darkness and shadows, hiding the madman who lived in the depths.

The jotunn had existed in the woods for as long as people could remember. Most believed he was a troll. Others claimed he was a deformed and deranged man who had been cast out of society.

Whatever the case, the forest wasn't safe. Every time someone ventured inside to hunt, they never came back. Tales abounded of dangerous traps and torturous snares. But no one knew for certain what haunted the woodland.

With only the few fields and hills left around Romsdal for hunting, the earl had laid claim to those for his personal hunting grounds, leaving none for anyone else. In the absence of being able to hunt, the villeins had petitioned for fishing rights. But the earl had staunchly refused, claiming that additional fishing by the tenant farmers would drain the fjord and harm the fishing industry. As a result, the villeins had nowhere to go for food when their stores ran low.

Apparently, the earl had decided he was finished living in fear of the madman and was ready to gain control of the forest, because upon the spring thaw last month, he'd made the proclamation that the man who could bring him the jotunn's head would be rewarded with freedom or a bag of silver.

"I'm strong," Frans said as we headed up the short incline toward the castle gatehouse. "The muscles I've gained from working the forge will finally be put to good use."

Still scrambling to keep up with him, I released a scoffing laugh. "Your muscles won't be a match for the madman, and you're a fool if you think so."

Frans shook his head. "He's likely old by now. And weak."

"And I suppose that's what the other three said before losing their lives." In the early weeks of the earl's challenge, many had clamored for the opportunity to try. But with each subsequent disappearance, the enthusiasm had faded. It had been over a sennight since anyone had offered to venture into the forest. Rumors were circulating that the earl was growing restless in waiting for volunteers, that he might soon begin forcing men to go in and hunt the madman.

"I'm also smart and quick." Frans slowed his pace as we passed into the outer bailey. "And I'm good with a slingshot, am I not?"

Because the earl didn't allow any of his subjects—whether paid domestics or bondmen and villeins—to carry swords or knives, some created makeshift weapons out of their tools. Others, like Frans, learned to use a slingshot so that they might have a means of defending themselves against foes.

"You know as well as I do that a slingshot will be worthless in the forest."

Frans glanced around, then lowered his voice. "I won't be unarmed." Frans had crafted a dagger of his own in secret. But even with a knife, the danger was too great.

"You can't take this responsibility upon yourself.

It's too risky."

"If it frees the land of the menace and gives the populace back the forest, it will be worth the risk."

"You are letting everything that happened with Gunnar goad you into it."

Halfway across the bailey within sight of the forge, Frans halted. "Since losing my savings, I have already been contemplating doing it. Gunnar's return is the nudge I needed."

"You have no need. I shall wait for you to save again."

As Gunnar strolled through the gatehouse, oozing his usual confidence and charm, Frans reached for my hand, lifted it to his lips, and placed a kiss upon my knuckles. "Perhaps I no longer wish to wait."

With Frans's kiss upon my skin, I should have experienced tingles, warmth, a fluttering, something. But I could conjure up nothing.

Frans was making a bold move to initiate physical contact so publicly, since he'd remained chaste thus far.

When he slid a sideways glance in Gunnar's direction, I understood what he was doing. He was staking his claim upon me, letting Gunnar know he needed to stay away from now on.

"I beg you not to go into the forest, Frans." I tightened my grip on him as he released the kiss and lowered our hands.

Underneath the mop of bushy brows, his serious eyes met mine.

"I haven't begged you for many things," I whispered. "But I beg you not to do this."

He opened his mouth to respond but hesitated.

I stuck my hand in my pocket and touched the shell I kept there at all times, the shell my twin sister Maiken had given me the last day I'd seen her alive. The purple fragments had chipped away over the years, reminding me of the tenuous nature of life, how fragile it was, and how easily I could lose someone I cared about. "Please. I can't lose you."

He seemed to test the sincerity of my words before responding. "Very well."

I expelled a tremulous breath.

"But I cannot guarantee that I won't consider it in the future."

I wanted to protest again, but I held it in and released him. Dusk was fast approaching, and I needed to return to the nursery with all haste. Nanna would get into trouble if I was late, and I couldn't let that happen.

With a nod of farewell, I scurried toward the lower-level side entrance for servants. My best hope for protecting Frans was figuring out how to fall in love with him so that I could speak the words to him truthfully. I had to do so quickly before Gunnar left, while there was still time to accept his offer.

The problem was that I needed to avoid Gunnar so that I didn't let any thoughts about him interfere with my mission.

Chapter 5

GUNNAR

MIKAELA DIDN'T LOVE FRANS.

The thought shouldn't have brought me such intense satisfaction, but it did, nonetheless.

I finished the contents of my mug and pushed back from the table. Across from me, Torvald paused in breaking his fast. He eyed my untouched platter of oatcakes, thick brown goat cheese, and slices of ham. Then he quirked a brow at me.

"What?" I tried to keep my tone as nonchalant as possible. "After feasting late last night, I have no appetite."

Having stabbed a piece of ham and cheese onto the tip of his knife, Torvald took a bite without saying anything. He needed only to raise his other brow and pierce me with his gray-blue eyes for me to know he didn't believe me.

With his hulking frame, the scar on his cheek, and his brooding mannerisms, Torvald made an imposing figure. No one gave Torvald any trouble. In fact, most people revered him just about as much as they revered King Ansgar.

In spite of his severity—perhaps even because of it—he'd been a good traveling companion these past months. His strictness balanced out my lightheartedness. He was silent and contemplative compared to my being talkative and impulsive. He thought deeply, while I pushed him to action.

Although we worked well together, we'd failed thus far to uncover the whereabouts of the chalice. And although I hadn't wanted to stay at Likness Castle with my brother—had suggested residing at one of the inns within the city—Torvald had convinced me that we couldn't anger Bernhard by turning down his offer to be his guests for the duration of our sojourn in Romsdal. We needed to keep him as an ally.

"Who is she?" Torvald's question was low and meant for my ears alone.

Even so, I glanced around the tables nearby to see who might be paying us heed. Thankfully, besides our squires and castle staff, the great hall was mostly deserted, since few guests were awake at the early hour.

"Believe it or not, there was no *she* last night." I pretended to fasten the top button of my tight-fitting cotehardie, having shed my chain mail in favor of more civilized and colorful garments.

I'd long ago realized I could avoid Bernhard's wrath by playing the role of the easy-going, troublemaking, womanizing brother. As such, I posed no threat to him. Thus last night, I'd spent most of the eve and well into the late hours resorting to my role as a ladies' man, staying busy flirting and conversing with the women, letting Bernhard believe I was as wayward as always.

When I'd made my exit with a lovely noblewoman at my side, he'd grinned his approval. Today he'd likely learn I'd done nothing more than escort the woman to her door before bidding her goodnight.

Of course, I'd perfected my excuses to women for why I never got serious and never made promises. And if Bernhard asked, I'd have a ready excuse for him too.

I'd learned to maintain my reputation without giving away the truth—that I had no desire for any woman, save one.

"I own to the fact that I left the feast with a beauty," I said. "But I was tired and didn't pursue anything further."

Torvald twisted his knife, peering at the remaining ham and cheese as if deciding which angle to devour next. More likely he was trying to decide if he believed me. After the past months of traveling together, he knew me better than most, that my womanizing was based on hearsay and nothing more. Though I flirted with maidens everywhere and stayed up too late, I never took advantage of the women and always returned to my room alone.

I stood and stretched, trying to remain casual, even though excitement thrummed louder with each passing moment at the prospect of seeing Mikaela again.

"The other beauty," Torvald stated.

With my arms high above my head, I froze.

"Who is she?" This time he lifted his gaze to mine, the intensity piercing me.

Was he referring to Mikaela? Of course, he'd seen me send my squire after her yesterday. When I held back from returning to the castle with everyone else, perhaps he'd assumed I intended to follow her for myself.

If Torvald had so easily discovered my secret, how

many others would?

'Twas best, as always, to downplay my feelings for Mikaela. Yet, Torvald wouldn't be so easily deceived. I would have to give him some information or draw more suspicion.

I lowered my arms and shrugged. "She's a childhood companion."

From the moment Mikaela had entered the nursery as a young girl to work with Nanna, I'd been smitten with her. At first, Nanna had been nervous about us playing together and forming a friendship, and she'd gone out of her way to keep Mikaela too busy for me.

But I'd managed to sneak around behind Nanna's back, until the day I brought Mikaela one of the kittens from the stables, the tiny gray-and-white one she'd adored and played with every chance she could get.

At the sight of the kitten in the nursery, Nanna had asked all kinds of questions and learned we were spending time together. Nanna had given us each a firm scolding and told me Mikaela was someone I could never have as a friend or anything else. At the time, I hadn't known what she meant, and her words had only stirred the desire to have Mikaela even more.

Eventually, Nanna had given up trying to keep us apart and allowed us to spend endless hours together. She'd been busy with my little sister Viola, and Mikaela had kept me occupied. I suppose she'd known I would eventually leave and that our friendship would come to an end.

"That's why you were quiet on the ride here." Torvald studied my face as though solving a riddle. "You were thinking about her."

"A little." What I meant was I'd spent *little* time thinking of anything else.

"You love her." His sharp gaze saw everything, likely saw the situation better than I saw it for myself.

My answer got lost somewhere inside. I couldn't recall a time when my infatuation with Mikaela hadn't existed. I loved talking with her, loved her zest for life, loved that she wasn't afraid of anything. But that didn't mean I loved her, did it?

Thankfully, Torvald said nothing more and tore off a hunk of ham and cheese.

My best course of action was to change the subject. "After you're done with your fare, we'll ride into town and begin questioning priests."

He nodded and chewed.

"Good. I shall meet you at the stables at half past the hour."

He swallowed, then picked up his ale and swished the liquid in a circular motion inside the mug. "I can wait. Take as long as you need."

Again, I paused. Did Torvald know I was going to visit Mikaela? Now, before the rest of the household stirred? Of course, Bernhard's children would already be awake. I needn't worry that I'd find her or them yet asleep.

Torvald took a sip.

I stared at him. Torvald had never once encouraged me to spend time with a woman. Most of the time he admonished me against it.

He placed his mug back onto the table and wiped his mouth with his sleeve. "When I said take as long as you need, I meant with her, not me." Was he hiding a grin?

I felt a grin twitching my lips. "Why? When you're such joyous company, I can hardly bear to pull myself away from you."

One of his rare smiles finally made an appearance.

With a chuckle, I strode off. If only I could figure out a way to see Mikaela without Nanna supervising every second. In fact, I suspected Nanna would hug me and talk to me for a few minutes before detecting my ulterior motives for visiting and shooing me out of the nursery.

It didn't matter. I wouldn't be in Romsdal long. Most likely, our quest here would end the same way it had at other places, with someone remembering when the chalice had once been within a Stavekirche or abbey before it had been moved to another secret location elsewhere in Norvegia.

The problem was that our time was running short, and the prospect of war loomed in the nigh future. With the spring thaw, we expected King Canute of neighboring Swaine to resume his efforts to take Norvegia's throne. Hailing from Norvegia's royal Oldenberg lineage, he believed he had more right to our country's throne than Ansgar. We could only pray that Ansgar's possession of the Sword of the Magi would deter Canute, but we didn't know for certain.

More importantly, time was running out because Queen Elisbet—Queen Lis, as she preferred to be called— had started bleeding from a curse supposedly passed down to the firstborn daughters in the royal family. And it was believed the chalice could heal her.

We'd been unable to discover the relic to save King Ulrik. Now Torvald and I, like Ansgar, were growing more desperate. We'd failed one king and couldn't fail another, especially Ansgar, who was like a brother to us.

As I wound through the passageways toward the wing of the castle reserved for the nursery, I picked up my pace. I was tempted to whistle the merry tune on the tip of my tongue. But I held it back, not wanting to alert anyone of my presence, especially Mikaela. I couldn't give her the chance to hide before I saw her.

Upon reaching the door to the several chambers where the children spent most of their time, I paused, my mind returning to the many years I'd lived in these very rooms. Nanna had always been a mixture of firm and tender, never afraid to discipline her charges, but always showering us with genuine love.

While my memories of my mother had faded over the years, I did remember that I'd never felt the same unconditional acceptance and love from her that I did from Nanna. Most of the time, I'd felt as though I was some sort of prize that she'd given my father as a second son.

The other thing I remembered about my mother was that she'd worn a veil of sadness every bit as real as the veil she wore over her hair. Even when she'd smiled at me, the sadness had lingered in the tilt of her lips and in the shadows of her eyes.

In some ways, her passing from my life had freed me to love Nanna without any more worry of hurting my mother's feelings.

Not bothering to knock, I cracked open the door and peeked inside. Two little blond-haired girls sat side by side on a bench in front of the hearth fire, one slightly taller than the other. Though their backs were facing me, I could see that both were already attired in simple but pretty tunics. And Mikaela stood behind them—her back also facing me—brushing the taller one's hair.

She was in the middle of telling the girl something but paused. "Good morning, Nanna. I thought I told you to slumber later so that you can rid yourself of your chill."

I stepped into the room and closed the door behind

me. "If only I could blame a chill for my sleeplessness last night."

She sucked in a sharp breath and then cast me a glance, the brush halfway through the sheen of hair. My nieces swiveled as well, their eyes widening at the sight of me.

"Instead, I blame you for keeping me awake." I flashed her a grin.

She cocked her head toward her charges, clearly warning me that I needed to keep my suggestive comments appropriate for innocent ears.

While I'd met my nephew, Bernhard's oldest son, during my last visit, I couldn't remember if his daughters had been born yet. Maybe one of them had been a babe.

"Dreams of you kept me awake," I stated. "On-ly dreams." I enunciated my words, although I wasn't sure why since my nieces weren't babbling infants. They had to be at least four and six years of age. Or maybe three and five. Surely old enough to talk.

Mikaela held up the brush like a weapon and started toward me. "Go away, Gunnar. I have no wish to see you any more today than I did yesterday."

"You'll be happy to know they were good dreams. Really good dreams." Every dream about her was a really good dream, but from the way she was lifting the brush, as though she intended to beat me from the room, it was clear she wasn't interested in hearing about my dreams or anything else.

When she was but a foot away, she stopped, brush at the ready. The brown of her eyes flashed with sparks of gold, the fires inside her easily combusting as usual, fires I took too much enjoyment in fanning. "You need to leave." Her whisper was menacing. "This is highly inappropriate."

"What's inappropriate about me coming to give Nanna a hug and to meet my nieces?" I asked in a loud whisper.

"Really? You expect me to believe that's why you're here?" Her whisper dropped a notch, almost coming out a growl.

"Yes." I cocked my brows in feigned innocence. "Don't tell me you think I came here to visit you."

Her mouth opened, but then her retort stalled.

"Oh," I whispered, again loudly. "I guess you were secretly thinking about me and wishing I'd make an appearance."

"No." A flush crept into her cheeks. "That's not true at all."

I was right. She had been thinking about me. But she was stubborn and would never admit it. My gaze snagged on a gray-and-white cat curled up in a corner chair. "I see you still have Grumpy."

"Happy."

"Yes, I am happy now that I'm here with you."

She rolled her eyes, but she was fighting back a smile. "No, his name is Happy."

"Why, exactly, did you name him Happy?"

"Because he made me happy."

"And . . . ?"

"That's all."

I pressed my lips together to keep from reminding her of her sweet declaration the day I'd delivered the kitten to this very room. *I'm naming him Happy because you made me happy.*

"Don't say anything else." Her whisper dropped in another warning.

I shrugged as if to demonstrate I had nothing else to say. "Also, why are we still whispering?"

She glanced over at the girls, who were watching our exchange, their eyes wide, their *innocent* ears still hearing every word. A burst of laughter escaped from Mikaela's lips, but she caught it in her hand.

Immediately my nieces smiled, although tentatively. They obviously took their cues from Mikaela.

I hadn't spent much time with Bernhard's wife, Sofia. But during the times I'd visited previously, as well as last night, I'd surmised that she was nearly as conniving and cruel as Bernhard. I'd learned she'd lost several babies during childbirth but was expecting again. Apparently, Bernhard was determined to have a second son.

As much as Mikaela and Nanna shielded their charges from the influence of their parents, even good nursemaids couldn't stop children from growing up and making poor choices. Bernhard had gone his own way, and from what I'd heard, his son was just like him, although now fostered out to another nobleman and no longer living at Likness Castle.

Though I'd had Nanna's gentle guidance and loving care, I hadn't exactly led a stellar life either.

"So," I said, turning my attention upon the girls. "Are these my nieces? Or are they angels visiting from heaven?"

My question earned giggles. And a widening smile from Mikaela, one that made her features come to life with a vibrance that never failed to light me up.

"If I had to guess, I'd say angels." I crossed to them and crouched. "You're too beautiful to be mere mortals."

Again, they giggled. They were miniature versions of their beautiful mother. It saddened me to think that one day Bernhard would barter them to the highest bidders regardless of their needs or wishes, just as my father had done to my two older sisters. Or confine them in a convent like my younger sister Viola.

"Do you angels have names?" I asked.

Their gazes darted to Mikaela, as though gaining her permission to speak.

"Let me guess." I tapped a finger against my lips, pretending to be deep in thought. Then I pointed at them. "You're Rikissa. And you must be Renate."

"Yes, how did you know?" the taller girl asked in an awed whisper while the younger one curled closer to her sister.

"As Mikaela knows, I'm incredibly intelligent. Not to mention witty, handsome, and strong—"

"And he has a very big head."

"That too."

Mikaela was still smiling.

Energy coursed through me in a way I hadn't felt since the day I'd ridden away from her. Being with her always made me feel as though I could accomplish anything I set my mind to doing. "Now that we've established that you're both angels, can you guess who I am?"

"You're Uncle Gunnar." Rikissa spoke solemnly. "Nanna told us you were coming for a visit."

I pretended to look around to see if anyone was spying on us. "Did she also tell you my true identity?"

Both girls shook their heads.

I leaned in, and they did likewise. I had to bite back my mirth at how adorable they were. "Amongst my fellow Knights of Brethren, I'm renowned as the Slayer."

"The Slayer?" Mikaela's voice took on an incredulous tone.

"Yes." I tossed her what I hoped was my most censuring look, although I was having a difficult time keeping a straight face. "I'm known for slaying . . . well, hearts."

Mikaela snorted.

I straightened and pretended to take offense. "I beg your pardon."

Even though she slapped her fists to her hips and attempted to glare, her eyes danced with merriment. "We will not be calling you Slayer. Not now, and not ever."

I pressed my hands to my heart as though she'd wounded me.

The girls' eyes bounced between Mikaela and me, trying but failing to keep up with our conversation.

I bit back my laughter and spoke as sincerely to them as I could manage. "I give you permission to call me Slayer—"

Mikaela shook her head, pinching her mouth closed.

"Or Happy?" I inched up an eyebrow.

"Uncle Happy?" Rikissa offered.

Mikaela tried to keep her lips together, but laughter pushed out, and in the next moment we were all laughing, the beautiful sound ringing in the chamber. As though sensing the laughter involved him, the cat stretched, jumped down, and waddled toward us.

"He approves," I remarked as the cat rubbed against my leg, drawing even more laughter.

Before I could offer another jest, the door swung open, and as it did so, the laughter trailed away, leaving a breath of tension in its place until Nanna stepped into the room. Then the smiles came back out, reminding me just how swiftly the mood could change. And just how dangerous my brother's house was.

I gave the cat a final pat before crossing to Nanna and enveloping her in a hug.

"Oh, Gunnar-boy." She wrapped me in her arms tenderly. The top of her head and the veil she wore over her graying hair only reached my chin. A petite woman like Mikaela, she'd always had more energy than someone double her size. "I was hoping I'd have the chance to see you this morn."

"Mikaela said you have a chill."

"Oh posh. I'm fine."

I could feel every bone of her ribs and every ridge of her spine through her garments. Even though she'd always been thin, she'd grown almost frail.

Nanna pulled back but held me in place, examining me from my head to my toes. Her warm eyes sparkled with delight, and I wish I'd made more of an effort to visit her over the past years. I could have, at the very least, come for a holiday. Instead, I'd accompanied my friends to their homes every time I'd been away from the king or court.

"You've grown."

"Yes, Mikaela has already informed me that my head is bigger." I tossed a grin her way.

But she'd turned her back on me and had resumed brushing Rikissa's hair.

Nanna's perusal ended with her gaze connecting with mine. Though her eyes remained welcoming, they also contained the same guarded warning as last time I'd seen her, when she'd sought me out to tell me that rumors were circulating about me and Mikaela being together.

"You cannot be seen with her again." Nanna's whisper had wobbled that dark night when she'd come to my chamber.

I'd wanted to protest. After kissing Mikaela at the hot spring earlier in the day, I'd had every intention of sneaking off to find her after everyone else was asleep for the night, hoping I could say farewell to her privately. I hadn't wanted to admit I was hoping I could claim another kiss, this one longer.

Nanna had grasped my arms and dug her fingers in. "Please, Gunnar. If you care about her, then you'll bring an end to the rumors. Tonight. Now."

The urgency in her voice had halted my easy dismissal of her suggestion.

"If Bernhard discovers she means something to you, he'll make her life miserable."

The harshly whispered words finally registered. And I'd known Nanna was right. I couldn't give Bernhard any reason to think Mikaela was special to me. He'd see how beautiful and vivacious she was. What if he ended up wanting her for himself? Or what if he used her, perhaps even harmed her, in order to make me do his bidding?

At the prospect, nausea had roiled around my stomach.

In all my interactions with her, I hadn't considered what might happen to her if Bernhard discovered my feelings. Instead, I'd been selfish, thinking only of the present.

"Promise you'll fix this and prove you aren't singling Mikaela out?" Nanna had asked.

I'd nodded, knowing exactly what I had to do to show Bernhard I had no lasting interest in Mikaela. I'd guessed the rumors would also eventually reach Mikaela. But I hadn't counted on her seeking me out and catching me in the middle of my charade. Once she had, I'd realized such a scene would prove to Bernhard even further that Mikaela meant nothing to me.

I only regretted I'd hurt Mikaela. Even though the hallway that night had been dark, there had been no hiding the confusion in her gasp and expression. I'd deserved her slap and her loathing, because I shouldn't have let my feelings for her cloud my judgment and put her in jeopardy in the first place.

Watching her stride stiffly away had been the hardest thing I'd ever done. I'd wanted to race after her and tell her the truth, that I hated myself for hurting her, that I would rather kiss her than anyone else, that I was only trying to keep her safe.

But I'd remained rooted to my spot, covering my stinging cheek, knowing it had to be the last contact I ever had with her.

Nanna had been wise to warn me then. And her warning now was every bit as wise.

Chapter
6

Gunnar

I AVOIDED MIKAELA FOR A TOTAL OF TWO DAYS.

I didn't plan to interact with her again, tried to keep busy with Torvald searching for the chalice, tried to remind myself of the peril I would bring to her if Bernhard learned of my feelings for her.

But I was too attuned to her presence, so that any time we were even remotely in the same area, I homed in on her as if she were the only one present. On the third morn, as I saddled my steed and readied to continue the search—which had, as usual, amounted to nothing—I watched Mikaela at the servants' entrance.

She stood talking with a younger woman, one who shared a family resemblance. I knew Mikaela had a large family, was the oldest child of five or six. She'd long ago lost her twin sister, and I guessed the maiden was one of her younger sisters, no doubt Kirstin, the closest in age to Mikaela.

Mikaela pushed a bowl into Kirstin's hands.

Kirstin shook her head and thrust the bowl back, but

Mikaela took a step away and folded her arms. The move only outlined all the more just how thin Mikaela was—almost as thin as Nanna.

I halted in tightening the cinch. . . .

Mikaela was giving away her food to her family. And so was Nanna.

In fact, I had no doubt the bowl was Mikaela's pottage, that she hadn't taken a bite of it and was instead making her sister eat it. And the wrapped bundle in her arm was probably most of her and Nanna's meal from the previous eve.

I straightened, anger shooting through me and stiffening my limbs. Mikaela and Nanna shouldn't have to choose between feeding themselves and caring for their family. But that's exactly what was happening and had likely been this way for weeks, since the stores from last harvest had run out.

The spring was always difficult, a hungering time. Until the vegetables began to grow, the villeins had little to eat from their own gardens and nothing to use for bartering at the market. They didn't have hunting or fishing rights—although some resorted to doing so illegally. If only they had the whole of Hardanger Forest at their disposal, they'd have an easier time surviving.

Shortly after arriving, I'd learned of Bernhard's plan to eliminate the jotunn who lived within the depths of the forest. While I agreed that it was past time to free the forest, especially for the poor people of Romsdal, I didn't like Bernhard's method of sending unarmed men to face the madman.

I'd wanted to offer Torvald's and my services instead. But Torvald had only shaken his head and kept me from rushing rashly into the forest. "We have an obligation to the king and queen first," he'd said. "Once we find the chalice, we can consider returning and assisting in killing the jotunn."

I'd reluctantly agreed with him, but now I couldn't stand back and do nothing while Mikaela and her family suffered from hunger.

As I stepped out of the shadows of the stables, a movement in the wide-open doorway of the forge nearby drew my attention. Holding a red-hot rod of steel, Frans was watching Mikaela and Kirstin too. He wore a long leather apron over his tunic, and his sleeves were rolled up to reveal his thickly muscled arms. Even at the early hour, his hair was already plastered to his head from the sweat and heat of the workshop.

How could Frans allow Mikaela to waste away from lack of nourishment? Why didn't he step in and do something to aid her?

His muscles flexed, and his eyes were dark beneath a furrowed brow.

Maybe he was helpless to change the situation. I suspected he'd probably already tried to convince Mikaela to take his daily rations. Knowing how stubborn Mikaela was, she'd never give in to him. But she would give in to me. I'd see to it.

I handed the reins of my steed to the nearest squire. "Tell Torvald I had an errand but shall be ready to go soon." I'd arrived at the stables early just so I could observe Mikaela from a distance without anyone realizing it. Even so, Torvald wouldn't mind waiting, especially once I informed him later that my delay had to do with *her*.

Of course, Torvald hadn't addressed the issue again. But I'd sensed him watching me keenly a time or two as though trying to understand what was going on in my head and why my eagerness of the first day had turned into avoidance.

I ducked out of the stables into the busy inner bailey. With servants drawing water, feeding livestock, and scrubbing laundry in the cool spring morn, I hoped to cross the yard without notice. But as with earlier when I'd made my appearance, all eyes turned my direction, even Mikaela's.

I wanted to glance at her with a smile or wink. But as I walked casually across the yard, I pretended not to notice her, just as I'd done on my way to the stables a short while ago. Once I disappeared within the confines of the castle, I sprinted forward, knowing I was taking a risk but not caring, not when Mikaela was suffering.

Bernhard stepped out of a stairwell, and we nearly collided. Taller than me by a few inches, he stumbled back and scowled, his eyes bloodshot, his hair unkempt, and his breath foul. From the rumpled condition of his leggings and tunic, he'd clearly just awoken and dragged himself out of bed without thought of grooming.

Though we both shared the same narrow build and thin features, his hair was lighter and his eyes a fairer blue than mine. He may have been handsome at one time, but the years of heavy imbibing had taken a toll.

He scowled at me. "Where are you going with such haste?"

I intended to return to the great hall and gather the fare I hadn't eaten, but telling Bernhard so would only arouse his suspicion. "Torvald and I are making ready to head out."

"And where will your little search take you today?"

I resented his condescending tone, one that indicated

he thought we were on a futile mission to find the chalice. If only we could have kept our business private as we had in the beginning. But with the weeks turning into months, more and more people had discovered we were seeking the chalice at the request of King Ansgar.

On the one hand, the openness of our quest had provided more clues as people came forward to give us hearsay or tips. On the other hand, we feared the renewed interest in the chalice had spurred others into hunting for it too. While we hadn't told anyone about the chalice's potential to heal, it was possible others already knew, and we didn't want it falling into the wrong hands—thieving gangs who might demand a high price in exchange for the relic, Ice Men who had threatened Queen Lis last autumn, or perhaps even spies working for King Canute.

We didn't think Rasmus was involved. The former Royal Sage hadn't been seen since he'd left Vordinberg after his scheming to harm King Ulrik and use the Sword of the Magi to put someone of his choosing on the Norvegian throne.

At first, we'd suspected Rasmus was hiding in Norvegia and was perhaps still plotting to take the throne from Ansgar. But over recent weeks since the ports had begun to open, we'd heard rumors Rasmus was in Swaine and had offered his wisdom to King Canute.

Whatever the case might be, Torvald and I had to find the chalice before anyone else did and especially before we were called away to fight another battle against King Canute.

"We are interviewing more priests at the abbey today." I offered Bernhard my standard answer. So far, we'd learned the chalice had been stored in the

Stavekirche for a number of years, but that at some point it had been moved. The question was whether it had been moved within Romsdal or elsewhere in Norvegia. Our hope was that one of the priests might be able to provide information to point us in the right direction.

"Did Father ever mention the chalice being in Romsdal?" I asked. If it had ever been in his safekeeping, what had he known about it? Had he guessed that it had the power to bring about healing?

Bernhard finished a noisy yawn. "He never spoke of it to me."

"What about our grandfather Jorg?" I'd never met our grandfather, but Bernhard had been a lad when Grandfather was still alive. "Did he have any tales of the relic?"

"None that I remember." His tone took on a bored note, and he started on his way, obviously finished with the conversation.

Our grandfather had been as renowned for his cruelty as our father. Apparently Jorg had only become the earl because his older brother Sven had died in a fire.

"Is it possible they would have stored it in the chapel here?"

"No, it's not here." Bernhard stopped, and his statement came out much too rapidly, containing an edge that almost sounded like a warning.

"I didn't think it was." I shrugged and started on my way now too, needing him to think I believed him. "If so, you would have found it by now."

Even as I projected a carefree spirit, my mind was already at work, piecing together Bernhard's reaction. Although he'd invited us to stay at Likness Castle, his response just now revealed that he felt threatened by the search. Perhaps he knew where the chalice was or already had it in his possession. Perhaps he hoped that by entertaining Torvald and me, he could distract us and keep us from prying too deeply.

Bernhard didn't linger in the passageway but hurried away. I did likewise and entered the great hall, returning to the table where I'd left my unfinished platter.

I had to find a way to explore the castle and talk to the servants without Bernhard being the wiser. The question was *how*?

Chapter 7

Mikaela

"Enok is growing impatient," Kirstin said softly as she finished scraping the last drop of pottage from the bowl.

"Tell him that soon enough we'll have plenty." I drew my cloak closer against the morning chill and pressed my stomach. I couldn't chance my sister hearing the rumbles of hunger lest she refuse to take the bundle of food home to the others. The only reason she ate the pottage was because she assumed it was an extra and didn't know it was mine.

But the cook, under strict guidelines from the castle steward, only allowed each of us a certain portion of food every day. I understood. If he didn't ration, then servants would take freely to give to their families, many of whom were suffering just like mine.

"He'll sneak away one night while we're asleep." Kirstin ran her finger over the bottom of the bowl. "And when we awaken, we'll find that he's gone to the earl and pledged to kill the jotunn."

At seventeen, our younger brother was volatile and impetuous. I feared he would run off to fight the jotunn more than I feared Frans would. I stuck my hand in my pocket and fingered the special shell, and my thoughts turned to Maiken's death. How could we bear another loss? "You can't let him."

"Father's forbidden him from going." Kirstin licked her finger. "But I don't know how he'll stop Enok."

My sister and I shared the same brown hair color and had similar brown eyes, but beyond that we were different in almost every way. Whereas I was petite and had more pointed and delicate features, she was tall and broad and sturdy. I was practical and level-headed, while she was easily swayed and emotional. I was responsible and self-reliant, but she needed others to keep her steady.

"If only the earl hadn't issued the challenge," I said wistfully. Perhaps the earl had known the hunger of his villeins would drive them to desperation this spring and make them more willing to sacrifice their lives.

"And Frans?" Kirstin glanced again toward the forge doorway. Moments ago, Frans had been obser-ving us, but he was no longer there. The red sparks flying in the air and clanking from inside meant he was hard at work again.

Gunnar had also been sneaking looks our way as he'd saddled his horse. Ever since he'd stepped outside and walked to the stables, I'd been keenly aware of his presence, as if my body had a special sensory organ that was made specially to detect him. Of course, I'd attempted to shut it down, block Gunnar out, and ignore him completely.

But when he'd crossed back into the castle, my

traitorous gaze had followed him anyway. And my traitorous heart had skipped faster, as if trying to get me to chase after him. I was much too desperate for a smile, for a teasing comment, for even just a word. In fact, ever since he'd come to the nursery the day after his arrival, I'd been waiting to see him again, secretly hoping he'd return.

Every time the nursery door opened, my skin tingled with anticipation, only to feel cold when he didn't come. I berated myself for how easily I was distracted by thoughts of him. And I spent the majority of my time reminding myself of the reasons why I had to ignore him. What other reason did I need besides the most obvious one—that I'd found him locked in the embrace of another woman and kissing her?

Of course, he'd never made pledges or promises to me that long-ago summer. He'd been free to embrace and kiss any woman he wanted. But I supposed more than anything, I'd been confused . . . and maybe still was over why he'd seemed sincere and genuinely interested in me and why he'd spent so much time seeking me out, when it hadn't meant anything to him.

"Frans," Kirstin persisted. "He hasn't mentioned accepting the challenge again, has he?"

I'd told Kirstin about Frans's desire to take the earl's challenge, and now I wished I hadn't so that she didn't have to worry about both Enok and Frans. "I'll watch out for Frans, and you look after Enok. We'll appoint ourselves their guardian angels."

Just the mention of angels took me back to Gunnar squatting in front of Riki and Rena, calling them angels. Seeing a strong knight like Gunnar lower himself and speak to them so sweetly had melted my insides.

No. I gave myself a mental slap. I couldn't think of Gunnar. I had to dwell on Frans. I needed to fall in love with him. I closed my eyes, pictured my dear friend, and attempted to feel love for him. But as with all the other times I'd tried over the past few days to evoke any heat, I couldn't do so. Not only wasn't there a spark, there wasn't any fuel either.

Kirstin finished cleaning the bowl and handed it back to me. I passed her the bundle of food to take with her to the thatched cottage my family lived in on the outskirts of Romsdal with the other villeins who farmed the lord's land.

She lingered only a few minutes longer before going on her way. As much as I enjoyed her visits every morn, I worried about her traveling about on her own. But she insisted on coming rather than sending Enok in her stead.

With a final wave, I retreated down the steps and to the lower level where the kitchen and storage rooms were located. The scent of herbs and vegetables and venison in a stew filled the passageway, and I faltered feeling suddenly dizzy. I stopped and braced myself against the wall.

The door of the storage room beside me swung open. I started forward, not wanting to be caught lingering lest anyone accuse me of trying to steal from the stores. But before I could make it past, a hand reached out, caught my arm, and began to drag me out of the hallway.

I jerked to free myself, and in the same instant I caught sight of Gunnar with a finger pressed against his lips cautioning me to remain silent. I ceased my struggling and allowed him to pull me into the room.

He closed the door behind us, and darkness would have encompassed us if not for the candle resting on a nearby barrel, illuminating a platter filled with all manner of meats and cheeses and breads.

I salivated just glimpsing it and rapidly turned my attention to him instead. "Are you making it your mission to scare me to death?"

I waited for a witty comeback, for his ready grin, for him to tease me about how easy I was to sneak up on. But his beautiful face was more serious than I'd ever seen it before. "No, I'm making it my mission to ensure that you have enough sustenance that you'll live."

"As you can see, I'm living." I reached for the door handle, unwilling to subject myself to his pity or the reminder of the difference in our stations.

He stepped more fully in front of the door and leaned against it. "You're giving your family almost all your food and leaving nothing for yourself."

"I don't need much." I lifted my chin and glared at him. "Now please step aside. I need to return to the nursery."

"Not until you eat some of the food I brought you." In the windowless room with only the light of the candle, his dark blue eyes were almost black. How could I resist, even if I wanted to?

I swayed.

"When's the last time you had something?" His voice was gruff even as he steadied me gently.

"Yesterday for supper. But I'm fine."

He growled something under his breath, then guided me toward the platter. "Eat."

I stared down at the food. I couldn't eat it, could I?

Doing so would only humiliate me and put me in his debt. "I can't."

He picked up one of the slices of cheese and held it against my lips. "Good, then you give me no choice but to feed you myself, which I shall gladly do."

"I don't want to be beholden—" As I opened my mouth to speak, he inserted the cheese. In doing so, his fingers brushed my lips.

The contact was brief, but it was enough to cause lightning to sizzle along my lips and throughout my body. I was too aware of the sparks to taste anything. Even so, I chewed and swallowed.

"Ready for more?" He lifted another wedge of cheese.

I reached up to take the piece from him. As much as I wanted to go on all morning letting him touch my lips, I couldn't. In fact, being anywhere near him was a big mistake.

"I can feed myself—" Before I could get the words out, he slid more cheese in, his fingers lingering on my lips longer this time.

I fumbled for his hand, needing to take the cheese away, needing to break free of his touch.

"Let me—" I murmured, but even then, he gave me another bite.

His lips twitched upward with the beginning of a smile.

"This isn't humorous—"

He shoveled in more. "You're making this easier than I anticipated."

"Stop."

He squeezed in the last of the cheese, his smile widening. "Keep on talking, and I'll have you fed in no time."

I wanted to say more, but I had to put a halt to his feeding me. It was much too intimate. As he raised a chunk of ham to my lips, I snagged it from him and popped the whole thing in.

"That's a good girl." He retrieved a slice of thick bread from the platter.

I glared at him but took the offering, all the while fighting against the need to cram it in my mouth ravenously. I would only get sick if I ate too quickly. I had to give my empty stomach proper time to adjust to having food in it.

"If anyone discovers you've given me this," I said between bites, "I'll get into trouble."

"It was the remainder of my meal, and I can do with it as I see fit."

I studied his face in the candlelight, solemn but irresistible. I swallowed my mouthful. "Why are you doing this for me?"

He picked up another piece of cheese. "I saw you giving your food to your sister and realized why you and Nanna are so hungry."

"What is it you expect of me in return? To become your next conquest?"

His head snapped up, and his eyes rounded. "What? No. Absolutely not. I expect nothing in return. Nothing."

"Then why?" I held his gaze, needing to know the truth.

He didn't look away. Instead, something smoldered in the depths of his eyes, something that reached out to stoke the embers inside me that I'd long tried to douse with anger.

As the warmth fanned to life inside me, I fought

against it. "Don't," I whispered.

"Don't what?" he whispered back.

I didn't want him stirring up longing that could never be requited. But I couldn't say that. "Don't . . . don't hurt me again."

He dropped his gaze away, letting his lashes fall. "I'm sorry for hurting you before. I didn't want to. But I had to do it."

"Had to do what?" Involve himself with another woman and reject me?

He shook his head curtly. "I promise I'll be careful not to hurt you."

"Thank you." Even though I wanted to hang on to my resentment, it was past time to forgive him and move forward. Besides, I'd heard rumors he and Torvald were searching for the sacred chalice on behalf of the king and queen. They would only stay until the clues took them elsewhere.

"We can be friends, can we not?" His voice contained a note of hope. "I loathe being your enemy."

I finished eating the piece of ham. I didn't have to remain his enemy. But could I really allow friendship to flourish between us? Would that be as dangerous for my heart as allowing attraction to grow? After all, what would stop friendship from overreaching, like runaway vines, twisting and turning and sliding beyond the fences set in place?

"How long will you be in Romsdal?" I asked.

"Another week. Two at most."

I wasn't disappointed at so short a time. Surely not. 'Twas as I'd thought. We wouldn't have many opportunities to interact with how busy we would both be. Conceding to friendship wouldn't harm anything.

"Then I agree to move from enemies to friends. But under two conditions."

He raked his fingers through his overlong hair, lifting it off his forehead and combing it back. I'd watched him do so many times in the past, and now as then, it made me want to comb my fingers there for myself. I'd never done so. But I'd certainly dreamed about it. I had no doubt his hair would flow through my fingers like fine silk.

He started to drop his hand, but then dragged it through his hair again, this time more slowly. "Condition number one?"

As I tore my gaze from his hair, his smug smile told me he'd noticed my reaction to his combing. It was the kind of smile that only made him look more roguish and appealing.

Heavens above. Already I was crossing the bounds of friendship. I shook my head. This wasn't going to work.

Before I could protest, he laughed lightly. "Friendship, Mikaela. That's all."

"Do you vow it?"

"Yes. And I accept your two conditions."

"You don't know them yet."

"I covet your friendship enough to do whatever you wish."

A thrill whispered through me, one I needed to silence. Friendship didn't involve thrills blowing through me, not even in small increments, especially not when I needed to make myself fall in love with Frans. "Very well. Condition number one: do not cross the line." I sliced the air between us.

Gunnar studied the space as though examining a

real line. "Am I allowed to do this?" He poked a finger through the boundary.

I swatted his hand. "No."

"This?" He shifted his boot under the imaginary boundary.

"Absolutely not." I couldn't contain a smile even as I toed his foot.

"Then I suppose you won't accept this either." He leaned closer, his shoulder dipping toward me.

I folded my arms and took a step away to keep from shoving him. I'd just informed him we couldn't touch. Maybe not in those exact words. But that's what *not crossing the line* meant. We had to keep our hands to ourselves.

He folded his arms, imitating me. "Condition number two?"

"If you're already testing condition number one, is there any hope you'll follow a second one?"

He shrugged and offered me a disarming smile, one that would have power to make a judge pardon any crime.

Nonetheless, I pressed on. "Condition number two: promise to tell your nieces a bedtime story every night while you're here."

Gunnar was a natural-born storyteller. When we were children, I'd loved listening to him invent tales. He had a way of embellishing the things that happened to him, making everything seem funnier and more absurd than it really was. After watching Riki and Rena come to life the other morn, I wanted them to have more time with their uncle. And they'd been asking about whether Gunnar would visit them again.

"A bedtime story? Every night?"

"You're right. What am I thinking? Such a feat would be much too strenuous for you." I loved taunting him.

From a new smile tugging at his lips, I guessed he loved my taunting too. "I may be rusty, but I think I can manage."

"You obviously won their hearts, though I don't know how." I did know how. It was the same way he won every female's heart everywhere he went. He was charming and sweet and funny.

"I'm glad I've won their hearts. If only I could as easily win yours." The playfulness of his tone and the twinkling in his eyes warned me not to take his words too seriously. Even so, I was half-tempted to tell him he had easily won my heart the last time he'd been home. And from the runaway tempo in my chest at the moment, he seemed to be winning my heart again.

I had to go. I started to tuck the remains of the piece of bread into my pocket.

"No." Gunnar's protest came out a growl. "Eat it now so that I can make sure you don't give it away to someone else."

I planned to offer it to Nanna, although I was certain she'd suggest saving it for the family. I lifted my chin and slid it the rest of the way into my pocket.

"Very well." Gunnar grabbed another piece of bread from the platter and handed it to me. "Then eat this."

My stomach gurgled with need, and I couldn't resist eating the slice while Gunnar wrapped the rest of the food on the platter into a towel.

He pressed it into my arms, and the stern set of his jaw warned me not to reject his offering. "I'll see you tonight for your story time."

"It's not for me. . . ."

He was already out the door and striding down the passageway without looking back. All I could do was stare after him. One week. Maybe two. And he'd walk out of my life again. I couldn't forget that.

Chapter 8

Mikaela

For the first time in weeks, my stomach wasn't gnawing with hunger. Gunnar's provisions earlier in the day had filled me up, and I'd had more energy throughout the afternoon and eve as a result.

Sitting on the bedframe, I bent and placed a goodnight kiss on little Rena's forehead then leaned over and kissed Riki before folding the coverlet around them more snuggly.

"When will Uncle Gunnar be here?" Rena peered at me with sad eyes.

I glanced to the chamber door again, wishing now I hadn't told the girls Gunnar was coming to see them and give them a story. But after his gift of food that I'd shared with Nanna, I'd expected him to keep his word. He'd been so kind and concerned and generous that we'd even had enough to save for Kirstin to take back to the family on the morrow.

Nanna hadn't been as happy to receive the food as I'd expected. And when she'd learned Gunnar planned to come to the nursery to say goodnight to Riki and Rena, she'd shaken her head and told me it was a bad idea.

Now she sat quietly in a chair by the hearth, her eyes closed. I'd explained she didn't need to stay, that she could go to bed as she usually did while I finished the evening routine with the two girls. But she'd insisted on being present in the room when Gunnar was there.

"I can tell you a tale." I brushed back the pale strands of Rena's hair.

"We've heard all your stories already." Riki stuck out her lip petulantly. At six, she was developing a stubbornness that I prayed I could yet curb.

"Then perhaps you can tell one to me tonight?"

Riki hesitated, but before she could give me an answer, the door swung open, and Gunnar stepped in, brightening the room immediately with his confidence and charm. His grin, his swagger, and his debonair garments only added to his attractiveness.

As Riki and Rena sat up, they watched him with an awe and excitement that reflected mine.

"How are all my favorite girls?" Gunnar's gaze landed upon the two in bed first before hopping to me then Nanna, who was now sitting forward, eyes open and smiling at the boy she'd raised.

Gunnar strode directly to Nanna, holding something behind his back. "I have something for you."

She sat forward. "I don't need anything but your sweet presence, Gunnar-boy."

He removed one hand and held out a small bowl filled to the brim with rich custard and drizzled with a purple sauce.

I gasped at the beauty of the sight.

Before Nanna could protest, Gunnar placed the bowl in her lap. "For you."

Then he turned his attention upon me and pulled his other hand out from behind his back to reveal a dish identical to the first.

I couldn't contain a second gasp or the delight that rushed through me. Riki and Rena mimicked my gasp, peering at Gunnar with an adoration that would have made me laugh if I hadn't been so stunned.

He wasted no time in crossing to the bed and delivering the second bowl to me. "And this is for you."

For me? Surely not. The mound of fluffy cream topped with what appeared to be a sugary plum sauce was the kind of food served to nobility and royalty, not a poor bondservant like me. "How? Where? I can't—"

"Torvald and I had no appetite for the dessert." Gunnar looked from Nanna to me, his happiness contagious. "I wanted you both to have them."

He fumbled in his doublet pocket before pulling out two spoons.

"This is very generous of you, Gunnar-boy." Nanna accepted the spoon but hesitated to put it in.

When Gunnar distributed the spoon to me, I had no such hesitations. I delved in and scooped up a mound into my mouth. As the delicacy flowed over my tongue, I closed my eyes and released a half-sigh, half-groan of pleasure.

I savored the soft texture, the tartness of the sauce, and the sweetness of the custard. When the bite melted and was gone, I opened my eyes to find Gunnar watching me with such stark wanting that my stomach did a strange and unexpected flip.

I slowly removed the spoon from my mouth and dipped it into the custard with more reservation this time. All the while, Gunnar watched my lips, causing my insides to somersault several more times.

"We've been waiting for a story, Uncle Gunnar." Riki kicked off her covers and started to scoot over, dragging Rena to make room for Gunnar next to them.

Gunnar finally tore his attention from me and glanced at the little girls as if he'd forgotten they were in the room. "Story?"

"Yes, for bedtime." Riki patted the spot beside her.

"Methinks we have all the entertainment we need watching Mikaela eat her custard."

Spoon in my mouth, I sucked every morsel from the second bite and held back another groan. I was making a spectacle of myself, but I didn't care. I'd never had such a treat before, and I wanted to relish every second of it.

Nanna cleared her throat loudly. She glanced between Gunnar and me, lines grooved into her forehead.

The look seemed to act like a prod to Gunnar's backside, and he stepped up to the bed. "I promised a story, and a story I shall deliver."

I stood, fighting the desire to crawl in next to my charges and let Gunnar tell me a tale too.

"Is that a good idea, Gunnar-boy?" Nanna had yet to take a bite of her custard.

I was nearly face to face with Gunnar.

His gaze affixed upon the spoon trapped between my lips. "I promise I won't stay long. My story is short." A smoldering in his eyes made my breath snag.

What was this happening between us? Was he thinking about my lips? About kissing me? Surely not.

"Let's make it very short." Nanna's voice was thin with worry.

It was becoming clearer by the second that Nanna didn't want Gunnar in the room. Was that why she'd waited here with me? So she could chase him away as quickly as possible?

My spine stiffened with the need to show her that we had nothing to fear from Gunnar, that he was a blessing to us. But I respected Nanna too much to defy her in any way.

I ducked my head and skirted around Gunnar.

"The story is for you, too, Mikaela." His tone was tinged with teasing, as though he sensed my inner conflict and knew I was putting distance between us. "It's about a daring knight who came upon a beautiful huldra in the forest."

Was he insinuating that he was the knight and I the woodland fairy? I didn't dare turn around and subject myself to any more of his charm and read an ulterior meaning in his expression. My heart was already beating too fast. If I looked at him again with his winsome smile and beckoning eyes, the pace of my heartbeat would surely send me into a faint.

"I already know how that story ends." I managed to walk calmly away.

The ropes holding up the mattress squeaked as Gunnar flopped onto the bed beside the girls. He grunted playfully, and they giggled, enjoying every second of his attention. If only their own father loved them and wanted to be with them. But Bernhard had never visited the girls in the nursery, not once in their short lives. Sofia came occasionally, but even then, she didn't stay long and was usually distracted.

"Eat, Nanna," I admonished as I lowered myself to the bench across from her and took another bite of my custard.

She stared down at her dish, untouched.

Gunnar had started his story, his voice as animated as I'd remembered. I chanced a glance toward the bed to the sight of his nieces curled against him, one under each arm. His broad shoulders were relaxed, his head back against the headboard, his long legs stretched out and crossed at the ankles, as comfortable as if he'd been telling stories to little girls his whole life.

My insides twisted with a strange need I hadn't wanted to acknowledge before, but that had been there regardless—the need to have my own babies. I wanted them to have a father just like Gunnar who didn't shy away from showing them attention, who cherished the women in his life.

Would Frans be that kind of father?

The question popped into my thoughts unbidden. Yes, Frans would be a good husband and father. Of that I had no doubt. But I could never picture him crawling into bed with our children, snuggling with them, and telling them stories.

Not that Frans needed to do that. . . .

I focused on my custard, savoring another bite. Frans was as different from Gunnar as pottage was from custard. While pottage might be bland at times, it was sturdy and filling and a hearty meal. Custard might be sweet, but it wouldn't provide sustenance for a lifetime, was instead a special treat, here today and gone tomorrow.

All the more reason why I needed to keep my attention upon Frans and work on loving him, so that I could speak the words to him honestly and gain the bride price money by the time Gunnar was ready to leave Romsdal.

Nanna finally slipped her spoon into the custard and lifted a small bite into her mouth. Was she worried someone would catch us eating food that wasn't ours? As she ate it and swallowed, I offered what I hoped was an encouraging smile. "Don't worry. Gunnar will keep us safe."

She nodded but didn't smile in return. "I hope you're right, Mikaela-girl. I hope you're right."

I couldn't have asked for a more perfect night, sitting next to the warmth of the fire, eating custard, and listening to Gunnar spin a tale about an enchanting huldra, a daring and brave woman who helped the knight escape from a troll who'd locked him away as his prisoner.

As the tale came to an end, Gunnar tickled and teased the girls, and I wasn't able to stop smiling as I watched them together. Their girly voices mingled with Gunnar's deep one. Their delicate faces were wreathed with delight below his tender one, their light blond heads contrasting with his dark hair. The sight left me nearly breathless with more of the strange need.

When Nanna squeezed my arm and asked me to go to the kitchen to retrieve a cup of warm mead to ease the aching in her chest, I left reluctantly. And even though I hurried, by the time I returned, Gunnar was gone, along with all traces of the custard.

Chapter 9

GUNNAR

Torvald finished reading the missive then let it fall to the floor while burying his face in his hands.

"Well?" I crossed to him and propped my foot on the bench beside him. At the early morning hour, neither of us had finished dressing and wore naught but our tunics and leggings.

Our chambers were next door to each other, and when a messenger had arrived breathless and disheveled from riding all night to deliver a letter to Torvald, I'd barged into his room. Only bad news came with such great haste, and I wanted to be present for my friend as the blow felled him.

My muscles tensed at the waiting. I wasn't by nature a patient man, but I forced myself to let Torvald tell me when he was ready.

The light of dawn making its way through the open window touched upon his bent head, highlighting his dejection. The air was cold, but in the months of traveling together, I'd learned Torvald preferred the cold and liked to slumber with his window open as oft as possible.

"'Tis news from home." His voice was so low I could hardly hear him.

"Your father?" Torvald rarely shared personal information about his family, but I knew enough. His father was frail and growing ever weaker, and a rift existed in the father-son relationship although I wasn't sure why. "Is he worse?"

Torvald released a sigh that was laden with immense sorrow. "'Tis a sickness of mind."

My thoughts spun back to the condition of King Ulrik last autumn when his mental faculties had deteriorated. The king had acted irrationally, impulsively, and put himself and the kingdom in danger. Was Torvald's father making rash decisions now too?

"He has called me home." Torvald spoke as if he'd been issued a death sentence.

I wanted to blurt out that Torvald need only write back and tell his father he was too busy, that he was on an important mission for the king. But again, I waited, wanting to support Torvald in whatever decision he made without putting undue pressure upon him.

"I am to leave with all haste."

"Do you want to go?"

"I have no choice in the matter."

"Then I shall go with you."

"No." Torvald sat up. "This will take two weeks. We cannot delay the search that long."

After a sennight of hunting for the chalice in Romsdal, we were no closer to finding it than we'd been when we first arrived. We'd eliminated almost every possible hiding place in the city and surrounding countryside. The only area we'd yet to scour was Likness Castle. But I hadn't discovered a way to probe without drawing my brother's attention and censure.

"While you're gone, I can stay and investigate the castle as best I'm able." I'd have to ingratiate myself to Bernhard, perhaps stay with him through the long hours of revelry and trick him into saying more than he normally would. I might even have to resort to searching in the dark of the night after Bernhard and the rest of the guests retired.

Torvald stood suddenly and paced to the window.

"So two weeks?" I asked. "Will that be sufficient for you to tend to your father?"

Torvald stared outside, his back rigid. "A fortnight will be sufficient . . . for me to wed the woman of my father's choosing."

"Wed?" I released a short laugh. "You're jesting."

"I wish I was. But I must get married to save the Wahlburg estate from ruination."

Whistling my surprise, I lowered myself to the bench. As the firstborn and only son, Torvald would someday inherit his father's lands and title. But as a man of twenty and five, Torvald was still young and had put his whole heart into serving the king. He'd made no secret he wasn't ready for marriage.

"My father has emptied the coffers and turned the family fortune into nothing." Torvald's tone was again low, but this time bitterness laced it.

"So, he would have you marry into wealth to replenish the fortune?"

"Yes."

What would this mean for Torvald as a Knight of Brethren? No rules existed preventing the elite knights from marrying. But the unspoken standard was that upon marriage, the knight would retire from the honored position. I couldn't imagine the Brethren without Torvald. He'd become more than just a fellow knight. He'd become my closest friend.

"I will not abandon this mission for the king." Torvald spun, his feet spread, anger hardening his features. "I will go home and do my duty. But then I shall return and continue our search until we find the chalice."

"'Tis a reasonable enough request to make of your father and new bride."

As a coveted Knight of Brethren and close companion to the king, Torvald was in a position to claim any woman he wanted. Clearly, his father had taken advantage of Torvald's popularity to secure a woman with a large dowry. His marriage would be more of a business arrangement than anything.

"Do you know the woman he has chosen for you?"

Torvald blew out a tense breath. "No, and 'tis of no significance to me."

I wouldn't be able to stand where Torvald was and enter into a marriage with a woman I neither knew nor cared about. Fortunately for me, as the second son, I didn't have the same pressure to make a good match. Yes, Bernhard had spoken several nights ago about trying to find me a wealthy and comely bride, but I'd jested with him about not wanting to settle down yet with just one woman.

He'd sneered and remarked that I didn't need to worry about settling down with just one woman, even after I was married. I'd laughed at his remark, but inside I'd been sick. The truth was, when I was finally ready to wed, I wanted to remain faithful and true to my wife, loving and serving her above all others. Unlike Bernhard, I intended to honor my marriage vows and the marriage bed forever.

Bernhard had thrown out several suggestions, maidens from especially wealthy families. He'd even offered to invite the families to visit Likness Castle in an effort to begin arrangements. But he hadn't pushed me overly hard. He wasn't ready yet to sever my connection with the king and the renown it brought. My rise to fame had elevated his status too, so that he'd been given a place on the Noble Council that convened several times a year in Vordinberg to discuss important matters of the country.

Regardless, I'd already decided not to enlist Bernhard's assistance with finding a spouse. I would find the right person on my own.

My mind jumped back to the past three nights in the nursery, sneaking Nanna and Mikaela food and desserts and telling stories to my nieces. That part of my day had become my favorite. In fact, even now, I was counting down the hours until I could see them again. I couldn't deny the time with them was something I wanted as a part of my future.

But I didn't allow myself to dwell too long on such thoughts. Mikaela wasn't someone I could ever have in my future. As a bondservant, she belonged to my brother. And even if I offered to purchase her, I feared what Bernhard would do to her if he learned of my interest in her.

In fact, I was already bringing too much attention her way, which was why I had to cease going to the nursery every night. Even though I'd promised Mikaela I would tell bedtime stories, Nanna had warned me again last eve that not only were the servants starting to talk but Rikissa and Renate had told Sofia I was visiting. It was only a matter of time before everyone saw past my blustering to realize I cared for Mikaela.

Deep inside I knew what I had to do. I needed to sever the ties with her just like I'd done the last time I was home. The best way to do that was to give Frans the money so he could pay the bride price. What did it matter if Mikaela loved him or not? She needed to marry him to be safe. The sooner the better, especially since I was unable to keep my distance from her.

"I pray you will find some happiness in your marriage," I finally said to Torvald. "You deserve it."

He gave a sharp nod. "I shall be back."

"And I'll be waiting for you."

I helped Torvald and his squires pack and ready their mounts. By mid-morning as I watched them leave through the castle gates, I couldn't shake a strange foreboding that perhaps I wouldn't see Torvald again.

After he disappeared from sight, I squared my shoulders and braced myself for what I should have done all along. I had to sever all ties with Mikaela and tell her I couldn't come any more to the nursery.

I rounded the keep into the gardens at the rear, knowing that's where I'd find Mikaela and the girls. I wasn't embarrassed that I already had their daily schedule and routine nearly memorized. I loved that whenever I thought about her, I could picture where she was and what she was doing.

Getting fresh air in the gardens every morn was an important part of her routine with her charges. As I came upon the stone benches and walkways closest to the castle, I searched amongst the raised vegetable and herb beds as well as the raised flower beds. Most of the greenery had only just sprouted. The gardener had to cover the sensitive shoots every night to protect them from frost. Even so, the plants were hardy and able to survive the harsh conditions—much like the villeins who lived on the land.

The dozens of fruit trees beyond the raised beds were beginning to blossom. Likewise, the raspberry, gooseberry, and red currant shrubs were flowering, and as a result, a sweet heaviness permeated the air.

Near a fountain in the center of the fruit trees, I glimpsed Rikissa, her face down in her hands as though she was silently crying.

I hastened my steps, and as I drew nearer, I realized she wasn't crying but was instead counting. At my approach, she paused and peeked up through her fingers at me. "Good day, Uncle. We are playing hide-and-seek. Would you like to join us?"

"Of course I would, Angel." I scanned the woodland and spotted Rena squatting behind a too-narrow tree trunk. But I couldn't find Mikaela anywhere.

"I'll give you thirty more seconds to hide." Rikissa dropped her head back down and covered her eyes. "One, two, three . . ."

I bounded off, scrutinizing the gardens again. The door of the tool shed was slightly ajar. Since the gardener was nowhere in sight and wouldn't have left the door open in his absence, I guessed that Mikaela was hiding there.

I veered toward it and slipped inside. The shadows were dark, but I easily spotted her.

"What are you doing?" she hissed.

Crowded with shovels and rakes and hoes, baskets and barrels, crocks of seeds, trays of seedlings, and much more, the floor space hardly had room for Mikaela, much less a full-grown man like myself.

Nevertheless, I pushed in, our bodies nearly touching. "Rikissa invited me to play your game."

"You can't hide in here with me." She shifted but bumped into a barrel.

"Why not?" My eyes began to adjust to the darkness, broken by the sliver of light coming in through the crack in the door.

"You need to find your own hiding place."

"I like this one."

"But I was here first."

Rikissa called out that she was beginning her search. I pressed a finger to Mikaela's lips to silence her.

At the touch she froze. Her only motion was to draw in a quick breath.

But it was enough to awaken every nerve in my body to the realization that she was close enough that I could feel the tickle of her hair against my chin and the graze of her chest against mine.

The air inside the shed suddenly felt hot, like the middle of summer without a breeze. I was unable to take my finger away from the soft curves of her lips, unable to step back, unable to form a coherent thought save one— she was the most vivid and beautiful woman in the world. I wanted nothing more than to trace every one of her features.

At the tremble of her lips, I gave in to the need. Gently, I started at her chin and drew a line up her cheek.

She didn't bat my hand away as I expected. Instead, she remained absolutely still, almost as if she was waiting for more.

Taking courage from her lack of protest, I skimmed her forehead, then traced her delicate eyebrows before caressing her nose.

Her lashes fell as though she relished my touch.

Did she? Was it possible I had the power to affect her the same way she did me?

A faint warning sounded at the back of my mind, but I ignored it, letting my fingers go where they wanted. And they wanted to trace her other cheek down to her chin before returning to her lips.

As I let myself graze her bottom lip, she parted her mouth. At the gush of warmth, my gut clenched with sudden and intense desire. I wanted to kiss her more than I wanted anything else in life. And from the increased tempo of her breathing, I could sense she wanted it too.

What harm could come of sharing a brief kiss here in the shed? No one would have to know. It would satisfy our curiosity. It would sate our longing. It might even bring an end to the undercurrent that had been building between us. Because ultimately, that was where this attraction had been leading all along, wasn't it? The inevitable culmination in a kiss?

With the pad of my thumb, I brushed her lip again. Then before I could rationalize what I was doing, I cupped her cheek. My other hand was already circling around the back of her neck, drawing her closer. In the same instant, I lowered my mouth to hers.

As our lips meshed, she released a murmuring. I paused, unwilling to continue if she objected in the slightest. In that brief instant, her hands slid up my chest, and her fingers dug into my tunic all while she pressed her mouth more fully against mine.

Her return kiss was the permission I needed to keep going. I released the latch on the longing I'd tried to keep shuttered away, and I melded my lips to hers. Time and space ceased to exist. All that mattered was this woman in my arms and the passion we shared.

As I deepened the kiss, she murmured again, and this time I knew it to be her pleasure. The sound, though soft, barreled into me, tied me up, and rendered me her prisoner. I was hers and could never belong to anyone else.

Why had I waited so long for this? Why had I ever resisted?

The squeak of hinges interrupted my haze, and bright sunlight spilled over me.

"Found you!" came a girlish voice.

Mikaela broke the kiss and shoved against me, releasing me and scrambling away from me in one swift motion.

I wanted to cling to her, wanted to groan out my frustration and need, wanted to slam the door shut and keep on kissing.

But Mikaela was already sidling past me.

Rikissa and Renate were both standing in the open doorway peering up at us.

"Do you have a hurt, Mikaela?" Renate asked, her eyes wide as she took in Mikaela's flushed face.

"No, love. I'm just fine." Her voice was breathless as she stepped outside.

No doubt about it. I'd made her feel something toward me. And I wanted to do it again.

"Then why was Uncle Gunnar kissing you if you don't have a hurt—"

Mikaela cupped a hand over the little girl's mouth. "Shhh. . . ."

Following Mikaela out of the shed, I couldn't hold back a smile. "Actually, Mikaela does have a *hurt*, and I'm guessing it will need tending again. Soon."

The girls glanced between the two of us.

Mikaela shook her head, avoiding eye contact with me. "Don't listen to Uncle Gunnar. He's just being silly—" Her attention locked in on someone standing at the edge of the gardens near the keep.

Frans.

He held himself rigidly, and the dark scowl above eyes radiating with pain said it all: he'd witnessed our kissing.

Wearing his blacksmith apron and holding tools in both hands, it was clear he'd come from the forge. But for what purpose? Had he followed me after I'd said farewell to Torvald? Had he suspected I'd been on a mission to find Mikaela?

What had my mission been in the first place? Hadn't I planned to tell her I would give her the money for the bride price regardless of whether she loved Frans? What had happened to my good intentions?

I held back a sigh, reality rushing in and rattling me. I'd been a fool to give leave to my impulsiveness. I thought I'd gotten better over recent years in learning self-control and being a stronger and better man.

Apparently, I was still weak when it came to Mikaela.

She released Renate and straightened, watching Frans with ever-widening eyes. What was she thinking? That she'd made a mistake in kissing me? That she'd hurt Frans? That now he wouldn't marry her?

I wanted to remind her again that Frans wasn't right for her. But I honestly couldn't think of any man who would be right for Mikaela. Except me.

My stomach churned with unease. I was being selfish. As usual. And I was undermining Mikaela's happiness and future with a good man. Frans might not be perfect for her. But he was the best option. It had been easy to see how much he loved her and that he'd do anything for her. They would live out their days working at Likness and finding happiness together. Who was I to stand in the way of that?

Frans stared at her but a moment longer before spinning and stomping away.

She didn't make a move to follow him even as her gaze trailed him until he rounded the castle and moved out of sight.

"Is Frans angry with you, Mikaela?" Rikissa asked.

Mikaela reached out and smoothed back the girl's flyaway blond strands, her fingers trembling. "Yes, I've caused him grief."

"I am to blame." I combed my hand through my hair, half wishing I could just pull it out. What was wrong with me that I was interfering with Mikaela and Frans? The only thing I truly wanted for her was that she be happy and stable and secure. Since it couldn't be with me, I had to ensure she found that with Frans.

"I acted without thinking." I turned what I hoped were apologetic eyes upon Mikaela. "And I shouldn't have—"

"Don't say it." Her tone dropped to a dangerous decibel.

If Frans had seen us kissing, who else had? I glanced around. No one else was present except Rikissa and Renate. I would have to figure out a way to bribe them into staying silent about what they'd seen.

"Renate's turn to count." Mikaela's voice was strained with forced cheerfulness. "Go on now, and the two of you play a round without me so I can finish speaking with your uncle."

"Is he going to kiss your hurt again?" Rikissa asked.

"No." Mikaela couldn't get the word out fast enough.

This time I didn't contradict her even though everything within me wanted to kiss her again. I'd already kissed her two times too many—once during my last visit home and just now.

That had to be enough. The two kisses would have to sustain me for the rest of my life.

Chapter 10

Mikaela

Had I really just kissed Gunnar?

As I watched Riki and Rena skip away hand in hand into the arbor, sparks were still flying through my body. I didn't dare look at Gunnar, but I was aware of each of his movements: the jabbing of his fingers into his hair, the shifting of his weight from one leg to the other, the clearing of his throat.

Gunnar seemed to be watching and waiting for Riki and Rena to disappear too. Did he intend to pull me back into the shed and kiss me again?

The sparks crackled into flames, and I was tempted to reach up and touch my lips. They felt swollen and changed from his kiss, and somehow, I sensed they'd never be the same again.

This kiss had been entirely different from the one he'd stolen from me five years ago. We'd been young and unsure, and the kiss had been so light and tender that it had barely qualified as a kiss, at least compared to what we'd just shared.

Oh heavens above. Nothing could compare with this one.

I stifled a sigh and forced myself not to push Gunnar into the shed, slam the door closed, and throw myself at him. Before I kissed him again, I had to do the right thing and talk to Frans.

I needed to apologize to him for kissing Gunnar without first bringing an end to our relationship. Even though Frans and I weren't betrothed or promised to each other, we'd had an understanding of a future together, and I regretted that I'd betrayed him. It was cruel of me, and I was ashamed that I'd hurt him.

But it was all too clear I couldn't marry him. I'd tried all week to make myself love him. But something inside resisted the idea, perhaps always had. Was it the same something that had secretly been relieved when he hadn't been able to pay the bride price after the fire? I hadn't wanted to admit the relief even to myself, but how could I deny it any longer? Especially with how I felt about Gunnar.

And how, exactly, did I feel about Gunnar?

I slanted him a sideways look. His brow was furrowed, his eyes troubled. He'd apologized for kissing me and had taken the blame for Frans's anger upon himself, was likely already making plans to speak with Frans.

"I'll talk to Frans," I said quietly. "I'll explain to him that—that—" What? What was the nature of my relationship now with Gunnar? With each passing day, I'd sensed my feelings changing. With how considerate he'd been in continuing to give me food, with the desserts every eve, with the stories he told more for me than the girls, with the teasing and smiles in passing—all of it reminded me of what I'd always loved about him, how thoughtful, caring, sweet, and funny he was.

Surely the kiss meant he wanted to be with me. And I could no longer deny how much I wanted to be with him. I'd already tried on that account and failed at it miserably.

The truth was, the more I was around Gunnar, the more I realized he was everything I needed in a man. Yes, I'd labeled him as my enemy. And I'd tried to hate him.

But I couldn't any longer.

Gunnar pulled at the shed door, closing it firmly, clearly having no plans to take me back inside. "When you speak with Frans, tell him I'm giving you the money for the bride price."

"What?" Why would I need the money now? After this kiss . . .

"I'm taking away my stipulation that you need to love him." Gunnar stared into the distance, still not meeting my gaze. "I'll give you the money without any conditions. It's what I should have done all along, and I'm sorry I didn't."

I stared at Gunnar, at his jaw working up and down, at the pounding pulse in his neck, at the rigidness of his shoulders. What was he saying? "You want me to marry Frans?"

"Yes."

I didn't understand. How could Gunnar kiss me so passionately one moment and in the next toss me into another man's arms? "You told me Frans will never make me happy."

"I was wrong."

"You said he was too serious and steady for me."

"You need someone serious and steady."

Unlike him? Was that really what Gunnar was hinting at? That he'd given me the wrong impression with our kiss? That just because we'd shared a moment of intimacy didn't mean I should start dreaming of a future with him?

My heart sank with a sickening thud. What had our kiss really meant? Maybe he'd seen me as nothing more than a challenge, another conquest, the same way I had been last time. And now that he'd made me like him—and gotten his kiss—he was ready to abandon me for the next maiden.

A gust of cold wind blew through me, putting out the sparks that had reignited for Gunnar. I fisted my hands on my hips and faced him squarely. "You have no need for me now that I've given you the affection you seek?"

He dropped his head and his shoulders. "No, Mikaela, it's not like that."

"If you weren't using me again, then what were you doing?"

"I wasn't using you." His voice contained a note of desperation, one I wanted to believe. Even so, he was cutting me out of his life again. I didn't understand it, but I wouldn't allow him to do it to me first.

"I've changed my mind. I have no wish to hear your excuses. Please just begone and do not seek me out again." Without waiting for him to speak, I started toward the arbor where the girls were still playing hide-and-seek. From their laughter and smiles as they chased each other, they were oblivious to the way Gunnar had broken and stomped on my heart for the second time.

Hot tears burned the backs of my eyes, but I angrily blinked them away. I wouldn't cry now, not anywhere near him where he could see my sorrow.

"I will give you and Frans the money," he called after me.

More tears threatened to spill over.

"I shall bring it to you tonight."

I didn't halt. "Leave it with Nanna."

He didn't say anything more. And later, when I glanced toward the shed, he was gone.

Late that eve when Gunnar came to the nursery to tell Riki and Rena a bedtime story, I hurried into the adjacent chamber designated for the girls' play area. I pretended to organize and clean, but all the while I fought back the despair that had been plaguing me since his rejection in the garden.

After he was gone and the girls were asleep, I returned to the bedchamber. Nanna wearily stood from her chair beside the hearth and held out a leather pouch. "Gunnar left this for you." Her eyes held a hundred questions that I didn't want to answer.

I gave her the only response I could. "He's giving Frans and me the money we need for the bride price."

"I see."

I took it, feeling the weight as if it were a heavy sack of barley instead of a fistful of coins. I'd yet to seek out Frans and explain what he'd seen earlier in the garden. And I needed to do so soon. Frans would forgive my mistake. He was a good man and would put it behind him, moving forward as though nothing had happened.

But how could I move forward? Frans deserved a better woman, one who loved him totally and completely, not someone like me who harbored affection for another man—even if unwillingly. I didn't want to have feelings for Gunnar. Had tried not to for many years. But the truth had become all too clear with his return—I wouldn't be able to stop caring about him. Not now. Not for a long time. Maybe not ever.

Nanna's kind gaze rested upon me. "'Tis for the best to marry Frans, Mikaela-girl."

I couldn't shed the acute sadness I'd been battling all day. If only Gunnar hadn't strolled back into my life with such power and appeal. If only I'd guarded my heart more carefully from falling for him.

Perhaps the best option was to remain single and avoid both men. With a sigh, I held the pouch out to Nanna. "I can't take it."

She crossed her arms. "You must."

"If you don't give it back to Gunnar, then I will."

Nanna's thin face contained a haggardness I hadn't noticed there before—dark circles under her eyes, more lines in her forehead. "If you think by waiting, you'll have any hope of Gunnar marrying you, you'll be very disappointed."

Had my feelings for Gunnar been that obvious to Nanna? "I'm not waiting for Gunnar. He made it clear today I am nothing to him." Nothing more than another woman to woo.

"Good."

"Good?" My chest squeezed at Nanna's easy

dismissal of my feelings.

"He's dangerous for you, Mikaela. And 'tis best to sever all ties now before rumors spread about his affection for you."

"If rumors spread, they'll be full of pity, since I've once again fallen for his charm when he had no thought to cherishing my affection in return."

"And that's for the best."

"My humiliation?"

"Yes. As hard as it is in the short term, 'tis what will protect you."

"Protect me?"

"The safest course is for you to marry Frans."

This conversation was growing stranger by the moment. "What does my safety have to do with this?"

Nanna pressed her lips together as though she had nothing more to say.

Was someone out to harm me? And if so, why? "'Tis clear you're worried about me. If you wish for me to marry Frans for my safety, then you must speak truthfully with me."

Nanna remained silent.

In the big bed, one of the girls released a soft snore. The firelight on the hearth was dying. And 'twas time for Nanna and me to roll out our pallets and sleep. Mornings always came too early.

As late as the hour was growing, I doubted I'd be able to slumber, not with how much was on my mind. Nevertheless, I placed the pouch on Nanna's chair and stepped back. "I cannot take it. I implore you to please return it to him on the morrow."

I started toward the chest in the corner where we kept our few belongings, including our pallets and blankets.

"The danger is from the earl." Nanna's low response halted me mid-room.

For several seconds all I could picture was Lola, standing at the cliff's edge, the stone tied to her feet, her eyes flashing with defiance. Visions of the woman had haunted my dreams this past week. The peril from the earl was real and 'twas no phantom. But what did marrying Frans have to do with saving me from such danger?

Nanna cocked her head at the bed, then began to walk toward the connecting chamber. I trailed after her. Enough light from the bedchamber cascaded through the doorway so that I could see Nanna standing in the far corner, away from doors and anyone who could hear us.

She drew me close, and even then when she spoke, her voice was a mere whisper. "You are the earl's property, and he won't give you away to Gunnar."

Protest rose swiftly, from whence I knew not. "If Gunnar truly cared about me, he would buy my freedom." Was that what I really believed? Was that why I'd been so disappointed in his rejection again?

"Because Gunnar cares about you, he knows he has to keep away from you."

"Why must he stay away from me but not other women?"

"You're different."

The raging of questions inside me came to a halt.

Something deep inside me had sensed our attraction was real, that we shared a genuine connection, that I hadn't imagined the interest in his eyes or the force pulling us together. The trouble was I'd never known if he felt that way about me alone, or if he had this kind of connection with multiple women.

"How do you know I'm different?"

"He's always cared for you. Always. Even from your youngest of days."

I shook my head. "I once caught him with another woman."

Nanna released a weary breath. "He made a show of being with her to keep the earl from suspecting how much he liked you."

"No—"

"Yes. The night before his last departure, I made him do it."

My response dried up, and I could only stare at Nanna's dear face.

"I warned him to stay away from you then, and I told him to stay away this time as well." Even as she whispered the words, she lifted her chin as though daring me to be angry with her.

I tried to process Nanna's confession, but my mind was spinning too fast. "Why?" It was the only question I could think to ask. "Why would you keep us apart?"

"If the earl discovers Gunnar's affection for you, you'll no longer be safe here."

"I'm a strong woman—"

She cut me off with an impatient wave of her hand. "It doesn't matter how strong you are, the earl will keep you his prisoner in order to exert control over Gunnar."

"Gunnar's strong too."

"Gunnar's feelings for you run deep. All Bernhard needs to do is threaten to harm you, and he'll have control of Gunnar for life."

I wanted to take satisfaction from Nanna's

assurance about Gunnar's feelings for me. But another part of me couldn't quite believe her. Gunnar had never made any declarations of his affection. What if Nanna was mistaken or had misread Gunnar's intentions?

Whatever the case, I needed to use more caution. The earl was already callous and uncaring enough toward Gunnar. I didn't want Gunnar to face worse treatment at his brother's hands.

Perhaps Nanna had been right all along to discourage our friendship. The less time Gunnar and I spent together, the less people would talk and spread rumors.

As if sensing my acceptance of what must be, Nanna reached for my hand and squeezed it between her two boney ones, her skin cold and clammy. "That's why the safest thing for you and Gunnar is if you marry Frans."

I swallowed the lump that was forming in my throat. "I don't know if Frans will want to marry me now...."

"He loves you—"

"He saw me—well, he saw Gunnar and me—earlier today—"

Nanna's brow rose.

"We kissed."

Her face didn't register surprise, but she gave a sharp shake of her head as though frustrated. "Did anyone else see you?"

"I don't think so."

She stared unseeingly into the darkness of the room, thinking quietly for several moments before speaking. "I'll instruct Gunnar to make a show of being with another woman tonight and then not to seek you out again here in the nursery or anywhere." I shook my head, but she cut me off. "On the morrow, you'll go to Frans, tell him what a fool you were, and beg him to take the bride money and marry you with all haste."

I didn't want Gunnar to make a show of liking another woman. And I didn't want to be with another man, even Frans. But what other choice did I have? I'd been born into the earl's family and would remain his until the day I died.

The frustration deep inside swelled up, making me want to cry out. The system was unfair, the injustices too pervasive. And I burned with the need to bring about changes.

But how could I help others when I couldn't begin to help myself?

And if what Nanna said was true, then not even Gunnar could help me. He was bound by the laws of the land and the customs that had been in place for centuries. Worse, he was rendered helpless by the cruelty of his brother, the same way we all were.

Whatever the future held, I didn't want to hurt Frans again. "I cannot ask Frans to marry me, not when I won't be able to give him my whole heart."

Nanna cradled my cheek. "Maybe he will be satisfied with having only as much love as you can give."

Why must either Frans or I settle for less than true love? And why couldn't we fight for more?

My questions begged to be spoken, but I knew my grandmother had survived these many years by not asking questions, by doing as she was told, and by finding ways to survive amidst the unfairness.

If I followed her example, I would remain safe. But could I be satisfied with that? Or was I destined for more?

Chapter 11

GUNNAR

I DUCKED INTO A DARK ALLEY AND GLANCED BEHIND ME. I searched the blackness but didn't see anyone.

Tonight, I'd done my best to elude Bernhard's spies—spies following Torvald and me all week. At the last tavern I'd visited, I'd made a point of staggering outside with a woman tucked against my body. I'd disappeared into the inn next door with her. After paying her to tell everyone I'd spent the night there, I'd escaped out a back window and made my way here, to this alley in the poorest slums of the city.

I needed the news of my debauchery to reach the castle and Bernhard. Nanna had instructed me to make a scene with a woman and keep the attention off Mikaela, and hopefully this ruse would suffice.

I loathed the prospect of hurting Mikaela if she learned of my so-called revelry. But even if I hurt her in the short term, she would be safer this way.

If only I'd learned my lesson the last time I'd been home. Instead, I'd made the same mistake again and was bringing her more heartache.

Since walking away from her in the gardens, I'd beaten myself up over the kiss at least a hundred times. I hadn't planned to go to the nursery later for story time, had tried to stay away, but I'd decided I needed to visit Rikissa and Renate.

Upon my appearance, Mikaela had rushed from the room, clearly not wishing to see me. I'd longed to chase after her, pull her into my arms, and tell her I didn't want her to marry Frans. In fact, the very thought of her being with Frans wrenched at my insides and tore me apart. And it hadn't made any difference how many times I'd reminded myself that he loved her and would take good care of her.

Instead of thinking on Mikaela and Frans, I'd resolved to put them from my mind and focus on the mission, so that by the time Torvald returned we would have more clues.

Now in the early morning hour, with the city asleep and only the thieves and troublemakers awake, I prayed I'd reach my destination without Bernhard learning of where I'd gone.

The stench of garbage wafted heavily in the stale air of the narrow alley. The rot and refuse sat in heaps, home to vermin of every kind. Even as I stepped carefully over a pile, a rat scurried out with a frightened squeak, its claws scratching the stone pavement.

I paused, knife at the ready, my extra one stuffed into my boot. I'd already fended off one drunk thief, and I would fight others yet before the night was over. If only I could know for sure the man whom I sought was still alive.

He'd been called Eggum when he'd been a servant in

my grandfather's household. But no one I'd spoken to in the taverns knew of an Eggum. The only man who had possibly once worked in the castle was an old beggar by the name of Oslo.

If Oslo was Eggum, then he would be the only one left from those who'd served in my grandfather Jorg's household during the time of the purge. All the others were dead or gone.

The purge had come to my attention after spending the greater part of the day—after the kiss—talking with staff who remembered my father and knew of my grandfather.

Some had mentioned a frightening purge, a time when my grandfather had hanged at least two dozen people after indicting them in a plot to overthrow him by colluding with the jotunn.

I'd pressed for more information, but the staff had been adamant that they didn't know anything else. The chilling tale and their hesitancy had only sparked my curiosity all the more, leading me to seek out anyone who might have more information.

Could Eggum help me make sense of my grandfather's purge? 'Twas likely a false lead and nothing more. I was probably wasting time investigating. But in the search for the chalice, Torvald and I hadn't overlooked anything, even the oddest of clues. We wanted to be thorough, because when it came to the ancient relics, the stories, strange events, and superstitions were usually important.

Besides, after my interaction with Bernhard about the chalice, I'd become convinced there was more to uncover about the sacred relic and its connection to my family.

I tiptoed past the ramshackle buildings, most of which looked like they could collapse with the slightest breeze.

The wattle and daub walls were broken away in places, the roofs nothing more than a thin covering of molding hay, and the shutters and doors either entirely off or ajar.

As I counted the shacks for the fifth one that supposedly belonged to an old half-blind beggar named Oslo, a slouched shadow appeared in the doorway.

I settled my knife more firmly in my gloved hand. "You Eggum?"

"No. Go away," the man whispered harshly.

His response was defensive, telling me I'd found the man I sought. How had he known I was coming? Had he heard me stepping through refuse, though I'd done everything I could to remain stealthy?

I reached into my leather pouch and extracted several coins. "I'll pay you well for any information you give me."

The moon was shrouded in a mist, but it provided enough light that I could see the man's scraggly beard that reached halfway down his chest and his equally long hair that hadn't seen a comb or washing in years. His clothing was stained and tattered, and he wore rags around his feet.

I jangled the coins.

"Fine. Come in." He retreated into his hovel.

I ducked into Eggum's shack. It was dark, but embers glowed in a stone pit at the center. I was surprised to see that the one room was tidy, consisting of a crate-table creation with a three-legged stool. A couple of battered and blackened pots hung from hooks in the wall.

He motioned me toward the stool.

I wanted to stand and remain alert, but refusing his kind gesture to take the only seat would be rude, so I sat down.

"I know you're Sir Gunnar, one of the Knights of

Brethren." Eggum crouched in front of the embers and began to stir them with a rod.

Of course my identity had proceeded me into the slums. I couldn't expect to trespass in this part of town without every single outcast knowing about it.

I might as well get right to the point of my visit. "You served my grandfather."

Eggum didn't answer but neither did he deny it.

"I want to know more about my grandfather's purge, specifically why he accused a group of his domestics of trying to overthrow him." I let the coins clank through my fingers to remind him of what he stood to gain.

"Your grandfather was a cruel man, just as cruel as your father and your brother."

I'd heard enough stories to know the legacy of cruelty was true. "I will not disagree with you on that score. But did the people do as he accused them, collude with the jotunn?"

Eggum pushed at the embers. "They secretly met with the jotunn at the forest edge and bargained with him to come out and destroy your grandfather."

His answer was too rehearsed to be true.

"Why bargain with the jotunn? If the jotunn is so dangerous, why would they want to encourage him to come to their aid?"

Eggum was quiet, still stirring the embers.

"I need to know the truth." I sensed his answer was pivotal.

He lowered his head, and his response came out a mumble. "They believed he was the rightful heir to the earldom and wanted him to take your grandfather's place."

My fingers twisting the coins came to a halt. "Are you

telling me they believed the jotunn was my grandfather's older brother, Sven?"

"'Twas but a rumor."

Sven had been badly burned and disfigured in a fire as a child and had died. Or at least that was the tale I'd been told.

But what if he hadn't died after all? Had his family sent him away into the forest as an outcast in order to take the earldom from him?

And yet, how could Sven—my great uncle—be the jotunn? Hardanger Forest had been uninhabitable, dangerous, and haunted by a jotunn long before my grandfather and his brother's time. Maybe instead of one jotunn, the forest was made up of many madmen. "Do you think the jotunn is Sven?"

"No. I believe the jotunn is a troll who escaped from the underworld and made his home in the forest." The answer came too quickly, as if he'd spoken it many times over the years. No doubt the answer had once kept him from losing his life with the others my grandfather had purged.

Obviously, my grandfather had felt threatened in some way by the madman living in Hardanger Forest, or he wouldn't have felt the need to eliminate his servants.

Silence settled around the hovel as I tried to process what Eggum's revelation meant. Was the mysterious monster of Hardanger Forest my great uncle or someone else altogether?

"I know you're searching for the sacred chalice." Eggum leaned forward, his whisper dropping so that I could barely hear it.

"News gets around."

"The jotunn has it." Again, the words were barely audible.

I opened my mouth to speak, then shut it. I hadn't been expecting such news, to say the least. And now a hundred more questions crowded my mind.

Eggum kept his head down. "I was cleaning in the chapel when I saw the priest take it from the altar."

Was this old beggar speaking the truth? With as much as the chalice had been moved from church to chapel to abbey, I didn't doubt the chalice had changed locations from Romsdal's Stavekirche to the chapel in Likness Castle. "You're sure you saw the chalice?"

Eggum nodded. "The priest put it into a sack and took it with him to the edge of Hardanger Forest."

"And how do you know the jotunn possesses it?" I kept my voice as low as Eggum's. If this was true, the information I was receiving was too important for anyone else to know.

"When the priest returned, he didn't have the bag."

"Maybe he tossed it in the forest."

"Or maybe he gave it to the jotunn."

My blood began to pump with a strange sense of anticipation. Was I getting close to a discovery?

Eggum could very well be deluded and simply spinning a story so I would give him the coins. But if this old servant was right, I'd just made a huge step forward.

"Why would the priest give the jotunn the sacred relic?" I voiced the question, although I didn't expect Eggum to know the answer.

"For safekeeping?"

What if the priest had known about the possibility that the chalice could bring healing? If he'd believed the jotunn was my grandfather's brother Sven, perhaps he'd thought the chalice would help restore the brother to sound body and mind so that he could return to Romsdal and take his rightful place as leader. Obviously, that hadn't happened, and it could very well be another myth surrounding the chalice—just one more of the many I'd heard.

"My grandfather learned of their communication with this jotunn, believed it was his brother, and then hung the priest along with the others?"

"Yes."

"Did he know about the chalice?"

"He never mentioned it. No one ever mentioned it."

I raced to make sense of all I'd learned. "Have you told anyone else what you've revealed to me?"

Eggum hesitated. "Just one person."

"Who?"

"He seemed to be a learned man."

A learned man? As in a wiseman? A Sage? My pulse thudded an extra beat. "What more can you tell me about him?"

"He was tall and thin with dark hair and dark eyes."

What if the mysterious visitor had been Rasmus? Such a description could fit any number of men, including the Royal Sage. If Rasmus still had spies living in the royal residence, it was possible they'd informed him of Ansgar's quest for the chalice and his deployment of Torvald and me to that end.

"When did he come?"

"Late last autumn."

If Rasmus had been searching ahead of us, he very well could have put the clues of the chalice's whereabouts together more quickly than we had. Maybe he'd already discovered the chalice within the depths of Hardanger Forest.

But how? With as dangerous as the forest and the jotunn had become over the years? No one ever made it out alive. The failed efforts of Bernhard's bondservants over recent weeks to go in and eliminate the jotunn were proof of that.

At the scratching and scurrying of another rat on the flimsy roof above, I placed the coins on the table and stood. I'd gained what I needed from this visit.

"You have been a great help."

He rose, too, and swiped up the coins as though they might disappear—or perhaps he feared I was taunting him and would take them back.

I dug into my leather pouch, withdrew three more, and set them firmly on the table. "I am not my brother, nor my father, nor my grandfather."

He stared at the additional money but held back.

"I regret you were cast out of service so callously upon your old age. You deserved more from my family after so many years of faithful service."

Without waiting for his reply, I ducked back into the alley. 'Twould not be long ere dawn broke, and I needed to be at the inn by first light.

As I made my way cautiously through the slum, my mind replayed the conversation with Eggum, especially the part about Rasmus. While I didn't know for sure he'd been to Romsdal, I couldn't think of any other learned man who would have a reason to seek out the chalice.

Surely Rasmus knew of the legends of the chalice's healing power and would guess why Ansgar wanted the sacred relic. In fact, knowing how much Ansgar loved Queen Lis, no doubt Rasmus wanted the chalice to thwart Ansgar and cause him turmoil.

The question plagued me again. Had Rasmus already discovered the chalice? If he had, wouldn't he flaunt it? Or attempt to bargain with Ansgar?

But since Rasmus was silent on the matter, that meant he was most certainly still looking for it. But how? Did he have someone else searching on his behalf? Someone as twisted and devious as he was?

Someone twisted and devious like Bernhard.

My footsteps tripped over each other, and my heart plunged. Why else, after years of not caring about the madman of Hardanger Forest, would Bernhard suddenly decide to eliminate the jotunn?

What had Rasmus promised Bernhard for doing the deed? I shuddered to think of what Rasmus might be scheming and Bernhard's place in it.

I had to foil them. And the only way to do it was to go into the forest and find the chalice before they did.

Chapter 12

Mikaela

I had to talk with Frans, but I'd been procrastinating.

Even now, my steps slowed as I passed by the storeroom where Gunnar had fed me. My mind filled with the image of his face as he'd watched me eat, his eyes alight with humor, his lips curled up in a smile, his long fingers combing back his hair.

The ache in my heart pulsed anew, so much that I had to stop and press my hand to my chest.

Why did things have to be this way? I shouldn't have to worry about Bernhard learning about Gunnar and me. But all night, I'd flopped around restlessly on my pallet, imagining the ways Bernhard would torture me to make Gunnar comply with whatever he wanted.

All I had to do was think back on the punishments Bernhard had given others for my resolve to grow stronger. I wouldn't make Gunnar a prisoner to Bernhard. I wanted him to be free.

In order to do that, I had to get married. Once I belonged to another man, neither Gunnar nor

Bernhard would concern themselves with me. Yet, the more I thought about marrying Frans for selfish reasons, the more I loathed myself.

"I'll learn to love Frans and give him all that I can." My whisper was strangled as I exited through the door. Sunlight warmed my head but couldn't chase away my chill. Although I was tempted to delay again, I set my sights upon the open doors of the forge. The fire in the big oven wasn't glowing as brightly today, and the shop seemed quieter than usual.

As a matter of fact, the entire bailey seemed quieter.

I took in the deserted courtyard and the chores undone—the axe left in a log near the fuel shed, a goose half plucked, a rug needing to be beaten.

A strange sense of unease cascaded across my nerves. Where was everyone?

I started toward the forge, lengthening my stride, pushing aside my concern. Surely Bernhard hadn't found another of his subjects to punish, had he? Was he even now at the cliff outside the castle getting ready to throw someone else to their death in the fjord below?

"Frans?" I called as I closed the distance.

He usually saw me before I noticed him. This morn after I'd delivered the bundle of food to Kirstin, he'd been in the doorway watching our interaction. I hadn't been able to see his face in the shadows, but his body had been tense, his movements stilted.

I stepped into the forge and paused. The bellows were contracted. Both anvils were empty. The tongs, swages, and fullers were hung neatly on the wall. And no one was in sight. Not even Valter. Only the scent of charcoal remained.

Valter and Frans had obviously gone out to witness whatever Bernhard was doing. Why hadn't I been required to go?

I ducked back outside into the bright sunshine. Shielding my eyes, I spotted one of the kitchen boys racing across the yard toward a side gate, feet and head bare. "Where are you off to?"

He didn't pause and instead tossed his answer over his shoulder. "The master is sending someone new into Hardanger Forest."

Before I could question him further, he exited the bailey, likely eager to watch the departure just as we had for the others who'd taken the earl's challenge to kill the jotunn.

Who was the foolish man this time?

The smiling face of my younger brother filled my mind. What if Enok had volunteered?

I rushed forward, my chest pounding with sudden urgency. Enok was too young. He knew nothing of hunting or trapping or of self-defense. Yes, he'd perfected the use of a slingshot like Frans, but he was deluded if he thought he could overtake the jotunn with a mere slingshot when men much stronger and more experienced had failed.

I hastened out onto the trail that led to the north of the castle. It wound down a rocky cliffside. A hundred feet away from the forest, much of the castle staff had gathered for the occasion. The sight made my stomach roil. How could we stand back and keep sending more of our men into the forest to be destroyed? We had to stop the madness. The prize wasn't worth the risk. Surely we could find a better, safer way to bring about our freedom.

I would speak up this time. I had to. I'd stayed silent long enough.

As I reached level ground, I bunched my skirt to keep it from tangling in my legs, and then I ran. The trail was wider and easier, but by the time I arrived, I was gasping for air. I paused to draw in a breath, and those standing closest cast me a pitying glance, one that set my pulse racing again.

It had to be Enok.

With growing desperation, I pushed my way through the crowd, the knowing nods only adding to my panic. When I reached the forefront, I found myself standing beside Valter. He was staring into the overgrown forest, tears streaming down his leathery cheeks.

I scanned the open grassy area between the crowd and the dark forest. No one had left yet, had they?

"Stop!" I called.

More pitying eyes turned my way.

Valter took hold of my arm as though he would collapse without my aid.

My body ceased to function and a strange quiet settled over me, like the kind before a storm. I slowed my search, seeing each face, even that of the earl standing with his friends and advisors to the side. I was drawing unwanted attention. But at the moment, panic was twisting within me, and I couldn't bring myself under control like I knew I should.

"Frans?" His name escaped from my now-trembling lips.

Where was Frans? Why wasn't he standing beside Valter? I prayed desperately that he was in town on an errand. Or maybe he was resting in his bed above the forge.

Valter's fingers tightened around my arm even as a clamp tightened around my heart.

"No." I pressed a hand against my mouth, afraid I was going to be sick.

Another hand grasped my other arm, this belonging to my friend Ami.

Valter's tears continued to streak his cheeks, and as he met my gaze, my heart lurched into my throat. Frans had gone into the forest. Innocent, hard-working, trustworthy, kind, and dependable Frans.

"No! Tell him to come back!" I scanned the woodland, looking for him, his sturdy frame, his broad shoulders, anything. I had the sudden and overwhelming need to chase after him. He couldn't be that far in. I needed to catch up and tell him to stop.

I jerked against Valter and Ami. "Leave me be. I'm going after him."

The two held me fast.

I struggled again, tears now wetting my cheeks. "This is my fault!" I should have been faithful, should have kept my feelings for Gunnar from overruling common sense, and most certainly should have refrained from kissing him.

If only I'd told Frans I'd been wrong sooner. If only I'd assured him that I would try harder to love him the way he deserved. But now I was too late. How would I be able to live with myself knowing I'd been the cause of Frans's death?

From the corner of my eye, I could see the earl and one of his companions, the Sagacite Pontus, leaning together, watching me, and having a discussion.

I had to cease making such a commotion.

As if sensing the same, Valter drew me against his

burly body and began to lead me away from the gathering. I buried my face against Valter's cloak and clung to him, sobbing now openly. Several other friends joined in shielding me.

They knew me well. They understood my growing need to give voice to my demands for justice and fairness. And they only wanted to keep me safe so that I wouldn't find myself the earl's next victim.

However, no matter how well I may have averted trouble this time, I had the feeling a confrontation with the earl was inevitable.

Chapter 13

I AWOKE TO A SHARP PROD IN MY SIDE. I PRIED OPEN AN EYE TO SEE afternoon sunshine slanting through the open shutters of my chamber.

From the angle of the light, I guessed I'd slept five or six hours after returning from my visit to Eggum in the slums. Before falling into bed, I'd made sure to start rumors regarding my revelry so that Bernhard would believe I was as wild as always. I didn't want him suspecting I'd been investigating the chalice and now knew his true purpose for sending men into the forest to kill the jotunn.

In fact, the more I'd thought about Bernhard's scheme, the more I'd realized I had to pretend I knew nothing about it. Otherwise, Bernhard would devise obstacles to keep me from getting the chalice before he did.

Thus, in addition to rumors about my night of carousing, I'd decided to spread the word that I'd had no luck finding the chalice in Romsdal and was traveling to a new location. I intended to make a show of leaving on the morrow, ride out a distance, but circle around and enter the forest under the cover of darkness.

I also had to send a secret missive to Torvald, alerting him to my suspicion and plan. Even with my special training and skills as a Brethren, I didn't know what I'd face. If anything happened to me, I needed Torvald to know about the jotunn and the chalice. Then he could muster assistance and complete the mission.

Part of me considered journeying to Vordinberg, consulting with the king and his advisors, and amassing an army to storm the forest. But if Bernhard learned of such a plan, he'd round up his knights, squires, and bondservants and launch his own attack first, causing even more deaths.

For now, I'd venture in a short way by myself. If nothing else, I'd scout the forest and decipher exactly how dangerous the conditions were. If the threats were insurmountable, I'd retreat and wait to consult with Torvald before proceeding with the search.

I shifted under my covers to get more comfortable, but another poke against my ribs drew me up in bed, my fingers gripping my knife handle.

At the sight of Nanna at my bedside, I relaxed and blew out a breath. "Nanna, what are you doing—"

"Shhh." She glanced toward the closed door, and something in her eyes warned me she didn't want anyone to know she was in my room.

This had to do with Mikaela. Whenever Nanna sought me out this way, it always had to do with Mikaela. Usually Nanna warning me to stay away.

"I vow it. I haven't seen her all day," I whispered even though no one else was in my chamber. A servant had already come and gone. The garments I'd left beside my bed were picked up, the rushes fresh, and the chamber pot clean. A freshly-laundered set of clothing awaited me on the chest at the end of the bed.

"You need to make her see reason. Please." Nanna's voice wobbled with a desperation I didn't understand but that needled me, nonetheless.

"You asked me not to seek her out again."

"But you're the only one who can stop her."

"Stop her from what?"

Nanna peered around the room again. She'd always been extra cautious about Mikaela. But now that I was older—and wiser—I could appreciate how much Nanna had done to care for and shield her granddaughter over the years.

I reached for Nanna's hand only to find that she was trembling. Another needle pricked me. Something was amiss.

"What's happened, Nanna?"

Her fingers grasped mine tightly. "Frans accepted the earl's challenge to kill the jotunn. He went into the forest this morn."

I shook my head. What was Frans thinking? He was no match for the jotunn. He'd end up dead just like everyone else who'd gone in. "What a fool. Why would he do such a thing?"

"Frans saw you and Mikaela together yesterday, and Mikaela thinks he lost the will to live. She blames herself."

A fist seemed to slam into my chest, knocking the air from my lungs. If anyone was to blame for yesterday's moment of passion in the shed, I was. I'd sought Mikaela out. I'd initiated the kiss. I'd lost self-control. Not her.

Either way, Frans shouldn't have offered himself up.

He had to know he'd cause Mikaela heartache.

I released Nanna's hand and tossed aside my covers. I didn't care that I was indecent in my breeches. I needed to make this situation right. I grabbed my tunic from the top of the stack of garments on the chest and jerked it over my head.

"I believe she intends to go into the forest and call him back."

"Only over my dead body." I grabbed my leggings and stockings. There was no way in heaven or earth I'd allow Mikaela to rush off into Hardanger Forest after Frans. I'd tie her up and lock her away before she had the chance.

Nanna nodded but couldn't hide the tears that filled her eyes. "You know how stubborn she is."

"And you know I'm more stubborn."

"That's why I came. I need you to convince her not to go."

And so the conversation had come full circle. I was the only one who had the power to stop her. Even then, I wasn't sure I'd be able to. But I had to try.

"I'll be taking the girls to visit their mother." Nanna wiped at the wetness on her cheeks. "While I'm away, you must go to her."

"I will." I had to get to her soon. She might even be sneaking off to leave while Nanna was with me. I shoved my foot into my stocking.

"Do *whatever* you have to, Gunnar-boy. Kiss her again if you must."

Tugging up a stocking and hopping on one leg, I paused.

Nanna nodded as though to confirm her permission. She was truly desperate if she was advocating my kissing Mikaela. Even so, I couldn't pursue such intimacy again. I wouldn't lead Mikaela on, not even for this.

"I can't—"

"I'm told she drew the earl's attention at the forest's edge. And now that he's aware of her, he'll single her out."

My blood ran cold. I couldn't let that happen.

"She's too beautiful and full of life," Nanna continued, "and he won't be able to resist."

"You're right." I was surprised Mikaela had gone this long without Bernhard's notice.

My thoughts jumbled in a frantic race to find a solution for keeping Mikaela from falling into Bernhard's clutches.

As I finished with my stockings, Nanna handed me my doublet. "She won't be safe here in Romsdal anymore. Not after this."

I slipped into the doublet. "I'll think of something." But what?

"The best thing for you to do is buy her freedom from Bernhard, take her away, and marry her."

Marry her? I stumbled over myself and grabbed on to the edge of the bed to stay upright.

"Take her with you to Vordinberg and implore the king to grant her sanctuary."

Could I really do such a thing? For several pattering heartbeats, excitement charged through me at the prospect. I hadn't wanted to consider marriage previously. But with Mikaela? If I could have her as my wife, I'd wed her at this very moment.

My blood pulsed with a sharp and bold need. I wanted Mikaela. I always had. Dare I consider Nanna's proposition?

Nanna reached for both of my hands, her eyes turning

tender. "I tried to keep you away from her for her safety."

"I understand—"

"You love her, Gunnar-boy. You always have."

I wanted to deny her. But how could I when the truth of her words resonated deep within me?

"I thought if she married Frans that she'd settle down and be protected. But after today, she'll never be safe here again." Nanna's voice grew low and urgent. "Now you're the only person who can protect her."

But at what cost? Bernhard wouldn't easily relinquish any of his bondservants, especially not after setting his intentions upon one as beautiful as Mikaela. If I offered him everything I had for her, he'd hold onto her just to spite me. And even if I secretly stole her away, Bernhard would eventually learn of my connection to her.

Once word of my deception reached him, he'd seek vengeance, and most likely he'd bring difficulties to her kin, starting with Nanna and then hurting her father and mother and siblings. He'd punish them all.

"Don't worry about me." Nanna pressed a hand to my cheek, likely seeing the anxiety warring in my eyes. "I can take care of myself."

"I can't risk bringing harm to you or your family," I whispered. "And I know Mikaela will never want to risk it either."

Nanna let her hand fall away, and her shoulders slumped. She knew as well as I did that the battle with Bernhard would be far too dangerous for everyone. But the fact was, we could no longer sit back and do nothing.

"I vow that I'll find a way to protect Mikaela." I buttoned my doublet, not caring if I was getting each one looped.

"I trust you, Gunnar-boy. You'll figure it out."

If only there was a way to be with Mikaela without destroying all the people we loved.

"And you'll keep her from going after Frans?"

"Yes, I shall go in her stead." Since I'd already planned to set forth into the forest, I would simply do so a day earlier.

After Nanna left as quietly as she'd arrived, I hastened through the remainder of my grooming. Then I made my way to the part of the castle with the nursery. As I slipped silently inside the bedchamber, I found Mikaela doing exactly what I'd expected. She was kneeling beside her trunk and hastily packing her bag now that Nanna had left with the girls.

"Where are you going?" I whispered, closing the door behind me.

Her startled gaze darted to me, and she shoved her sack behind her. "'Tis not your concern."

Her eyes were rimmed with red and her cheeks wet with fresh tears.

At the sight of her distress, an ache pulsed through my chest. I wanted to cross to her, draw her in my arms, and comfort her. But I held myself back, knowing she wouldn't welcome me right now. Not after I'd walked away from her yesterday.

"I heard about Frans."

She shifted her face away, fiddling with something inside the trunk before closing it.

"I'm sorry. I hold myself responsible, and I shall go in after him and do my best to bring him back."

"I won't let you throw away your life too." Her response was sharp.

"I'm the one who incited him to leave, and I'll be the one to rescue him."

She stood and slung her bag over her shoulder, no longer bothering to hide her intentions. "No. I drove him to it, and I'll be the one rescuing him." She lifted her dainty chin, and her amber eyes flashed with defiance.

I loved her feistiness and her fire and her determination. But at this moment, I would win this battle, and I aimed to do it by *any* means possible. Including kissing her. I had Nanna's permission to do so, and I couldn't let so generous a gesture of goodwill go to waste.

Chapter 14

Mikaela

I needed to make my way into the forest now, while Nanna and the girls were occupied elsewhere. But from the firm set of Gunnar's mouth and the clamp of his jaw, I guessed he wasn't going to make this easy for me.

"Please leave." I'd located the knife I'd hidden within the depths of the chest, the knife Gunnar had given to me years ago, one he'd told me to use if anyone threatened me. I would need it today as I went into the forest.

"I'm not leaving. At least not until I tie you to the bedpost, where you'll remain until I return." His normally playful eyes held no mirth.

"You wouldn't dare."

"I would dare." He took a step toward me.

I took a step back. "You have no authority over me and cannot stop me."

"You're right. I don't have authority and am glad of it." He continued advancing with a confidence and determination I didn't understand.

I retreated again but bumped into the wall with no place to go.

Ever since I'd left the forest edge earlier in the day, I'd been racked with despondency and guilt. I'd done little else but think on what I could do to rectify the horrible situation I'd created with Frans. I'd decided I had to go in, search for him, and tell him I was sorry. 'Twas likely the only way to save him. And with each moment I delayed, I feared I would be too late.

If only Gunnar hadn't decided to interfere. If only he wasn't threatening to go into the woods after Frans. I didn't know how I could bear losing him in addition to Frans.

Gunnar didn't stop until he was directly in front of me, less than a hand's span away. His doublet was only halfway buttoned, one of his stockings unlaced, and his hair disheveled. But he'd never looked more handsome . . . dangerously so.

I didn't want to have this undeniable attraction to Gunnar any longer. I had to resist it. Even more, I had to find a way to put an end to it.

With what I hoped was a haughty air, I glared at him. "You need not concern yourself with me. I am nothing to you."

Before I could move away, he braced his hands against the wall on either side of me.

I should have felt trapped. But my disloyal heart gave another fast beat.

His gaze was unrelenting. "You are everything to me."

My breath caught. What did he mean?

"You are the only maiden who has ever meant

anything to me." His voice dropped as did his gaze, which affixed upon my mouth. "And you will always be the only one."

I flattened my palms to the wall to keep from sliding down under the power of his words and his eyes. His nickname as the Slayer was entirely appropriate. He was slaying me by stirring up my desire for him when it was best left undisturbed.

How could he come in here and do this to me again? Yes, I understood from everything Nanna had told me that Gunnar cared about me. She claimed his feelings ran deep. But I couldn't so easily put aside my long-held belief that he was a womanizer who would use me and leave me at will.

And even if he wasn't the ladies' man everyone believed him to be, I couldn't give way to my attraction to him, because nothing good could come of it. It would only put us both in danger.

"Don't do this, Gunnar," I whispered.

"Do what?" He leaned in, and his long, thick lashes fell halfway.

"You know what."

"What?" His voice turned husky. "Kiss the woman I love?"

Love? Before I could process his question, he closed the distance and fused his lips to mine. The kiss wasn't tender or soft or sweet. Instead, it was hard and demanding and passionate.

I knew I ought to push him away, but my fingers found his tunic. I dug in and kissed him back with the same fervor. And as the kiss deepened, I found myself soaring with him above the problems and turmoil and obstacles. We were swirling together in a flight I didn't want to come to an end. I longed to stay above it all like this with him forever.

But before the kiss could take us too far away, he gentled the pressure, tenderly softening, until he was hardly touching me.

I wanted to groan and chase after him, demanding that he take me away again, but before I could drag him back, he shifted and rested his forehead on the wall, his labored breath echoing in my ear.

My chest rose and fell in the same ragged rhythm. He'd told me he loved me and then kissed me. What did all of this mean to him?

A part of me simply wanted to take pleasure in this stolen moment. But another part—the part that had been hurt by him before—couldn't rest. It demanded answers.

"Is this one of your tactics for slaying a woman?" I asked. "Tell her you love her and then kiss her?"

He still braced his arms on either side of me. I needed to push him away, free myself from being ensnared in his hold, and put distance between us. But I closed my eyes instead, and simply basked in his nearness, the strength and warmth and power that almost seemed to wrap around me.

He didn't move either. "This is no tactic, Mikaela. If anyone has done the slaying, 'tis you."

The low rumble of his voice made my insides flutter so that my fingers tightened in his tunic again.

"I meant what I said." He brushed his cheek against mine, the stubble on his jaw rough but delectable.

"What exactly did you mean?" I forced my hands to stay right where they were instead of running them over his face the way I wanted to.

"You are the only maiden I've ever loved." His whisper echoed in the hollow of my ear.

Every time he spoke, I was having more difficulty thinking coherently. But somehow, I managed to squeeze out a small protest. "No. I can't be."

"Yes. You are and always will be the only maiden for me."

Oh heavens above. Being here with him. Like this. It was like traveling to paradise for just a few minutes. And I didn't want to return to earth.

But the fact was, reality had a grip on both of us and was already tugging us out of this perfect moment where just the two of us existed.

"I want to find a way for us to be together." His whisper contained a desperation that planted my feet back on the ground and reminded me of the peril to both of us if anyone discovered how much we cared about each other. No, I hadn't told him I loved him in return. I was still too scared to say the words. But in my deepest of hearts, I couldn't deny that what I felt for him was love.

"We can't let Bernhard find out." Even now, I trembled at the prospect of a servant opening the door and discovering me with Gunnar.

He brushed his cheek against mine once more. "That's why I was with the woman last time I left—"

"I know. Nanna told me." All I wanted was to wrap my arms around him and never let him go, despite my fears.

"I regret that I led her on and deceived you. While I blame it on my desire to protect you, I have no excuse."

"I understand now, and I forgive you."

He pressed a kiss against my ear.

The touch sent delight shimmying over my skin.

"After this morn, there are rumors that Bernhard has taken notice of you."

I shuddered. I regretted the outburst, but I'd been distraught. Only Gunnar's presence with me now had been able to calm me.

"You must stay in the nursery," he whispered against my temple. "Go nowhere and see no one until I'm able to work out a plan to get you away from here."

"Away from here?"

"I intend to purchase your freedom from Bernhard, but I must do so without endangering Nanna or the rest of your kin."

I'd only thought about what Bernhard would do to Gunnar and hadn't considered the ramifications to my family. But Gunnar was right. We had to worry about them too. If we angered Bernhard, he wouldn't hesitate to harm the people we loved in order to make us do his bidding. In fact, I suspected if Gunnar revealed his interest in me now, Bernhard would only desire me all the more.

"Any hope for a future between us seems impossible."

"I will find a way." He lifted a hand away from the wall, as though making ready to go. "I must."

I clung to him, not ready for this moment to end.

"Let us be clear on one other item." He pulled back enough to look in my face and trail a finger down my cheek.

My breath hitched at the tenderness of the caress. "What item?"

He made a path down my neck, ending at my collar

bone. "You will stay here while I go after Frans."

"I don't know . . ."

He skimmed the length of my neck up to my chin, then to my lips. "I'm better trained and equipped to travel into the forest and find Frans than you."

His touch distracted me—likely what he intended to do. In fact, knowing Gunnar, this had been his objective all along—cornering and disabling me in any way he could. And he'd done it. I was a puddle of melted tallow.

"I will bring Frans back." He kept his finger pressed against my mouth as though to stop me from protesting. "But you must know, I have no wish for you to marry him. I never have and only encouraged it because I thought it was the honorable thing to do."

"I have only encouraged it because I was selfish, and for that I owe him an apology I hope I'll be able to give him."

Gunnar's blue eyes were dark without a star in sight, the most serious I'd ever seen them. "'Tis not fair to ask you to wait for me, for us, until we can be together. But I would wait a lifetime for you, if I must."

My throat constricted with thick emotion. Instead of speaking—which would only sound desperate and incoherent—I pulled his finger away from my lips and rose to capture his mouth. I didn't care if I was being too bold. I wanted him to know I would wait for him forever too.

As I offered him my kiss, he accepted, melding with me in a consuming moment that was much too short. Even as I started to wind my arms around his neck to deepen the kiss and embrace him longer, he broke the connection and set me away from him.

His gaze smoldered, but he took a large step backward, then another.

I had the urge to grab him, to force him to stay, to never leave me. But if anyone could rescue Frans, Gunnar could do it. I had to let him try.

"I refuse to say farewell." He retreated several more steps toward the door. "If I don't say farewell, then it won't be."

"You'll be back by nightfall."

"And if I'm not, I shall return on the morrow sometime."

As his hand closed around the door handle, I clutched the wall to keep myself from running after him. Prolonging the parting would do neither of us any good.

His gaze swept over me slowly from head to foot, as though he was painting a picture to take with him. Then he turned, opened the door, and left without another word.

At the click of the door closing, I slid to the floor. A cry of both amazement and misery pushed for release, and I pressed my fist to my lips to hold it in.

Had Gunnar really declared his desire to be with me? After so many years of fighting this attraction, denying it, and trying to foster my animosity toward Gunnar, he'd eliminated all my defenses in but a few minutes' time.

I leaned my head back and closed my eyes, replaying his kisses, his whispers, and his declaration: *You are the only maiden I've ever loved . . . You are and always will be the only maiden for me.*

Was this real? Or was this another one of his ploys?

No matter what it was, I was totally and thoroughly

ensnared and didn't want to free myself. I wanted to be his, even if only for these few stolen moments. Maybe that made me a weak woman. But the alternative was worse—living without him at all.

Perhaps eventually he'd be able to find a way to outsmart Bernhard so that we could love each other openly without consequences to ourselves and my family. But even if I had to live the rest of my life secretly loving Gunnar, I knew I would.

Chapter 15

Mikaela

I didn't see or hear from Gunnar again, but the rumors circulating through the castle reached me by eventide that he'd gone into the forest to aid Frans.

I received the news as calmly as I could but hadn't been able to hide my shaking hands from Nanna. She raised her brow at me but didn't say anything, for which I was grateful. After she'd forbidden me to have any further interactions with Gunnar, I didn't want her to know I'd kissed him again and had practically pledged myself to him.

At some point, I needed to tell her I couldn't go through with marrying Frans. But first Gunnar had to find Frans. Although Gunnar had assured me that he would bring Frans out, I was under no illusion his task would be easy, since Frans already had a six-to-eight-hour head start.

"Finish the last bite, Renate," I said as I scraped the final spoonful of the thick stew. She and Rikissa sat at the table in their chamber where they took most of their meals. When they turned sixteen, they would start eating in the great hall and begin the process of mingling with suitors in preparation for their coming-of-age balls. Until then, Nanna and I were in charge of their meals and manners.

"I am done." Rena wiggled on the bench, ready to get down and play, bored from her long hour of sitting with her mother and having to behave properly.

I held the spoon out to her. "Before you decide to waste your food, I want you to think about all the villeins, my family included, who are hungry and would love to have this bite."

Rena, at three, was too young to understand the difficulties. But I took every opportunity I could to inform her and Riki of the true plight, hoping I might instill in them sensitivity and insight into what life was like for many people who served the earl.

Nanna had done the same with all the children in her care over the years, including Gunnar. She claimed that changes began with small steps, and she worked tirelessly to influence the children to live honorably, to look out for the needs of others, to be generous and kind and unselfish.

Though I'd followed her methods, at times I grew impatient and wished for bigger and more practical ways to make a difference.

Yes, our influence over Rena and Riki was important. I didn't deny that. But we couldn't stop there. The problem was, I didn't know how to do more. Perhaps others who'd come before me had also wanted to find ways to change our pitiful circumstances but hadn't known how either. Maybe even Nanna had once been like me and resigned herself to doing the little she could the best way she knew how.

If only that were enough for me. . . .

As Rena opened up and ate her last bite obediently, Riki swallowed her final mouthful and peered up at me. "You look pretty."

"Thank you." I smoothed a hand down her long braid, plaited just like mine.

"Uncle Gunnar will think you look pretty too."

I paused. How should I respond?

"Last night he said he cannot visit us anymore." Riki folded her hands in her lap, watching me expectantly. "But if you ask him to, he will listen to you."

"Uncle Gunnar can't come," Nanna cut in from where she stood in front of the hearth sweeping ashes. "He had to go away for a day or two." She caught my gaze as though to warn me not to say anything about Gunnar going into the forest. As young as the girls were, they knew about the jotunn. They'd overheard their mother conversing about the madman and had been frightened ever since.

At an urgent tapping on the chamber door, I froze. What tidings were upon us now? I wasn't sure I wanted to know.

As the door opened a crack, my friend Ami peeked through. While she outwardly appeared composed, her eyes held a warning. "Your sister Kirstin is at the servants' door. She's upset and is asking for you."

Kirstin was here? My pulse picked up speed. She never came any other time except in the mornings. Something must have happened.

Nanna stopped sweeping, a groove forming in her

forehead. "Hurry on down to her."

I nodded and hastened from the room, following Ami as she led the way through passageways and down a series of stairways until we reached the lower level. At the end of the long hallway, Kirstin stood just inside the door, leaning against the wall.

When she saw me, she released a soft sob and ran toward me.

My heartbeat sped even faster. Had something happened to Enok or Father? "What is amiss?" I asked as I opened my arms to her.

She flung herself at me, now openly crying.

Ami, thankfully, ducked out of sight.

I gathered Kirstin closer, my blood running cold at all the possibilities of things that could be wrong. I was desperate to know, almost frantic. But I drew in a calming breath. I was the strong one, the one who had access to resources my family didn't, the one everyone looked to for answers. I had to remain steadfast now.

"Tell me the news," I said, stroking her hair.

She huffed and pulled away almost angrily. "You already knew, and you didn't tell me."

"Knew what?"

"That Frans went into the forest." Her face crumpled.

"I found out this morn."

"You should have sent me word right away of his plans." Her voice broke. "Instead, I had to find out from Enok just now."

I could only stare at my younger sister. Although she was more emotional than I was, I couldn't make sense of this outburst and why she was so upset.

"What difference would it have made if I'd told you

earlier or not?"

She sniffled and wiped at her splotchy cheeks. "I would have figured out a way to make Frans stay back."

"I didn't know he was going in until he'd already left." That wasn't entirely true. He'd mentioned the possibility. And after his witnessing my kiss with Gunnar in the garden, I should have predicted he'd go. "Now Gunnar has gone into the forest to aid him."

Though my heart quavered at the prospect of Gunnar deep in the woods by now, I had to trust that as one of the strongest and best knights in the land, he could accomplish more than others had been able to do.

"If you cared at all about Frans the way you should, this wouldn't have happened." Kirstin's wobbly voice contained a note of censure I hadn't heard there before.

The truth of the matter was that she was right. If I had truly cared about Frans, he wouldn't have left. "He deserves someone better than me."

"He deserves someone who loves him." Her tears started flowing again. "Someone like—someone like . . ."

My mind halted its frantic racing, and I stared at Kirstin's anguished expression. Suddenly I knew why Kirstin came every morn instead of Enok, why she lingered and watched the forge, why she asked about Frans so oft, why she was here at this very moment.

"Frans deserves someone like you, Kirstin. Someone who loves him." If Gunnar brought back Frans alive, I would spend the rest of my earthly days doing my best to persuade Frans to love Kirstin instead of me. Surely once he was made aware of her adoration, he'd forget about me and let himself love Kirstin instead.

Kirstin sniffled. "You're not angry with me?"

"Why would I be angry?" I couldn't be, not when my affection belonged to Gunnar. "You are the better woman for Frans, and I regret I didn't conclude that sooner."

"It wouldn't have mattered." Kirstin's voice dropped to an agonized whisper. "He loves you and has no interest in any other woman."

"He may believe he cares for me, but if—when—I'm able to next speak with him, I'll inform him that he needs to marry you, that you'll love and cherish him in a way that I can't."

"Truly?" Tears glistened in her eyes.

"Truly." Even if Gunnar hadn't made his confessions to me earlier, I realized now I had to let Frans go so that he could have a wife who would be able to give him her whole heart and not just pieces. He deserved that, even if he didn't yet know it.

"I told myself I would never say anything," Kirstin whispered. "I told myself I only wanted his happiness. And if marrying you made him happy, then that was what was necessary."

"Maybe he thought marrying me would fulfill him. But ultimately, he'll find more satisfaction in being with someone who adores him."

Kirstin nodded and then peeked at me, as though to gauge whether I meant what I was saying.

I pressed my hands on either side of her cheeks and forced her to look directly at me. "I mean it, Kirstin. I don't love Frans, and I know now I can't marry him."

"Then who will you marry? Is there someone else?"

For the briefest of moments, I was tempted to divulge everything Gunnar had told me earlier. But I couldn't. Not even to my sister. "Don't worry about me. I have my work with the girls, and erelong Lady Sofia will have another babe to keep me busy."

Maybe I would never have a normal life. Maybe I would always be waiting for Gunnar's visits home. Maybe a few days or weeks with him would be all I'd get. While it would never be enough, I would cherish the moments anyway.

Kirstin studied my face a second longer, as though sensing more was going on inside me than I'd shared. I released her and stepped away, needing her to believe me. "Have no fear for me."

"I would never want to step in the way of your happiness. You know that, do you not?"

"And I would never want to step in the way of yours."

She glanced to the door at the end of the passageway leading outside before swallowing hard. "Then I hope you'll understand why I must go into the forest after Frans."

"What?" I clasped her arm. "No. Absolutely not." It didn't matter if I'd considered the same thing. I wouldn't allow Kirstin to go in. She was too naïve, inexperienced, and untested. I, on the other hand, had developed a sense of wariness, alertness, and caution after living in the earl's house for so many years.

Kirstin clutched my arm in return. "When Enok spoke of going in after the jotunn, he said the fables speak of women defeating the trolls, never a man."

"They're called fables for a reason. Because no one

knows for certain their merit."

"When Enok was making plans to accept the earl's challenge, he asked me to secretly go with him because he thought I might be able to help."

I oft found my ire rising at my foolish younger brother. And this was one of those times. "How could he? That's entirely selfish of him."

"Trolls are distracted by beautiful women, especially those wearing red."

"Perhaps. But what if that doesn't work? And anyway, everyone says the real peril isn't from the jotunn but from the deadly traps throughout the forest."

"No one knows for certain if there are traps." Kirstin finished drying her cheeks and pulled herself up to her full height. "But either way, I want to offer my help to the men."

Had I been hasty in letting Gunnar go by himself? Should I have insisted on accompanying him? Maybe Kirstin was right, that a woman ought to go along. But *she* wasn't that woman. "No. You can't."

"You don't understand, Mikaela." Her eyes welled again with tears. "The man you love isn't in the forest facing death."

If only she knew how wrong she was.

Her lips quivered. "If you were in my position, you'd want to go in too."

"It's too dangerous."

"But Enok says the jotunn won't harm a woman—"

"No!" The word echoed in the empty hallway. I glanced around and then lowered my voice. "You're not going."

She stiffened, and her eyes flashed. "I'm leaving

whether you want me to or not. If I can do something to help, then I have to try." She spun and began to walk away, determination in each firm step.

I had to stop her. She wouldn't last a dozen paces into the forest. Not that I would either. But I had a better chance than she did. "You're not going," I said again, "because I am."

My statement brought her to a halt. This time when she turned to look at me, her eyes were wide and distressed. I could see the protest formulating, and I spoke before she could, offering the same reasoning that I had to Gunnar. "I'm the one who brought this trouble to Frans, and I should be the one to rectify it."

"I'm brave enough, Mikaela."

"Of course you're brave enough. But of the two of us, I'll be able to navigate through the dangers of the forest and pay better attention to the details around me."

"But—"

"And I have a knife." I patted my pocket, feeling the long length of the blade in its sheath.

She took a rapid step back, her gaze darting to the closed doors as though to make sure no one heard my mention of the illegal weapon. "You could give it to me."

I shook my head, pressed my lips together, and said no more. I was willing to take the risk of punishment for having the knife, but I wouldn't let Kirstin.

After several heartbeats, Kirstin released a sigh laced with defeat. "Very well."

"I'll need your cloak so that I might leave the castle as you. Then no one will be the wiser as to my going into the forest."

She began to shed the garment. "What would you have me do?"

"You will stay here with Nanna until I return."

The plan was risky. If Riki or Rena spoke of my absence, if one of the other servants noticed, or if anyone saw Kirstin, we would heap trouble upon ourselves. But I had no choice, not if I wanted to keep Kirstin away from this immediate danger.

Besides, if there was even a slim chance that as a woman I had an advantage against the jotunn, how could I not use it to help Gunnar and Frans?

Chapter 16

A SKELETON DANGLED UPSIDE DOWN FROM A GNARLED BIRCH tree, the chains of a rusted snare wrapped securely around the ankle. Another victim who'd fallen prey to the vicious traps hidden all throughout the forest.

I stared through the fading daylight at the gruesome sight, only one of the many horrors I'd witnessed over the past hours of searching for Frans.

I'd made slow progress, carefully cutting back the foliage with each step, not only to make sure I wasn't ensnared in a trap, but also so that I could use my cleared footpath to find my way safely back out of the forest.

So far, I'd managed to stay on Frans's trail, which appeared to be an old deer path. Since he was such a big man, I'd been able to track him fairly easily. A time or two, he'd veered in a direction I hadn't expected, but I always picked back up the clues—the crushed leaves, a boot print, a broken twig, bent branches.

"Where are you, Frans?" I scanned the landscape, which was more overgrowth of trees, shrubs, vines, lichen, and windfall. The shadows were growing with the passing of the day.

Erelong, I would need to stop, clear an area, and make camp.

Although I wanted to keep going, traveling was already difficult enough by daylight, and I couldn't take any chances in the dark.

Not only were all sizes of snares buried beneath the leaves and dirt of the forest floor, but several skeletons were caught in foothold traps. 'Twas likely the clamp jaws had been laced with poison, killing the person before they could pull themselves free.

If that wasn't bad enough, there were also pits with human remains in them. Some trapped the person in such tight quarters that they couldn't move. Others were wider but too deep to climb out of. And still another pit had been lined with tree limbs that were shaven into dangerous points, no doubt impaling anyone who fell inside.

It was clear that each step I took was perilous. It was also clear the jotunn had spent countless days and hours working on the traps, as though he had no better way to occupy his time.

Had he created the maze of traps to protect the chalice? Was that the real reason for the difficulty? If nothing else, he'd scared people from venturing in and had been left mostly undisturbed these many years.

What did he think of the men who'd come in recently? And now Frans? If the jotunn had any wits about him— and with the complexity of the traps, he seemed smart enough—then he would soon realize something had changed the status quo. Perhaps he'd believe he was in jeopardy and would create more havoc in the forest to deter this new influx.

I skimmed the blades of grass in front of me and traced a finger along Frans's bootstep in the soft earth beneath the growth. I hadn't seen any other prints save those of animals. And I guessed the jotunn used his traps not only to keep out unwanted people but also to trap wild creatures to provide sustenance for himself.

Using my knife, I cut back more branches and twigs. Frans was taking some care as he wound through the forest. But with how cleverly the jotunn had disguised the traps, I could only pray Frans wouldn't get caught. If he had, I hoped I would find him in time and could free him.

At the very least, I'd stopped Mikaela from coming into the forest after Frans. I shuddered to think of her navigating the woodland by herself.

She was safe for now. But for how long? How long would I be able to hide my love for her from Bernhard? How long before he figured out I cared about her above anyone else?

I feared the day when that would happen. And a sense of urgency had prodded me all day since seeing her—an urgency to work quickly in coming up with a plan to protect both her and her kin.

A strange, strangled cry stopped me. I paused in my cutting and strained to listen. Was it Frans? From what I'd gathered, a total of four men, including Frans, had been sent out. It was possible—although not likely—that one or more of the first three were still alive somewhere.

For a long moment, I held myself motionless. But nothing moved around me, not even a breeze.

I continued forward, surveying each inch, testing each step. I had to work faster and get farther before darkness fell. I sawed off another branch, my muscles tense, my body ready to spring at the least threat.

My thoughts returned to my conversation with Eggum, as they had oft since I'd visited with him in the early morning hours. Was the old servant right in insinuating the jotunn was my grandfather's brother, my great uncle Sven? If so, had Sven gone mad from his injuries and being rejected by his family?

If the priest and other castle staff had sought him out and hoped he would take control of Romsdal, perhaps he'd been an honorable man. And yet, if he'd once been decent, he no longer was. No decent man could trap innocent men and leave them to die dangling from tree limbs or suffering in deep pits.

Another agonized cry resounded, this time louder.

I froze, my knife in the middle of slicing a stalk. Someone was nearby. He was in pain, that much was clear. But at least he was still alive.

What direction had the sound come from? Cautiously I straightened. "Who's there?"

Again, silence settled over the dense woodland.

"Is anyone there?" I raised my voice. I didn't care if the jotunn knew I was in the forest. Maybe I could even draw him out of hiding to engage in hand-to-hand combat. Yes, I'd heard he was vicious. The legends spoke of his strength. But I would fare better fighting him than dodging his traps.

"Frans?" I waited several heartbeats. Hearing nothing in response, I resumed cutting my way through the brush.

"Help." The call came more distinctly. "Help."

Though I hadn't spoken to Frans oft during my childhood or my visits home, I recognized his voice.

"Frans? It's me. Gunnar."

"Gunnar?" The voice was hollow, as if he was stuck in

a barrel. "What are you doing here?"

"Mikaela wanted to come after you. But I wouldn't let her and came in her stead." That was partially true. He didn't need to know I'd been planning to explore the forest anyway. No one needed to know what I suspected about the chalice.

"Where are you?" I scanned high and low but didn't see a sign of him anywhere.

"I fell into a hole. One of my legs is broken."

I tried to follow the sound of his voice, clipping the brush carefully and pressing the ground ahead with the tip of my sword to assess for foothold traps, snares, or depressions in the earth.

"Keep talking."

He groaned.

"What else hurts?"

"My other leg landed on a pike. The tip pierced through my boot into my heel. Deep."

I cringed. "Can you staunch the bleeding?"

"I can't move my arms." His voice faded, and I guessed he was losing consciousness.

I adjusted my steps, whacking the foliage faster. If he'd lost a great deal of blood, then I needed to get him out of the forest tonight.

"How long have you been trapped?" I needed him to stay conscious more than I needed the answer.

"Forever." The word ended on another groan.

"I'm almost there." I slashed several branches. "Stay with me."

He didn't respond.

"Frans?" I pushed aside a tangle of brush. Had he fallen unconscious? With the pain he was suffering, unconsciousness would give him a much needed reprieve.

I made it a few more steps before I finally saw the dark rim of earth just ahead. From what I could tell, a thin layer of branches and leaves had been placed over the trap to disguise it.

Why hadn't he noticed? Or tested the spot? He'd obviously traveled cautiously up to that point.

I inched closer. As I stepped near the edge and leaned to look into the hole, something coiled around my ankle. Before I could jump back, I found myself being dragged along the ground, flipped upside down, and jerked up through the air.

In the next instant, I was hanging head down from a high limb of a tall oak, a snare tightening painfully around my calf.

Chapter 17

Mikaela

I watched each step I took, staying to the path I'd discovered—one I guessed Frans or Gunnar had carved.

The deeper I wound into Hardanger Forest, the more I understood just how foolish I would have been to go in after Frans on my own. I'd only needed to see the first skeleton in a hole to understand how dangerous the jotunn really was. Of course, I'd heard and believed the tales. But now that I was seeing the horrible way that men had died, the reality of what Frans and Gunnar had gone into turned my blood cold.

I'd been the cause of them both rushing into this tangle of terror. If either of them died here, I'd hold myself accountable.

I carried a tallow candle to give me some light, especially since daylight was fast fading. I'd also brought along a torch to ignite once darkness fell, among a few other provisions I'd packed in a sack now slung across my shoulder.

After leaving Kirstin in the castle, I'd exited through the main gate, hustling along and taking care to hide my face. Thankfully, no one had questioned my departure or noticed me crossing toward the forest.

I'd traveled for a couple of hours at least. And I still hadn't seen or heard either Gunnar or Frans. I intended to keep going all night if necessary. I wouldn't stop until I found them.

The earl's challenge to kill the jotunn was ill-fated. If anyone could survive the traps and dangerous forest, how would they find the madman in the midst of the dark growth?

Even now at this very moment, the jotunn could be following me and waiting to attack me. I halted and shuddered, drawing my cloak more securely around my shoulders. I lifted my candle, examining every shadow and wishing I was anyplace else but here.

How had Nanna reacted when she'd learned Kirstin was in the nursery instead of me? I'd warned Kirstin not to tell Nanna what I'd done. But Kirstin wouldn't be able to hold in the secret for long, and I regretted the pain my going would cause Nanna. After so many years of making it her life's mission to protect me, I'd slipped beyond her grasp. And now there was nothing she could do to come to my aid.

The truth was that I'd been slipping from her grasp well before today. Of course, I admired her for spending her life making sure I was secure and well fed in the nursery. She'd done all she could to help the rest of my family too, not only giving them food when she could, but finding other ways to supply them with provisions.

But it had never been enough . . . at least not for

me. The pulsing need to do more pounded louder within me. Not just for my family, but for all those who lived in oppression.

As my candlelight touched upon the remains of a human hanging by one leg from a rusted chain in a tree overhead, I gasped and pressed my free hand over my mouth.

What was I doing here?

Even on this well-cut path, I was taking too many risks going any farther. I needed to stop now before something happened and Gunnar and Frans ended up needing to rescue me.

However, if I returned to Kirstin without news of Frans, she'd head into the forest herself. I'd have to tie her up and make sure she didn't go. Gunnar's warning about tying me to the bedpost came rushing back into my mind. Now I understood how he'd felt and why he'd threatened to do so.

Twisting my head away from the skeleton, I breathed out my frustration and let my shoulders sag. I had to go back.

Chapter 18

GUNNAR

BLOOD RUSHED TO MY HEAD AS I HUNG UPSIDE DOWN, AND MY sword began to slip from its sheath. With quick reflexes, I grabbed it so that I was holding my knife in one hand and sword in the other. I needed to have everything at my disposal as I worked at freeing myself.

From up high, I had a clear view of Frans. A foot from the surface, his shoulders were wedged tightly in the hole. His broad girth had likely saved his life by keeping him from plunging farther down onto the sharply pointed limbs. His head lolled to one side. He'd passed out again, just as I'd thought. There was nothing he could do to come to my aid anyway.

The chain around my calf was already tearing through my legging and burning against my skin. It wouldn't be long before it dug into my flesh and cut off circulation. And it wouldn't be long before I'd grow dizzy, nauseous, and perhaps lose consciousness.

If I had any hope of saving myself and Frans, I had to act right away.

Could I cut my way free? I glanced at the chain, then discarded that idea. I wouldn't be able to hack through the snare around my leg without harming myself. Even if I could somehow grasp the chain dangling from the limb, I wouldn't be able to saw the iron links.

What if I could climb my way out? I was at least a dozen feet away from the trunk and at least a dozen feet from the limb above. I couldn't reach either easily. No doubt the jotunn had planned it that way.

Even so, getting to the trunk seemed to be my best option. If I could propel myself close enough to the tree, I'd be able to use my sword or knife to stab into the bark and climb up to the limb. In doing so, I would pull the chain even more painfully against my leg. But I had to try it.

I swayed my body, gaining some movement. With the motion, the snare pinched tighter. Pain shot down my leg. Gritting my teeth, I forced my torso to swing back and forth like a pendulum, getting ever wider.

"Gunnar?" Frans's weak voice came from below.

"I stepped into the snare." Probably the one Frans had been avoiding when he'd fallen in the hidden hole.

Frans groaned.

"I'll get free." At least, I hoped I would before I fell unconscious.

I stretched out my sword as far as my arm could reach, and as I swung toward the tree, it grazed the trunk. A few more swings, and I'd be able to stab it.

Though my leg burned where the chain wrapped around my flesh, I wriggled to gain even more movement.

"If you free yourself," Frans said breathlessly, "I want you to marry Mikaela and take her away from Romsdal."

He was giving me his dying wishes. I'd heard such

wishes uttered before on the battlefield. And I wasn't ready to accept them. "Stay with me, Frans. Don't give up yet."

As my body tilted back toward the tree, my sword scraped closer but not enough that I could plunge it in.

"She loves you." Frans's voice didn't contain any bitterness or despair. Only resignation.

Even if Mikaela had responded positively to my ardor and declaration of love, she hadn't said the words in return. Her feelings, the situation, our future—it was all precarious and could be destroyed with just one wrong move. But I took comfort from Frans's assertion and prayed it was true.

"As much as I tried to deny it," he continued, "I've always known she cared about you more than me."

"You're a good man, Frans—"

"I saw the relief in her face when I had to forfeit the money that I was saving for the bride price. But I held on to her anyway."

"You've only done what you think is best for her. And I respect that."

"She'll never be truly happy unless she's with you."

I wished I were in another place having this discussion instead of swaying upside down in an ever-darkening forest. I couldn't savor his declarations, could only tuck them away and hope I'd have the opportunity to test them for myself at some point.

As the burning in my leg turned into torturous fire, I bit back a groan and forced myself to swing wider. Nearing the tree, I aimed and thrust the sword. I couldn't risk wedging it too deeply so that I wouldn't be able to pull it free.

The tip made contact, and this time, it stuck.

The chain above jerked hard against my calf, and an agonized cry slipped out.

"What happened?" Frans called.

I swallowed the bile that pushed into my throat and took a deep breath. "I'm starting my climb up the tree."

With the weight of my entire body pulling on my trapped leg, I needed to take the pressure off. I stabbed my knife into the tree above the sword. Then I rested my upper body strength upon the hilts of the sword and knife, giving my leg a brief respite. After a moment, I gauged the distance up the trunk until I reached the limb. "I'll be down in a few minutes."

When silence met me, I could only hope he hadn't given up the will to live yet.

My arms strained to keep hold of the sword and knife. But with as much speed as I could muster, I began the process of unhooking one weapon at a time and climbing my way up the trunk. Because the knife was shorter, wedging it took an extra effort that pulled on my leg. But with each climb higher, the pressure of the chain loosened until at last, I reached the limb.

I latched onto the branch and breathed out my relief. The snare was still wrapped tightly around my calf, but the pain was more bearable.

With a final heft, I pulled myself to a sitting position on the limb. It was thicker than I'd realized, and if I needed to saw through it, my task would be difficult. Nevertheless, I was one step closer to freeing myself.

I had a sweeping view of the forest below. Though the fading light and dense vegetation made the view difficult, I could see the outlines of several more dangling skeletons.

This forest truly was deadly. I'd been as foolish as

Frans to believe I could navigate it alone. Once I freed Frans, I'd take him out to safety and then wait for Torvald before coming in again after the chalice. Surely together, we'd be able to plot a strategy to outwit the jotunn and his traps.

I scooted down the limb until I reached the length of the chain. I dragged it up along with my leg. Even in the dimness, I glimpsed the oozing blood and the mangled flesh where the snare circled my calf.

Taking stock of the type of slip knot, I jostled the links, trying to loosen them. Each movement chafed my already raw skin. But I plied at the chain, needing to free myself.

In my periphery, I caught a movement on the ground. I halted my efforts and held myself stationary, scanning the undergrowth for anyone or anything that might prove a new threat. Only eerie silence and stillness met me. Even so, the hairs on the back of my neck prickled, and I sensed Frans and I were no longer alone.

Chapter 19

GUNNAR

I WAITED, KNIFE poised and ready to throw.

Frans remained unconscious and quiet. And this time, I wanted him to stay that way until I could determine who—or what—was lurking nearby.

After long minutes and a final survey of the forest, I resumed my efforts to remove the snare from my leg. As much as I needed to remain stealthy to hide my position in the tree, I also had to liberate myself so that in turn, I could free Frans. His life depended upon my skill and speed.

I tried to minimize the noise. But the chain was rusty and clanked with the slightest movement. All the while I loosened the links, I pulled away pieces of my clothing and bits of my skin. Blood coated my fingers, making them slick and cumbersome.

Even so, I managed to release the snare's hold little by little, until at last I had enough leeway to slip it down my leg and ankle then over my boot. I used my knife to slice off part of my tunic, then wrapped the linen around my calf and tied it tight. It would have to suffice as a bandage for now.

Sheathing my sword and knife, I began to climb down. I couldn't bear weight upon my injured leg and had to go slow. Halfway down, the same strange feeling came over me. We were being watched.

I stopped and glanced around. At a rustle in the bushes ahead, I tensed. Without taking my attention from the spot, I lowered myself the rest of the distance.

A branch shifted, and I caught the glow of what appeared to be eyes.

Was it a wild creature? Or was it the jotunn? More importantly, what kind of threat did it pose?

I crawled away from the tree toward the hole where Frans was trapped, dragging the loose chain with me. With each inch forward, I used my sword to clear a path and make sure I didn't find myself caught in another snare.

"Frans?" I whispered as I reached the edge of the hole. "Can you hear me?"

Only silence came from within.

I prayed he wasn't dead and was still merely unconscious. Either way, I wouldn't leave him behind.

Carefully I lowered the chain, not wanting to jar him and cause him to slip farther down. Before I could secure Frans, the branches ahead parted and a grizzled creature stepped through. Stoop-shouldered, with a long beard and stringy gray hair, he was bare save for tattered leggings. Even his feet were unclad and dirty. He reminded me of the beggar Eggum—weak and thin and unkempt.

Was this the jotunn that had been terrorizing the forest all these years?

I climbed unsteadily to my feet, unsheathing my sword.

At the sight of my weapon, the creature took a step back.

My attention lifted to his face, which was misshapen with a patchwork of taut scars. The scars, while dirty, were a splotchy red, the same color I'd witnessed on a fellow knight who'd once burned his arm.

Was this my grandfather's brother after all? Had Eggum speculated correctly?

This man—if he was a man—certainly looked old enough.

The only thing I could do was ask. "Sven? Sven Likness?"

He didn't respond. But something changed in his expression, telling me I'd guessed right.

"I'm Gunnar Likness, grandson of Jorg, your brother."

He watched me warily.

Maybe I shouldn't have mentioned my relation to Jorg, especially since he'd taken the earldom away from Sven. No doubt Sven loathed Jorg and any of his relatives. Perhaps he'd charge at me and push me into another hidden trap nearby.

"Why are you here?" The man's voice was raspy, as though from disuse.

I glanced down to Frans. "I came to rescue this man. If you'll let me free him, I'll be on my way."

Sven tilted his head as though examining me. Was he planning how best to attack me?

"Why save him? Why not save yourself?"

"I would save both of us."

"He is dying." The threaded voice was hardly a whisper.

"But he's not dead yet." Frans's bare head hung forward, his hat nowhere in sight.

"He is clearly but a servant, and you are his lord. Why does his life matter?"

I didn't have a ready answer. Yes, I'd come on this rescue mission partly for Mikaela, because Frans was Mikaela's friend, and I'd do anything to make Mikaela happy. And of course, I'd wanted to keep her out of the forest and away from danger.

Even so, I knew his life mattered too.

I wasn't lord of Likness Castle or Earl of Romsdal, and as the second-born son, I had no power to govern the people who worked for my family. But I'd always done what I could in little ways, and deep in my heart, I cared about them, many of whom, like Frans, I'd known my whole life.

"Frans has served my family faithfully these many years," I finally said, meeting Sven's narrowed gaze. "He deserves my service to him in return. And this is the least I can do."

Sven held my gaze, almost as though he'd taken me captive. "You are different than your father and his father before him."

"I have tried to be, although I fear I have failed too oft in that regard."

He glanced over his shoulder. "You will not have long to free your servant before the master of the forest arrives to enslave you."

Master of the forest? "Then you are not the jotunn?"

He shook his head and began to limp forward on his bare feet. "He enslaves those who are able to free themselves from his traps. The rest he leaves to die and rot."

"And how does he enslave them?" I wasn't sure I wanted to know, but the question slipped out anyway.

Sven again peered in the direction he'd come, and then lowered his head and voice. "The jotunn has the power to issue curses. And because you have freed yourself, he will bind you to him and the forest forever."

"I won't let him curse me."

"Then you must leave your servant and flee before the jotunn sets eyes upon you. Once his gaze links with yours, you will be cursed." Sven's low, hoarse voice turned urgent.

My muscles tensed with the need to escape. Even if I managed to pull Frans out of his trap without harming him further, there was a good chance he'd die anyway from the blood loss. Besides, in his current condition, he wouldn't be able to walk well. He'd slow down our retreat.

I knelt beside Frans again, touched his lips, and felt his breath. He was still alive.

No matter what might happen to me, I couldn't leave him behind. Not even if that meant I ended up enslaved to the jotunn.

I clutched the chain and began once again winding it past Frans's shoulder so that I could finish looping it around his arm.

In the next instant, Sven crouched on the ground on the opposite side of the hole. "Grab him under the arm, and together we shall endeavor to pull him up."

I didn't question Sven and his offer of help. Instead, I tucked both hands under Frans's armpit at the same time that Sven grasped Frans's other side, and together we hefted Frans.

The young man didn't budge.

"His foot." I strained with all my strength. "It's stuck on the pike."

The muscles in Sven's thin arms stretched taut as he worked just as hard to loosen Frans.

"How many have escaped the jotunn's traps?" I asked with a grunt.

"Only one before you."

I paused. "You?"

He nodded.

If Eggum had been correct, then Sven had been but a young man when he'd been cast into the forest by his kin. Somehow, he'd managed to free himself from the jotunn's traps just as I had. "How has the jotunn cursed you?"

"I am bound to live my remaining days in the forest as his servant. If I attempt to leave, I shall bleed to death."

"Have you tried to leave?"

Sven held firmly to Frans. "I did once many years ago."

"And what happened?"

"As I neared the forest edge, blood began to flow from my mouth and nose."

My skin prickled, and I scanned the dark forest around us. If the jotunn was real, then I was in even more danger than I'd realized.

"My family did not want me as the next earl anyway."

"From what I'm told, brave men rose up and risked their lives to restore you to your true place." The men my grandfather had eliminated in his purge.

Sven shook his head sadly. "They came to the forest edge to plead with me, believing I would make a better ruler than my brother. When I spoke of my curse and inability to leave, they tried to exchange something of value to the jotunn for my freedom."

"The sacred chalice?"

Sven's head snapped up. "That is why you, your servant, and the others have come recently? To seek the chalice?"

If I spoke the truth, would he abandon me and hand me over to the jotunn before I could make an escape? If I lied, I sensed I would only heap more trouble upon myself. "My brother, the earl, pursues the chalice for his own gain and has sent men into the forest promising reward to anyone who kills the jotunn."

Sven's mouth pinched into a line.

"I do not wish to assist my brother in his selfish ambition. Rather, I am on a mission for the king. He seeks the chalice to save his beloved queen from a bleeding curse."

Sven seemed to digest my news, likely not knowing much of what was going on in the rest of the kingdom. "Then you are not here to save this man after all but instead to find the chalice?"

"I own to wanting the chalice for the king. But I wouldn't save one life—the queen's—only to forfeit another." I nodded at Frans.

In the ever-darkening shadows, Sven studied me, as though searching for the truth. Though his face was dirty and disfigured, I saw in him the man he'd once been—a good man who'd been sorely rejected by his kin.

At a shout in the distance, Sven resumed his tugging against Frans with more effort. "We must make haste."

I bent and did likewise, and this time we managed to lift Frans an inch or so. The movement jarred him awake. His eyes flew open, and he moaned.

"Hold still now." I spoke quietly to Frans, hoping he wouldn't scream out his pain and draw the jotunn our way more rapidly.

Frans turned startled eyes upon me. "You're free?" His voice was weak and breathless.

"Yes. Now it's your turn." I nodded at Sven, and we both hauled upward again. The exertion must have been enough to free Frans's foot from the pike, because we drew him up and out of the hole in one swift move. In the process, Frans released an agonized cry, and then passed out again.

As we laid him flat, the darkness mostly hid the mangled condition of his foot as well as the broken bone in his opposite leg. But I saw enough to know I had to tend to both before I could move him any further.

I sliced a strip from my tunic. But Sven intervened before I could wrap it around Frans's foot. "I'll do the doctoring. You find two sturdy branches and tie your cloak them. You'll need a litter to carry him out."

I didn't hesitate. I handed over the strip and cut another. Then I began sawing the nearest limb.

Another shout rent the air, this one nearer. Sven didn't pause in his wrapping of Frans's foot. I guessed he was accustomed to the jotunn's rage, a rage I would soon experience.

But I sliced faster, until at last, I snapped the branch free. I wasted no time in reaching for a second limb and sawing it. My leg ached, but in comparison to Frans's injuries, I couldn't complain. Even so, I prayed I would be able to move swiftly through the forest and outrun the jotunn.

"Why didn't the jotunn set you free in exchange for the chalice?" The question tumbled out as I broke the second limb and began tying my cloak to it.

Sven had finished binding Frans's foot and was now working at strapping a thick piece of branch to Frans's other leg, likely to keep the broken bone from doing more damage during the transport out of the forest. For a moment, I didn't think he would answer me. But then his response came, low and raspy. "It did not provide the healing he sought for his pain."

I finished tying one end of my cloak and used my teeth to tighten the knot. The sacred chalice had been used by Christ himself during the Last Supper. Even though Maxim had found evidence pointing toward its healing capabilities, none of us knew for certain if it truly could work miracles.

If it hadn't brought the jotunn healing, maybe we were on a useless mission.

"Regardless of the outcome," I said, "the jotunn should have kept his part of the bargain and set you free."

Sven released a mirthless laugh. "The jotunn is a liar and a thief and has no honor."

"So, he kept the chalice?"

"Yes, he has hidden it away so deeply in the earth, no man will be able to retrieve it."

At a roaring call and the crashing of brush drawing nigh, Sven hefted Frans and dragged him onto the makeshift litter. "You must go. Now."

I helped to situate Frans. "What else will the jotunn accept as an exchange for your freedom?"

Sven attempted to shove me forward. "Do not worry about me. I am an old man now. And I shall live out my days here."

I didn't budge. "Tell me what he will accept."

"No. Now go."

"I won't leave until you speak of it."

We stood now, face to face. Sven was taller than me by several inches. His features, though scarred and deformed, contained a kindness I'd overlooked when I'd first seen him. Perhaps that was how it always was—we tended to focus upon the outward appearances of people and miss the true beauty of their character as a result.

Sven's gaze darted in the direction of the approaching jotunn. Then with a frustrated growl, he spoke. "If a person cannot give him something of great worth, then he will accept one life in exchange for another."

"Someone can take your place?"

"Yes, but I will never allow it."

Chapter 20

Mikaela

The sounds grew louder, and as I turned a bend and held up my light, it fell upon Gunnar.

At the sight of him standing in the path, a cry of relief escaped, and I nearly crumpled to the ground.

The torch I'd lit several moments ago revealed him to be safe and solid, except for a strip of linen around his lower leg. He was holding the ends of two limbs, his cloak tied across them forming a stretcher. A person's head was barely visible above the edge of the cloak, but I could see enough to know it was Frans.

My relief swelled, and this time I sank to my knees.

"Mikaela?" Gunnar took me in, his beautiful face filling with surprise. "What in the name of the holy saints are you doing here?"

Only then did I notice another man standing beside him, attired in rags and his face disfigured. He shot a look over his shoulder then pushed Gunnar aside to pick up the litter in his stead. "We have to keep moving."

Who was this man? He couldn't be the fierce jotunn everyone feared, otherwise he wouldn't be helping Gunnar and Frans.

Gunnar started toward me. The light from the torch revealed strips of ripped tunic wrapped around his calf. Already the linen was saturated in dark red blood. Whatever had happened, he'd been badly injured.

"I told you not to come into the forest." Gunnar's voice rose with both anger and a note of desperation. As he reached my side, he grasped my arm and tugged me to my feet. "You shouldn't be here."

"I know. I came to keep my sister Kirstin from rushing in. She was devastated to hear about Frans." And I'd come hoping to somehow help Gunnar. But I didn't say so. I already looked foolish enough for thinking I could somehow face the forest and come out unscathed when no one else had been able to do so for decades.

I'd tried to make myself turn around and go back, but with voices and cries ahead on the trail, I hadn't been able to walk away. All I'd been able to think about was that Gunnar was in need and that I might be the only one who could save him.

Gunnar began to tug me forward. "The jotunn is coming, and we can't let him see any of us."

As much as I wanted to stop and find out what had happened to Frans, I stumbled along behind Gunnar. "Who is this man helping you?"

"He's my great uncle Sven."

"Your uncle?"

"He was cast out by his kin long ago after he suffered severe burns in a fire."

I'd never heard about an uncle being cast out. But

perhaps it was part of the forbidden family history, the parts of the past that no one was allowed to talk about. "What's he doing here?"

"He's a prisoner of the jotunn." Gunnar's voice was hard and frustrated.

"Make haste." Sven spoke breathlessly behind me, clearly struggling to carry Frans's weight.

Gunnar moved faster so that I had to jog to keep up. "The jotunn will curse and enslave me if he catches me."

"Curse and enslave?"

"Yes, just like Sven. After he set himself free from the trap, the jotunn cursed him so that he can never leave the forest without bleeding to death first."

I tried to digest Gunnar's hastily spoken explanation, but the only part that I could focus on was that the jotunn had cursed Sven and now would likely curse and enslave Gunnar.

Sven steadily fell behind us. "I think you should carry Frans and let me guide the young woman."

Gunnar nodded. Even as they made the switch, curses and shouting bellowed nearer, almost as if we were being chased by a crowd of drunken woodcutters brandishing their axes. Gunnar picked up the litter and Frans as if he weighed no more than a baby fox. And Sven took hold of my arm, guiding me through the thick overgrowth but staying to the path Gunnar had previously cut as my torchlight guided the way.

"Perhaps Gunnar should go ahead," I offered. "Since he is most in danger from the jotunn."

"Everyone is in danger from the jotunn," Sven murmured, his breathing already labored. "Even if he does not bind you to the forest as his slave, he can curse anyone who provokes him."

"Then we will not provoke him."

"You already have by being here, and now you must get out of the forest as quickly as possible."

"And you too."

"Not me. I must stay."

"Surely we can find a way to help you escape from the jotunn's curse."

Holding on to my arm and directing me from behind, Sven pushed me faster. His lack of response meant only one thing: he had no intention of trying to escape with us.

"Is there any way at all we can help you break free from the jotunn?" I couldn't imagine what his life had been like in this dangerous forest, living under the control of the jotunn.

"Do not worry about me—"

"He cannot keep you here forever."

"He already has."

This man wasn't much older than Nanna. Maybe sixty years of age. How long had he lived here? Years? Maybe decades? Whatever the amount, he deserved to be set free.

Kirstin's admonition about the jotunn—trolls—being distracted by beautiful women echoed through my mind, as it had since I'd left. What would the jotunn think if he saw me? Would he tear me asunder? Or would I be able to distract him long enough for Sven to break free and go to safety with Gunnar and Frans? Even if Sven did break free, how could he survive leaving the forest without bleeding to death?

The narrow path wound past a deep pit, and I kept myself from looking down inside, knowing I'd see more skeletons.

"What will the jotunn do to you for helping us escape?" I asked Sven.

"He will keep me alive. He always does."

"But he'll torture you, won't he?"

Only Sven's labored breathing filled the space between us. His silence was answer enough.

"Gunnar, please. Can you think of a way to help Sven?" I glanced over my shoulder to find Gunnar struggling to keep up, his limp more pronounced. His leg was injured worse than I'd realized.

"I'm getting you!" came the enraged shouting from behind us. "You can't get away!"

Gunnar was breathing hard too, his muscles straining under the weight of his burden. "Sven, I need you to drag Frans for a little while."

Sven shook his head. "I know what you are thinking, that you will hand yourself over to the jotunn in exchange for my freedom."

"I'm growing weary." Gunnar's voice lacked conviction, which told me Sven was right. Gunnar was noble enough to make such a sacrifice. Just as he'd been noble enough to put his life in danger by coming after Frans.

"You are the true Earl of Romsdal," Gunnar insisted.

"Not anymore—"

"You have more right to the land and title than my brother. If you're free, you could rule with kindness instead of cruelty."

What if Sven were given the opportunity to rule? Would he do as Gunnar suggested and make life better for the people in his land? Surely his assistance now in this deadly situation proved he would make a better leader than Bernhard.

Keen yearning shot through me. Oh for a time of peace and plenty for all of us, a time when we no longer had to live in constant fear and hunger and control over every detail of our lives.

"Would the jotunn accept such an exchange?" I asked.

"'Tis likely with one so young as Gunnar. Yes."

Was that why Sven had given the task of carrying the litter to Gunnar? Perhaps Sven had guessed that as long as Gunnar was needed to save Frans, he wouldn't allow himself to fall behind and get captured by the jotunn.

My chest constricted at the prospect that Gunnar would enslave himself to the jotunn and experience the rest of his life cursed and imprisoned here in Hardanger Forest.

I couldn't let it happen. I loved him too much.

Yes, I loved Gunnar. Fully and completely. Without reservation. And I would do anything to save him. If the rumors about the jotunn with women were true, then I had a better chance of surviving captivity than Gunnar did.

With a shrug, I broke free of Sven and squeezed past Gunnar and Frans.

"Mikaela, no!" Gunnar's shout filled the night air, and he lunged after me. "No!"

I hefted my skirt and began to run.

"Release me!" Gunnar yelled. And I knew that Sven had stopped Gunnar. I didn't know how, but I prayed Sven would hold him long enough.

In the next instant, a giant-like man broke through the brush. Bald except for a tuft of white hair at the top of his scalp, he was swinging the trunk of a tree like a club, knocking down everything in his path. I thudded against his obese middle and fell to the ground in front of him. He raised the trunk above me, as if I were nothing but a bug he hoped to crush.

Chapter 21

GUNNAR

"LET ME GO!" I WRESTLED AGAINST SVEN, BUT AFTER YEARS OF fighting for his survival, my great uncle was stronger than I'd anticipated. And with my leg injury, I was weaker than I'd realized. Within seconds, he shoved me ahead of himself and wrestled me to the ground, pressing against my injured leg and causing me more torment—in order to force me into compliance.

"Fie upon you!" My heart bucked inside me just as hard as my body, demanding that I free myself and run to Mikaela's rescue. The thought of her facing the jotunn by herself drove me into a frenzy, so that all I could think about was getting to her.

Frans moaned softly but didn't awaken. If only he would, so that he could help me convince Sven to let me save Mikaela.

Sven's elbow dug into the middle of my back, keeping me down.

"Don't do this." With my face against the leaves and brush, I could hardly breathe. Had I misjudged Sven and taken him as an ally when he was my foe? Was he working in conjunction with the jotunn, hoping to win my favor so that I'd let down my guard?

"Be quiet and cease struggling." Sven's low voice resounded near my ear, and somehow he managed to bend my arm behind my back and wedge it upward sharply. "If the jotunn does not see you and link gazes, he cannot curse you."

"I don't care if he curses me. I'm not letting Mikaela put her life at risk." I twisted with a strong jerk, but Sven yanked at my arm, the pain tearing through me and blinding me.

"The jotunn won't harm a woman," Sven said evenly, almost calmly. "Especially one as beautiful as yours."

Blinking back a wave of nausea, I paused in my thrashing. "How can you be certain?"

"After these many years of watching him, I have learned his weakness is women." Sven's grip remained tight. "I would not have allowed the woman you love to present herself to the jotunn if I did not know it was so."

I closed my eyes and tried to swallow my panic. But it was lodged in my throat and wouldn't budge. We were in the darkness and no longer on the path I'd carved during the long journey into the forest. I feared moving to the left or right lest I find myself in another snare. Was that another one of Sven's tactics to make me do his bidding?

I spat out the dirt and leaves I'd inhaled. Even if I was angry with Sven and wanted to lash out at him, I sensed deep inside that he hadn't brought us this far only to betray us. He truly wanted me to leave the forest unharmed.

Somewhere behind me, I heard Mikaela again. And it was clear she was speaking with the jotunn.

"I have an offer for you," she called.

"Who are you?" the jotunn demanded in a hollow, almost childlike voice.

"My name is Mikaela, and I want to make an exchange for Sven."

I started to release a yell of protest, but Sven shoved my face back into the ground, cutting off the sound. I fought against him again, my pulse pounding with renewed urgency.

"Stop." Sven spoke quietly in my ear. "I will never let her exchange herself for me. I vow it."

The sincerity in my great uncle's whisper brought my frantic protest to a halt.

"She is providing you with the much-needed time to get away. When I release you, I want you to take your servant and run."

I shook my head. "I'll never leave without her."

"You cannot let her distraction be for naught." More protest crowded for release, but Sven continued before I could speak it. "Once you have a fair start, I shall step in and force Mikaela to go."

I didn't know if I could make myself move forward without her.

"This is the only way." Sven's voice was harsh. "With your injury and with the weight of the servant, you will never escape from the jotunn without a sizeable lead."

"I can't."

"You must."

I could see the logic behind the plan. But could I truly trust that he would make sure Mikaela didn't come to harm?

"Let me do this." His tone was laced with a plea. "I have had to stand helplessly by and watch people suffer for too many years. I need to do this now. Please."

I was wasting precious time fighting with Sven, time I could be using to make my getaway with Frans. The logical part of me knew I had to go. But my heart was ripping from my chest at the prospect of leaving Mikaela behind to an unknown fate.

"There have only been a few women who have come into the forest in the time I've lived here. The jotunn becomes addled at the merest sight of a fair maiden, even from afar, and cannot think clearly."

"What if he curses her?" I had only to think about Queen Lis suffering from a bleeding curse and her mother dying from the same to know that curses were real and deadly. Was it possible the royal family curse had come from a jotunn?

"I shall ensure she is gone before he has the chance to speak a curse."

I lifted a plea heavenward for help, then nodded. "Very well. I'll leave with Frans. But if she isn't out of the forest by the time the moon crests overhead in the sky, I'll return and fight for her."

"She will follow. I shall make sure of it."

Drawing in a deep breath, I pushed against Sven. This time he loosened his grip and released me.

For a fraction of an instant as I rose, I debated defying him and racing back toward the jotunn and Mikaela. But from the calmness of the conversation the two were having, I sensed Sven was right, that the jotunn wouldn't harm her.

"You'll make sure she is safe on her way out?"

"You have my word."

Mikaela's torch gave enough illumination to outline the trail I'd cut. Once I reached the boundary of her light,

I'd have to stop, use my flint, and make fire for a torch of my own so that I didn't fall into another deadly trap.

"Go now." Sven directed me toward the litter with Frans.

Once more I hesitated, regretting I couldn't help him get away. My only hope was to discuss the situation with Maxim and Princess Elinor. Maybe they would have suggestions for how to overcome the jotunn's curse. Then when I returned to Hardanger Forest for the chalice, I'd be able to assist him.

"You must never come back into the forest for me," he whispered as though reading my mind.

I didn't reply. Instead, I stepped in front of the litter, picked up the two limbs, and began to move down the path, leaving my heart behind with Mikaela.

Chapter 22

Mikaela

I clasped my hands tightly to the torch keep the jotunn from seeing my shaking. I needed him to see me as a maiden who exuded confidence and control.

He'd dropped the thick branch he'd been using to clear a path through the woods. With how large and clumsy he appeared, how did he avoid falling into his own pits and traps?

He stood at least a head above the tallest man I'd ever known and was at least twice the girth. His tunic was a patchwork of material, poorly sewn and threadbare, and his boots were open at the toes, revealing long curled toenails. Scars ran up and down his arms and neck and covered his face. They appeared to be pockmarks of some kind, perhaps from a disease he'd once experienced?

Was he really a jotunn, a legendary troll from the underworld? Or was he another outcast like Sven? A man despised by the world for his outward appearance and sent away to live in solitude?

It didn't matter what his origin was. Right now, my mission was to protect Gunnar and Frans, and in the process, make an exchange to gain Sven's freedom.

The jotunn peered down at me, one of his eyes half closed, the other blinking hard against the light from my torch.

I lifted it higher, tossing off my hood and letting the jotunn get a clear view of me.

He cocked his head. "You are pretty, lady." His voice was almost gentle.

"I seek Sven's freedom."

"Sven?"

Had he already forgotten about his slave? "I would like to make an exchange in order to break the curse and gain freedom for Sven."

"I will do anything for you, lady." He didn't take his blinking gaze from me.

"What exchange will you accept as fair?"

"Anything."

I'd expected him to demand that I stay with him the rest of my life and become his slave in Sven's place. I hadn't given myself time to think through the repercussions of such an exchange. All I'd known was that for once, I'd been given an opportunity to do something tangible to make a difference. I had the possibility of setting Sven free from the nightmare he'd existed in for endless years. And in setting Sven free, I also had the chance to set my people free from Bernhard's reign.

I suspected Bernhard wouldn't easily relinquish his position. With Sven's facial scars, the people would likely be afraid of him. But I had to hold out hope that somehow, some way, Gunnar would be able to wrest the earldom from Bernhard and give it to Sven.

"We need to stall the jotunn for a few more minutes," came Sven's low voice from somewhere in the brush behind me. "Long enough to give my nephew time to escape with his servant."

I breathed out my relief that Gunnar was leaving with Frans. With their injuries, the trek out of the forest would be difficult, and they would need all the extra time we could provide for them.

A moment later, Sven parted the branches and stepped into the light beside me. "Offer him something of great value."

The jotunn didn't take his attention from me, almost as if Sven were invisible. Nanna's warning reverberated through my mind, that the more invisible a person remained, the safer he or she would be. I understood that she'd only wanted to protect me, but I couldn't remain invisible any longer.

I had to do whatever it took to free Sven. But what did I have that was of great value? I had nothing except the knife Gunnar had given me. And . . .

My hand dropped to my pocket and my fingers found the lump inside—the shell that had once belonged to my twin sister Maiken.

I immediately hid my hand behind my back again. I couldn't give it up. It wouldn't mean anything to this jotunn even if it meant everything to me. Surely I could think of something else to give him.

"You are so pretty, lady." He spoke just as gently as before.

Would he accept a lock of my hair? My cloak? My shoes? But even as I went through the list of possibilities, my mind circled back to the treasure in my pocket. Even though the jotunn said he would accept anything, I suspected the worth depended upon what it meant to the bearer of the item rather than its monetary value.

"I will give you the thing that is most important to me."

"You will?" The jotunn's voice contained hope, as if he truly desired the gift.

Beside me, Sven shifted, no doubt ready to act if I gave something he didn't approve of.

"Yes." I took a deep breath and willed myself to have courage. "'Tis the one thing I have kept with me every day of my life and have never parted with."

"Anything, lady."

I handed the torch to Sven, then slipped my hand through the slit in my skirt and found the pocket I wore underneath. I reached inside and let my fingers settle around the smooth, worn mussel shell. It was my last connection with my twin sister.

It was the only thing of hers I had. She'd given it to me the spring day Nanna had come down from Likness Castle to take me away to work with her in the nursery when I'd been but a girl of five.

Huddled on the dirt floor of our hovel, Maiken and I had been listless with hunger, hardly able to move to keep warmth in our limbs. As Nanna had ducked into the dank one-room hut, she'd passed by Mother lying on a pallet cradling Kirstin, trying to keep her warm.

Father hadn't been home, had been gone with other villeins to find extra work along the docks in exchange for fish.

Nanna stopped in front of the two of us. She crouched and brushed first Maiken's cheek, then mine, studying us. "My assistant nursemaid has died, and I've been given permission to bring one of my granddaughters into service."

Her eyes held a sadness I didn't understand at the time.

"Take Mikaela." My mother pushed up to her elbow. "Maiken is stronger, and I have need of her help here."

As the second-born twin, I'd always been more petite than my sister, weaker, sicker.

"Are you well, Mikaela?" Nanna asked, this time feeling my forehead.

I stifled a cough that tickled my throat. I wanted to go with Nanna to the castle, where I would be away from the cold and hunger. So, even though I felt miserable, I nodded.

Nanna shifted to Maiken. "And you, Maiken. Are you well?"

My sister tightened her arms around me and squeezed me hard. She had always been sturdy, never getting sick, never complaining, never suffering the way I did. She gave a pretend cough. "No, Nanna. You must take Mikaela."

Nanna studied us both again, sighed, and then held out a hand to me. "Come, Mikaela."

I rose, but before I could extricate myself from Maiken's embrace, she pressed something into my hands. When I felt the smooth shape, I tried to give it back to her. Although blue mussel shells lined the shores of every part of Norvegia's coast, this was a rare purple one, believed to act as a shield of protection to the one who possessed it. Maiken had discovered it last spring after the snowmelt. And she'd kept it close ever since.

I shook my head, unwilling to take the special item from her.

She closed my fingers over the shell and squeezed her hand around mine. "Keep it near. Every time you miss being home, take it out and think of me."

Now, in the chill of the forest, I fingered the smooth shell, then pulled it out of my pocket.

The jotunn still hadn't taken his eyes from me, was watching me with the reverence given to a queen, not a servant.

"This truly is the only thing I own that means anything to me." I held it out, unable to pry my fingers up from the shell.

The jotunn stuck out his hand, thick with short beefy fingers.

I drew in a sharp breath, then forced my fingers to release the shell, displaying it in the palm of my hand. "It once belonged to my sister. My twin sister."

"Where is she now?"

"Dead."

Little had I known how much I would miss my sister when I'd walked out the door with a too-big sack filled with the few possessions I owned. Little had I known that was the last time I'd see Maiken alive. Little had I known she would die a month later from inhaling too much smoke after the thatch of our home caught on fire.

It just as easily could have been me who stayed behind and died from breathing the smoke. In fact, most of my life I'd blamed myself for my twin sister's death, knowing she'd given me the coveted position in the castle when she should have taken it for herself.

Why had she done it? The question had haunted

me for so many years along with the guilt. If only she'd gone with Nanna instead of me. But I'd been selfish, taken the easy way, and walked away willingly. At the very least I should have left Maiken the shell. I didn't know if the promises of protection were real, but I could have insisted she keep it.

The jotunn reached out to take my most treasured possession from me, but I closed my fingers around it again. "First, before I give you this, you must free Sven from being your slave."

"I free him." The jotunn didn't take his eyes from my hand.

"And set him free from the curse." I knew so little about Sven's curse and how it had come about. But I did know that I had to bargain for breaking the curse too, or Sven's freedom wouldn't do him any good, not if he bled to death.

"The curse once spoken cannot be broken." The words tumbled from the jotunn's mouth, likely a saying he'd heard from ages past.

So, there was no hope for Sven? No hope for the people of Romsdal? Or was this all some kind of hoax the jotunn had made up? After all, why did the jotunn have the power to utter curses on people? Who had given him such authority, and were the curses real?

"Tell him to cancel the curse by issuing a new one," Sven whispered, a thread of hope in his voice. "Tell him to pass the bleeding curse to the firstborn sons in my direct family line."

I didn't think Sven had ever married or had children, so the curse would be useless. But would the jotunn realize it?

The jotunn shuffled and looked away. Was I losing

his attention? How long before he lost interest in me altogether?

Sven nudged me, as though sensing the change in the jotunn's interest as well.

"You may not be able to break the curse," I said, "but you can pass it along. Let the curse go to the firstborn sons in Sven's direct family line."

The jotunn frowned and pressed a hand to his head.

"If you do, I'll give you this." I opened my fingers from around the shell again.

He reached down with a snarl and swiped up the tree limb he'd been wielding when he almost hit me.

"Please!" I called, suddenly growing desperate to have his strange, oddly-shaped eyes back upon me.

He glanced down at me and paused. "You're so pretty, lady."

"Please pass the curse away from Sven and onto his firstborn sons and grandsons. If you do, this shell will be yours to remind you of me forever."

"Forever?"

"Yes." I held my breath and waited. "First you must pass the curse on."

He hesitated then spoke his words in a rush. "I pass the curse from Sven to the firstborn sons in his family."

Sven shook his head, but as the jotunn shifted to look at him, he dropped his sights. His shoulders slumped, and he offered no further protest.

My muscles tensed with the need to hang on to my shell and flee. I didn't want to give it to this madman. But I kept my outstretched hand steady.

As though sensing my turmoil, he placed his palm up, clearly expecting me to deliver it to him willingly.

I could do nothing less. I gingerly set the delicate shell onto his crushing hand. Perhaps in sacrificing it, I could finally find redemption for my selfishness those many years ago when I'd refused to sacrifice my comfort for my sister's.

He lifted it between two large fingers, examining it. "It's pretty, just like you."

"I pray it brings peace to your troubled soul."

He nodded, watching my face, testing my sincerity.

"The exchange has been made." Sven tugged my arm. "But he is not to be trusted, and we must go."

Before I could say farewell or offer a word of thanks, Sven twisted me around and jerked me forward.

"Wait!" the jotunn called. "Where are you going?"

I glanced behind me, but Sven was pulling me along hastily, and I could no longer see the jotunn.

"Run!" Sven's harsh whisper resounded in the air. "Run as fast as you possibly can."

In the next instant, I heard the jotunn's angry shouts filling the air and the thwacking of the tree limb against the brush and knew he was chasing us again.

Chapter 23

My injury pained me with each jarring movement. My arms ached from pulling Frans's heavy weight. And my lungs burned with the need for air.

But I forced myself to keep up the punishing pace—even though everything within me demanded that I go back for Mikaela. I wanted to trust Sven to protect her and get her away from the jotunn. But the truth was that I'd never truly trust anyone with her but myself.

I had to deposit Frans outside Hardanger Forest and get him help. Then I was going back in to retrieve Mikaela. I might not be able to rescue Sven tonight, but I had to make sure Mikaela was safe.

With my torch lighting the way, I could finally see the end of the forest. The woodland was beginning to thin out, the brush wasn't as thick, and there weren't any more traps.

The trip out hadn't taken me nearly as long as the one in. Even so, I'd travailed for the past hour. Thankfully, Frans had remained unconscious so that the jostling of his wounds didn't cause him undue suffering.

As I reached the edge of the woods and took in the dark grassy field that sloped up toward the castle, I released a pent-up breath. Once word spread that I'd rescued Frans, how would I explain my reason for going in after him? Especially to Bernhard?

A part of me wanted to find a way to avoid the coming conflict with him. Through it all, he was bound to learn of my connection to Mikaela and Frans. And he might even suspect I'd gone into the forest to look for the chalice.

Could I find suitable excuses to fool him as I'd been doing my whole life? Or was it finally time to stop playing a role and stand up to him?

I couldn't imagine being honest with Bernhard about anything. But the thought of having to remain duplicitous with him sent despair spiraling through me. If I could find a way to get Mikaela out of the forest, I didn't want to keep my love for her a secret any longer. In fact, I didn't know how I'd ever be able to let her out of my sight again.

I dragged the litter out of the woods at least a dozen paces before lowering it. I bent over and pressed my hands against my thighs, needing to stave off my dizziness and to catch my breath.

But at the slap of footsteps in the field, I straightened to find a young woman running in my direction. The sliver of moon didn't provide much light, but I recognized her as Kirstin, Mikaela's younger sister.

What was she doing out? Had she been waiting nearby since Mikaela had gone into the forest hours ago?

Upon reaching us, she halted and took in Frans now laid out on the ground, unmoving.

"Frans?" Her voice wobbled. "Is he . . .?"

"He's alive but injured."

She pressed a hand over her mouth, capturing a sob while at the same time falling to her knees beside him. She touched his arm gently while scanning his legs.

My brows shot up. 'Twas obvious Kirstin harbored feelings for Frans. Perhaps someday he might be able to stop loving Mikaela and find happiness with Kirstin instead.

I shook off the thoughts. None of that would matter if Frans didn't receive medical attention. "I need you to go get Valter and then fetch the physician."

"How bad is he?"

"One leg is broken and the other—well, it's not good." I wouldn't scare Kirstin with the details of the suffering Frans had endured. Or with the possibility he might lose that leg, maybe even his life.

"He's here. That's all that matters." She swiped at her cheeks.

"He needs help. Right away."

She glanced across the distance toward the castle's side entrance. "Nanna is waiting to let me in."

"Then go tell her to alert Valter. And when you find the physician, assure him I'll be the one to reimburse him for his fees."

She hesitated near Frans as though she was loath to leave his side.

"Make haste. He's suffered long enough."

With a nod, she stood and started back the way she'd come. After a dozen steps, she halted and spun. "Where is Mikaela?"

I nodded at the forest.

At the simple gesture, Kirstin wavered.

I jolted toward her, grabbing her arm to keep her from collapsing.

Kirstin closed her eyes. "This is my fault. I sent her in."

"I'll find her and bring her back." There was no other option. I'd get her out even if it killed me to do so.

"I should have gone in as I'd planned."

"If anyone can survive, she can." That's what I'd been telling myself over and over. And I prayed it was true. I pushed Kirstin gently toward the castle. "Now go. Get Frans help."

With tears now streaming down her cheeks, she stumbled forward.

Without waiting another moment, I spun, drew in a breath, and then plunged back into the forest. I held my torch out and started the way I'd come.

Somehow, someway, I'd free Mikaela from the jotunn, even if I had to bargain my soul to do so.

Chapter 24

Mikaela

I gasped for each breath, but I couldn't draw in enough air to satisfy my body. My muscles had turned as wobbly as custard, and I would have tripped and fallen by now if not for Sven holding me aloft. His grip upon my arm didn't waver. In fact, the longer we ran, the more he seemed to bear my weight, half-carrying me through the dangerous forest.

No matter how far we ran, the jotunn's crashing and cursing came only steps behind us. I didn't know what he would demand if he caught us, but I guessed that the next time I wouldn't be able to so easily distract him and sway him to do my bidding.

"We are almost there." Sven still held the torch.

"Please, God." I lifted a prayer that we would make it. Even more, I prayed Gunnar had survived his trip out of the forest with Frans.

"We must go faster, child." Sven tugged against me. "Just a little faster."

I tried to make my legs obey my command to

hasten their steps, but I was simply too worn from the hour or more of endless running.

"A light, ahead." Sven's breathlessness told me he was nearing the end of his endurance too.

A faint illumination broke through the branches.

"Mikaela?" came a familiar voice.

My heart tumbled over itself. Gunnar. He was still alive.

"Get back out of the forest, nephew!" Sven's shout echoed above the jotunn's noise. "You are not safe." Sven didn't have to elaborate for me to understand that because Gunnar had escaped from the trap, the jotunn would want Gunnar more than any of us.

I opened my mouth to add my warning to Sven's, but I couldn't formulate any words past my constricted airways.

The light didn't waver, only drew nearer. As it did, panic pushed up into my throat. After coming this far, we couldn't let the jotunn draw any of us under his strange control. With a burst of fresh determination, I pushed myself harder, picking up my pace.

Only a moment later, Gunnar came into view. He was sprinting toward us, still favoring his injured leg. With his sights set on the forest behind us, he tossed his torch into the brush over our shoulders. Fire sprang to life amidst the windfall. I prayed it would pose a barrier to the jotunn and that he wouldn't find a way around it.

Gunnar didn't wait to find out. Without a word of greeting, he scooped me up, tossed me over his shoulder, and sprinted back the way he'd come.

I couldn't squeeze out a sound. All I could do was grasp at his tunic and allow him to carry me. From my odd angle, I could see Sven's bare feet right behind Gunnar and realized then that the older man had slowed his pace for me and was now moving much faster.

Within seconds of sprinting, the jotunn's shouting and bellowing began to fade. And within another minute, the cracking of twigs and our labored breathing filled the silence.

As we finally broke through the last of the brush and reached the forest edge, Gunnar abruptly stopped. His chest was rising and falling with the exertion of carrying me. "I will come back for you, Sven. I vow I will find a way to break the jotunn's curse over you."

Sven didn't seem to be listening and jogged past Gunnar.

"Sven, wait!" Gunnar called as he placed my feet back on the ground. He lurched after Sven, but the older man was moving too rapidly and darted through the last of the tangled overgrowth into the clearing.

Gunnar grabbed my hand, and scrambled to follow Sven. Obviously, Gunnar didn't know that I'd bargained with the jotunn and asked him to free Sven of the curse and place it instead on his firstborn son.

Even with the exchange, I watched anxiously as Sven came to a standstill in the grassy field, his torch outstretched. So many questions filled my head. Had Sven really been cursed? Or had it only been a scare tactic the jotunn had used to keep him from leaving the forest? If the curse was true, would Sven fall over and die at any moment?

Not far away, Frans lay in his litter on the ground, still unconscious. The moonlight revealed agony in his face. And I knew we needed to get him help right away.

But first, we stopped beside Sven and watched him for any sign that he was still cursed.

Sven stood straight and waited too, clearly expecting something to happen at any moment.

"I take it you made a deal with the jotunn to release Sven's curse?" Gunnar's question was low and tense, as though he feared what I'd done.

I drew in a shaky breath and nodded. "I gave him Maiken's shell."

"The jotunn accepted it?" Although Gunnar knew what the shell meant to me, since I'd shared the story with him long ago when we'd been but children, I understood why he'd question the value of such an insignificant item to the jotunn.

"Yes. I required him to change the curse first."

"Change?"

"To pass it along to Sven's firstborn son."

Gunnar placed a hand on Sven's back. "How do you feel?"

"I have not tasted blood yet."

"Then perhaps you are safe." Gunnar's voice contained a note of hope.

The older man's chest was heaving, but he remained upright, his shoulders back, his chin high. From this angle, without his scars showing, his face appeared noble, almost regal in spite of his ragged garments and unkempt body and hair.

Even so, the April night was cold, and he was barely clothed. How had he survived the winters without freezing?

I shrugged out of my cloak and handed it to Sven. It wasn't thick or necessarily even warm. But it would provide a measure of decency until we found suitable garments for him.

He took the cloak and bowed his head. "Thank you, lady."

"I'm no more than a bondservant in the earl's house, my lord."

Sven met my gaze solemnly. "Never have I met a truer or braver lady than you."

If only he knew the truth, that I wasn't very brave and had allowed grievous things to happen to others. As much as I'd wanted to change the circumstances, I'd let helplessness hold me back. "I haven't been very brave before tonight."

"Neither have I." Sven wrapped the cloak around his torso and pulled the hood up. "But I believe one act of courage has the power to clear the path for more."

At the lights and the sound of voices coming from the side castle door, I knew I needed to put some distance between myself and Gunnar before anyone saw us together. But instead of letting me get away, Gunnar grasped my hand again and laced his fingers through mine, drawing me against his arm so that we were standing side by side.

"Kirstin was waiting when I came out." Gunnar narrowed his eyes upon the group coming our way. "I sent her to fetch Valter and the physician. But 'twould appear she's bringing half the castle with her."

The darkness obscured their faces, but from the tightening of Gunnar's muscles, I guessed Bernhard was among those coming down to greet us. What would he say about me going in after Frans? And what would he do when he discovered Sven's identity?

I attempted to pull my hand from Gunnar's.

He didn't release me.

"Please, Gunnar," I whispered. "We cannot let Bernhard see us together."

"I have cowered before my brother's bullying for too many years. It's past time that I stand up to him and stand up for myself."

I was tired of living in fear of Bernhard too. But in spite of the courage I'd just shown in the forest with the jotunn, my old fears crowded in, pushing aside the inspiration from Sven from moments ago.

Gunnar spun me to face him, and for the first time since the horror of the night began hours ago, I allowed myself to feast upon him in all his flawless beauty—his hair falling over his forehead, his high cheekbones, his full lips, and his eyes framed with long lashes. He was not only an incredible man on the outside, but he was equally as beautiful on the inside. Tonight, he'd shown himself to be the hero and daring knight who had earned a place among the Knights of Brethren.

If I'd ever doubted I could love him, those doubts were gone. I loved him beyond my wildest imagination. But that didn't erase my fear of what Bernhard would do once he learned of Gunnar's interest in me. I didn't want to put Gunnar or my family into jeopardy.

"I love you, Mikaela." Gunnar brushed a strand of hair away from my face and tucked it behind my ear. "When I wasn't sure if you'd make it out of the forest, I decided I don't want to wait for you any longer. I want to be together. Now and forever."

His declaration wound through me, tying my insides into dozens of knots that only he would ever be able to unravel. I was bound to him, but due to our circumstances, we didn't have the liberty to make our feelings for one another public yet.

I wanted to reach up and brush his hair back the same way he had with mine, but I forced my hand to remain at my side. "We need to find a way to keep you and my family safe first."

"I've let Bernhard dictate my actions for too long already. I can no longer pretend to be someone I am not around him. I must start being true to myself no matter the consequences."

I couldn't repress a shudder.

He rubbed my arms up and down. Without my cloak and now that I was no longer running, my body was feeling the effects of the frigid air. The friction of his hands over my sleeves should have warmed me a little, but I couldn't shake the coldness settling deep inside.

The voices drew nearer. With Sven still holding the torch, it served to illuminate Gunnar and me so that those coming down the path and crossing the grassy field could see us together.

"I have to do this," he said quietly, "so that I can learn to fight for what's right both on and off the battlefield. If I don't, I'll never be the man you deserve."

Gunnar, like the rest of the Knights of Brethren, was renowned for his fighting skills and his fierceness in battle. But he'd never stood up to his brother before. And perhaps doing so would take the most courage of all.

"I won't let Bernhard harm you or your kin," he insisted. "I vow it."

I swallowed the fear rising into my throat. If

Gunnar was willing to make a stand for what was right, then it was time for me to do so too.

I lifted to my toes and kissed his cheek. "I love you."

Chapter 25

GUNNAR

SHE LOVED ME. SHE'D SAID IT.

Even though I'd longed to hear her declaration of love, had hoped she felt the same way I did, I hadn't wanted to pressure her into saying it before she was ready.

Even now as she peered up at me, her ever-changing brown eyes radiated her love. She'd given up hiding it and was ready to embrace our future together no matter what difficulties would come our way.

Under other circumstances, I would have jumped and whooped then picked her up and swung her around until we were both dizzy and deliriously happy. But with Bernhard marching toward us with half a dozen of his guards, the celebratory mood was rapidly sucked out of me.

The coming encounter was rife with uncertainty, and Bernhard was unpredictable.

"Brother," Bernhard called, striding to the front of his knights, his long cloak swirling around his legs, his hood shielding his face from view. "I heard the rumors you had gone into Hardanger Forest, but I had not believed them until now."

Mikaela began to pull away from me, but I slipped my hand into hers again so that she couldn't sneak away. I wanted her by my side. In fact, henceforth, I didn't plan to let her go anywhere without me.

"You should have informed me of your plans." Bernhard's voice contained a forced lightheartedness that told me more than words that he was angry with me. In going into the forest without his permission or even without his knowledge, I'd slighted his leadership and his need to be in control.

"I had to act quicky." I tossed him the first excuse I could find, and then realized I was easily falling into my old habit of trying to placate him, saying and doing the things that would hold his ire at bay.

As he crossed the last steps toward me, he took in our connected hands before lifting his attention to Mikaela's face and studying her with interest.

I was tempted to blurt out that she was mine and I didn't want him looking at her ever again. Especially in that predatory way he had about him. But before I could figure out how to voice my demand, his gaze darted to Sven and then to Frans.

Kirstin was amongst those crowding around Frans along with Valter and several other domestics. Frans was beginning to stir, their voices seeming to coax him back to life.

"Tell me what happened." Bernhard pinned a glare upon me. His knights had spread out, raised their torches, and were peering into the forest as though they feared something might come barreling out at any moment. If they knew just how close the jotunn was, they'd likely race back to the castle. Although the jotunn had never been seen outside the forest, I feared what he was capable of doing now that he'd lost Sven and hadn't captured me.

For a few moments, I relayed the events of my trip into the forest to help Frans. Mikaela listened too, not yet having heard of my near-death experience in the jotunn's trap.

"Sven came to my aid with Frans." I nodded toward Sven, who'd knelt beside Frans and was assisting the others in binding his wound more tightly before readying to transport him. "He's our great uncle and has lived in the forest these many years as the jotunn's slave. We have just now set him free." Mikaela deserved the credit for freeing Sven, but I knew Bernhard wouldn't see her deed as praiseworthy.

"Great uncle?" Bernhard examined Sven again, this time with narrowed eyes. "How can you know for sure he is who he claims?"

"I have his word." A sliver of wariness pricked me. Ought I to move with more caution regarding Sven? "If his word is not enough, the burn scars on his face validate his identity."

"If he has worked with the jotunn all these years, what will keep him from harming us?" Bernhard's tone turned scoffing.

In the past I would have colluded with Bernhard while privately seeking to undermine him. But I had to speak up and be a voice of reason and truth. I straightened my shoulders. "He aided us from the forest and saved our lives. That is proof enough he is a good man."

"I suppose you consider yourself the expert, now that you have gone into the forest and survived." Tension oozed from Bernhard's tone.

My muscles tightened at the coming conflict I'd always worked so hard to avoid. "After the difficult life Sven's experienced, he deserves to spend his final days in peace and comfort."

"Knowing so little about him, you would have him live at Likness Castle amongst my wife and children?"

Where else would he live? It was his home. In fact, he had more right to live there than either Bernhard or myself. But saying so would only threaten Bernhard and make him more opposed. "Once you take the time to speak with Sven, you'll see you have nothing to fear."

"Perhaps you are right."

I almost startled at Bernhard's concession. I'd expected a harder battle, even swift retaliation. This could only mean one thing—that Bernhard was scheming, and I would need to be extra wary. "Sven is a kind man."

Bernhard rubbed a hand over his jaw. "Yes, and he may prove useful in telling us more about the jotunn's weaknesses and how best to defeat the creature."

Prove useful? I didn't like the sound of that, especially coming from Bernhard. Bernhard would manipulate, connive, and threaten with any means possible to get the information he wanted. And I didn't want him to do that to Sven. Besides, I knew why Bernhard wanted to kill the jotunn. So that he could have access to the chalice.

For an instant, I waged an inner debate whether to let Bernhard know I was aware that he was working with Rasmus to find the chalice. But I couldn't take the risk of him trying to stop my mission. For now, I had to pretend ignorance. Perhaps I would even have to take Sven away from Likness Castle and Romsdal and settle him someplace where he would be safe from Bernhard's wiles.

"Why did you go into the forest after the blacksmith?" Bernhard's question pierced swiftly, almost as though he'd read my thoughts about the chalice.

"I wanted to help him."

Bernhard glanced pointedly at my hand holding Mikaela's. "You went in to aid the man who intends to marry the maiden you are taken with? Why, when you could let him perish and eliminate your competition?"

I bristled at the callousness of Bernhard's suggestion. "Frans does not deserve to die."

"Gunnar has my love already." Beside me, Mikaela spoke quietly but with an undertone of anger. "There is no competition with Frans."

Bernhard lifted his chin and peered down at Mikaela with a look of contempt I'd seen all too oft when he addressed servants. "Hold your tongue, woman. You are nothing but Gunnar's newest mistress of the month."

"No. *You* hold your tongue, brother." My body tensed with the need to slam my fist into my brother's face.

Bernhard wasn't paying attention to me, however. Instead, his lips curved into a dangerous smirk. "When Gunnar is done with you, maybe I shall have you next."

Hot anger rushed through me, and I lunged. Mikaela was mine. If Bernhard ever touched her, I'd break his bones, slowly and painfully.

"Wait, Gunnar." Mikaela wrestled me back to her side.

My rage wasn't so easily contained. And I couldn't pretend that Bernhard's crude comment hadn't mattered even if I'd wanted to. "You will never have her. Mikaela is mine and mine alone."

Bernhard released a derisory laugh. "A tad possessive, aren't we?"

"Not a tad." I ground out the words through my

clenched teeth. "I'm very possessive of Mikaela since I plan to marry her just as soon as I can make the arrangements."

Beside me, Mikaela sucked in a breath. Even if Nanna had encouraged it of me, I hadn't yet brought it up with Mikaela. Maybe I was getting ahead of myself. But I'd told her I didn't want to wait for her any longer, that I wanted to be together both now and forever. Surely she understood that meant I intended to marry her. If not, I needed her to know that's what I meant.

I met her wide-eyed gaze. "I can think of nothing I want more than to marry you. Please, Mikaela, make me the happiest and most fortunate man to ever live by agreeing to wed me."

She studied my face before looking deeply into my soul. Her expressive eyes seemed to say this was all happening so fast, that I would change my mind in the morn, that we didn't need to rush.

But I shook my head. I would never change my mind about her. I'd waited for her for years already and didn't want to lose her. "Marry me? Tonight?"

Again, she was quiet, contemplative, as she watched me, an internal debate showing in her troubled eyes. Our marriage would be unconventional, perhaps even the first of its kind with a nobleman marrying one of his family's slaves. But since when had I ever done anything conventionally?

Apparently seeing the resolve within me, Mikaela squeezed my hand. "If you're sure."

"I've never been more sure of anything." We had many uncertainties to face ahead of us. But we'd work through the difficulties just as we were right now, by facing them head on instead of running away.

A smile tugged at the corners of her lips.

"Well done." Bernhard clapped, and his grin held a hard edge. "Such a touching performance."

Of course Bernhard wouldn't approve. He wanted to remain in charge of securing an advantageous match for me. But I wasn't his pawn, and it was past time for him to know it.

"Rest assured, brother. This was no performance." My voice dropped with the gravity and depth of my feelings. In comparison with the pretense that I'd kept up around Bernhard previously, this was indeed the truest I'd ever spoken or acted. "I intend to marry the woman of my choosing, with or without your consent."

Bernhard's smile fell away altogether. "You are forgetting one thing. This maiden belongs to me. I own her. Not you. And because she is my bondservant, I may do with her as I please."

I'd suspected I would have this battle, and to buy her freedom I was prepared to offer Bernhard everything I'd saved during the past years working for the king. Why stop there? Why not buy the freedom for each of her family members as well? It would take time to come up with enough to satisfy Bernhard for all of them, but I'd find a way.

"I will purchase her from you." My tone dared him to defy me. With my connection to the king, how could he refuse me without bringing censure upon himself?

"You were with a different woman last night. How am I to believe you are ready to marry this maiden tonight? With your womanizing, how is anyone to believe you care about her?" Bernhard's brow rose in a sharp challenge.

Did he know the truth about my pretenses with women? That I hadn't spent the night with any of them?

Or was he merely using my reputation now to show me how he could easily cast suspicion upon my love of Mikaela?

I tensed again. "You cannot keep me from Mikaela."

As though realizing he would not easily influence me, Bernhard shrugged. "We will have time later to work out an agreement that may be beneficial to us both."

I didn't like the insinuation that he would make me pay more than money for my chance to wed Mikaela, but I shrugged and turned away from him.

The others nearby began hoisting Frans toward the castle. Following behind, Sven hesitated, as though unsure whether to leave us with Bernhard or not. I would be outnumbered if Bernhard ordered his men to turn on me, especially since I was troubled by my leg injury and lacked my usual strength and agility.

I nodded to Sven and fell in step beside him with Mikaela. For now, I needed to use great caution with Bernhard. In being honest with him, I'd begun a new kind of battle, a battle over Mikaela. I prayed we wouldn't come to physical blows over her. But if that happened, I would make certain he knew there was nothing he'd be able to do to stop me from marrying the woman I loved.

Chapter 26

Mikaela

Gunnar had asked me to marry him. All the while we walked back to the castle, Gunnar's words whispered in my mind: *I can think of nothing I want more than to marry you ... make me the happiest and most fortunate man to ever live by agreeing to wed me.*

Only when Nanna met us at the side castle door did Gunnar release my hand. Even then, I could sense his reluctance.

Nanna hugged me tightly, her tears dampening my cheeks. "You shouldn't have gone in."

"I'm sorry for worrying you, Nanna."

I could admit the journey had been perilous. But if I had to do it all over again, I would have done the same thing. If I hadn't been there to distract the jotunn, the jotunn would have caught up to Gunnar as he made his escape with Frans. And what about Sven? Without my bargain, he would still be the jotunn's slave and cursed to remain in the forest.

As she released me, Gunnar wrapped his arm

around me, tucking me close to his side, making a statement of possession that everyone could see. I was surprised Nanna didn't raise a brow or hastily warn us to go our separate ways.

On the one hand, I was relieved Gunnar and I no longer had to hide our interest in each other now that he'd made his intentions toward me public. On the other hand, I didn't trust Bernhard. He was too calculating and wouldn't let Gunnar's defiance go unpunished. I just prayed Gunnar would find a way to avoid the brunt of his brother's wrath. And I wanted to trust that Gunnar would also find a means for keeping my family safe as well.

While I conversed with Nanna and shared the details of my trip into the forest, Gunnar stayed close by my side but spoke quietly with Sven. The older man still covered himself with my cloak, but the torches around the bailey revealed his dismal condition all too clearly—his tattered clothing, his filth, his scars. Those servants who'd risen from their beds—and even those peeking out of windows and doorways—watched him with fear and stayed well away.

Their aversion didn't surprise me, but I was saddened by it, nonetheless. I guessed people wouldn't accept his disfigurement now any more than they had when he'd been a youth. Would he forever be shunned because of his appearance?

When Sven headed for the forge to check on Frans, Gunnar's expression turned grave, his attention affixed upon Bernhard across the bailey, conferring with his guards. "I fear for Sven's safety here."

"I fear for him too." Had we brought him out of one danger only to place him into even greater peril? From the people? From Bernhard? Or both?

"Sven agrees with me that for now he must go away to some place where Bernhard cannot use him for his own ill gain."

Though Gunnar didn't say so, I suspected this had to do with the jotunn and the forest. Since Bernhard wanted to kill the jotunn, it was possible he'd coerce Sven into revealing information to gain the advantage over the jotunn. Knowing Bernhard, *coerce* was probably a kind term for what he was capable of doing.

Gunnar was wise to find a safe place for Sven, a place of solace and peace.

"I must instruct several of my trusted squires to leave before daybreak with Sven and ride as fast as they can to Vordinberg." The seriousness of Gunnar's tone told me this was a mission that could not fail.

And suddenly I knew. This had to do with the chalice. It was in Hardanger Forest.

At some point, Gunnar had figured that out. And that was why Bernhard was sending men to their deaths in the forest. He'd also learned of the chalice's location and was seeking it.

Why hadn't I realized the truth earlier?

Now, Sven was the only one who could divulge critical details regarding the whereabouts of the sacred relic.

My heart sank with the growing understanding that Gunnar would go back inside the forest again at some point. No matter the risk to himself, he was determined to fulfill his mission. I wanted to admire him for his loyalty and commitment to the king. But after having experienced the danger firsthand, I didn't want Gunnar returning to the forest ever again.

At the same time, perhaps with Sven's instructions, Gunnar and the other knights could attack the jotunn and put an end to the menace. After all, if someone didn't stop the madness, how many others would the earl send to their deaths? What about Enok and eager young men like him? I couldn't let them die simply because I wanted to keep Gunnar to myself.

"Do you also need to go to the king?" I asked softly. "To inform him of everything you have learned?"

With the torches lit around the battlement and inside the bailey to dispel the darkness of the night, they couldn't take away the darkness in Gunnar's eyes. He held my gaze as though trying to decide how much I knew.

I nodded. "Yes, I've figured it out."

He dropped his voice. "I will send a missive to the king with my squires, but I intend to tarry until Torvald's return."

I didn't know why the chalice was important, but clearly it was special if so many were willing to sacrifice their lives to obtain it.

He slanted a look at Bernhard still speaking with his guards. "Just as soon as I'm able, I will meet with Bernhard and purchase your freedom. Then we will be married."

"Married?" Nanna's whispered word carried to servants nearby, who paused to watch us.

Gunnar spread his feet as though daring Nanna to stop him. "I would be grateful if you would help Mikaela prepare. Once my wound is tended and I finish with all the arrangements, we will meet at the chapel."

For the first time since Gunnar had mentioned the

possibility of us getting married, I allowed myself to believe this was going to happen.

"Should I speak with Frans first?" I didn't know his state of consciousness. But I still needed to apologize to him.

Gunnar gently cupped my cheek. "When Frans and I were trapped, he gave me his blessing to marry you."

"He did?"

"He told me he's known all along you cared about me. And he said you'd never be happy unless you were with me."

A swell of emotion rose into my throat, pushing against it and making it ache. If Frans had given me his blessing, then I only needed Nanna's. "Nanna?"

She clutched her cloak closer about her frail body to ward off the chill of the night. "You will be safest as Gunnar's wife."

I'd expected more reluctance from her. Would she give me her blessing that easily?

"My only concern is what might happen to the rest of the family." Her forehead crinkled with worry lines, echoing the fear inside me. I couldn't run away and leave my family to pay the price for our angering Bernhard.

Gunnar reached for her hands. "I intend to pay Bernhard not only for Mikaela's freedom but for each member in your family."

Nanna shook her head sadly. "Oh, Gunnar-boy. You know that won't stop Bernhard from exacting vengeance any way he can upon us."

Gunnar offered her a slight grin. "I am not so proud that I won't use my connection with the king to my advantage. I'll assure Bernhard that I can petition the king regarding his place in the Noble Council. If he treats my wife's family with respect and kindness, I'll speak well of him to the king. If not, I'll make sure the king knows of his evil deeds."

Would such a tactic work with Bernhard? The lines in Nanna's face remained, but I wanted to believe we could begin to make changes for my family and find a way to do more for all the people of Romsdal.

Regardless, I wouldn't feel safe until the priest concluded the marriage ceremony.

"Let's make haste." Nanna linked her arm through mine and directed me forward. "The sooner the better." She was obviously feeling the same sense of urgency I was.

I hadn't gone far when Gunnar snagged my hand, tugged me free from Nanna, and twirled me back. Before I knew what he was doing, he bent in and captured my lips with his. The instant his mouth moved against mine, it unleashed everything I felt for him. I knew I needed him to be in my life more than I needed anything else.

I pressed back, kissing him with all the desperation that had grown over the past hours of trauma, nearly losing our lives and not knowing if we'd have any future, much less a future together. But before the kiss had the chance to truly begin, he broke it.

He released me and took a step away, his lids halfway down, his long lashes barely concealing his desire. "Just wanted you to have a taste of what's to come."

Flames sizzled across my skin, turning my face and my body hot so that I didn't miss my cloak one bit. Oh heavens above. I was almost embarrassed by how much I was looking forward to the wedding and his promise of more kissing.

Rather than give him the satisfaction of knowing how much he affected me, I pressed a kiss to his jaw while skimming my fingers along his neck down to his collar bone.

He sucked in a soft breath, one that told me I affected him as much as he did me.

I moved away, putting an arm's length between us. "That was so you don't make me wait too long."

His lips turned up into a disarmingly handsome grin. "I won't."

"Good."

"Good." He grinned at me a moment longer, his eyes filling with happiness—a happiness I'd put there. I wanted to spend the rest of my life making his blue eyes light up like that.

"Posh. Let's be on our way now." Nanna's tone contained irritation, but as she pulled me away from Gunnar, I could see her fighting back a smile.

Chapter 27

GUNNAR

I DIDN'T LIKE THE WAY BERNHARD'S GUARDS WERE WATCHING US. It meant only one thing: Bernhard didn't intend to let Sven get away.

As the heavy darkness of the night began to give way to predawn, I stood in the shadows of the stables with my squires while they finished saddling their horses along with an extra for Sven. Would they even make it through the gatehouse? Or would Bernhard prevent them from leaving?

Bernhard had already gone inside the keep, and I wanted to catch up to him before he retired to his chambers. I didn't have everything I owned with me, but I would pay him what I had and assure him I'd return with the remainder—more than enough to buy Mikaela's freedom.

However, an internal warning kept resounding inside, one that told me Sven wasn't safe and that I needed to personally ensure he stayed out of Bernhard's grasp.

"I don't have a good feeling about this," I whispered to

Sven as he finished doctoring my leg. He'd insisted on helping me after I'd directed the physician to tend to Frans first. Using a few basic supplies one of the servants had fetched for him, he'd set to work cleaning my injury and plastering it with a poultice before bandaging it.

Now, he tugged my legging down and stood. "Bernhard reminds me of my brother. Nothing he says is trustworthy."

Sven, on the other hand, was proving himself more honorable every moment I was with him. He hadn't given thought to himself or his own needs when arriving at the castle and had been more concerned with helping me.

I knew what I needed to do. I had to ride out with my squires and assist them in eluding Bernhard's men. I was familiar with the area better than any of them and could lead them for a short distance.

A part of me didn't want to leave Mikaela behind, even for an hour or two. I'd debated just taking her with me and riding to Vordinberg with Sven and my squires. But I suspected aiding in Sven's getaway would be dangerous, perhaps even involve a skirmish with Bernhard's men.

Besides, I would do best to remain in Romsdal where I could keep an eye on Bernhard and prevent him from sending any more men into the forest. And I had to come up with a plan for how Torvald and I could defeat the jotunn.

I sent a servant to Mikaela with a message about the delay. Then I assisted a groom in saddling my horse. Before the passing of the next hour, I was on my way with three of my squires and Sven. None of Bernhard's guards tried to stop us as we left the castle, and no one seemed to be following us as we rode along the outskirts of town toward the southern border of Romsdal and the trail that led south.

As we reached a fork in the road, the Moors of Many Lakes spread out before us in the ever-lightening dawn. Several small lakes amidst sparse forests and low-lying hills reflected the streaks in the sky. Lonely merlins flew overhead. And the throaty bellows of newly awakened frogs filled the air.

Again, I neither heard nor saw any of Bernhard's guards on our trail and guessed I'd worried for nothing. Perhaps Bernhard didn't plan to make use of Sven's knowledge of the jotunn after all.

"To be safe, ride through the center of the moorland." I spoke to my most trusted squire. "Stay clear of the road along the Blood River."

The river path was easier to traverse. But the moorlands would provide a more direct route to Vordinberg.

Before my squire could respond, an arrow whizzed through the air and narrowly missed embedding into his unprotected neck.

In an instant I surmised the situation. Bernhard had sent a courier ahead of us and alerted the guards on night watch. They'd positioned themselves at this particular intersection because they had the higher ground. Whichever route we chose, they would have an easy view and be able to take us out one by one until only Sven remained.

If we retreated, no doubt we would soon find ourselves facing a contingent of fighting men Bernhard sent to follow us. Eventually we would be trapped from both ways.

As another arrow flew toward us, I urged my horse off the path.

"This way!" I charged into the brush.

Such a move was dangerous, since the moors were notorious for swamps that could slow down a rider, even cause them to get stuck and stranded. But I'd completed my knight's training in the moorlands and could traverse the difficult terrain better than most.

"Keep close!" I shouted as I jumped a stream and ducked under a low branch.

Bernhard's men would be on our trail erelong. Many of them would be as experienced in the moorland as I was. Nevertheless, I intended to keep our lead and lose them in order to return to my bride as soon as I possibly could.

Chapter 28

Mikaela

"I would like to see you marry Uncle Gunnar," Riki said from her spot at the table where she was picking at her simple meal.

"Me, also." Rena twisted on the bench in front of me, peering up at me with pleading eyes.

I paused in brushing Rena's hair. The very notion of being related to them—even if just by marriage—was difficult to comprehend. I wished I could bring them both with me to the chapel. And I wished I could call my family to witness the wedding too. But I suspected we would have a simple ceremony to keep from rousing Bernhard's ire more than we already had.

Nanna had helped me to wash up and put on my best gown. She'd also styled my hair, leaving the majority of it down, braiding back two strips and winding them with ribbons. Even though I wasn't wearing anything fancy, I felt pretty.

A sweet anticipation thrummed through my blood. And at every pair of footsteps that passed by the nursery doors, I only grew more excited.

I glanced at Nanna across the room as she used a hot iron to press wrinkles out of the garments the girls had yet to don. She frowned at the closed door as if frustrated Gunnar hadn't yet returned.

Earlier, a messenger had brought us news that Gunnar planned to ride with Sven for a short distance to make sure he was able to get safely away from Romsdal. However, neither Nanna nor I had expected the ride to take so long. Now morning sunshine poured through the open shutters, revealing that dawn had already come and gone. What was taking Gunnar so long?

"After you marry Gunnar, will you still help take care of us?" Riki posed the question I'd been wondering myself.

"I will never stop visiting or loving you." I glided my hand over Rena's hair. I didn't expect that Bernhard and Sophia or any of the nobility would welcome me into their lives. But I doubted Gunnar would want me to continue working in the nursery as a domestic. I could only pray that Nanna would be able to win approval for Kirstin to take my place. Together the two would carry on the task of influencing the little girls for good.

Already we'd had a short visit from Kirstin that morn to let us know Frans had awoken and was doing better. The physician had set his broken leg and done his best to repair the damage from the pike. Frans hadn't needed his foot amputated, but only time would tell how much weight he would be able to bear on the injured heel. Kirstin had wept as she thanked me for going in and saving Frans's life. I prayed, given time,

Frans would forget about me and learn to love Kirstin in my stead.

At the rap of knuckles against the door, I paused, my pulse leaping with an extra beat. Had Gunnar returned?

The door swung open, and I held my breath, waiting for Gunnar to step inside with one of his handsome grins. He'd beckon to me with his half-lidded gaze, wrap his arms around me, and kiss me just as he had last night.

Instead of Gunnar, however, a guard poked his head into the room and surveyed the chamber before nodding at me. "Time to go." His tone was curt and allowed for no arguing.

Why hadn't Gunnar come directly to the nursery himself? Surely he would be eager to see me again and walk with me to the chapel?

I hesitated.

"We've come to escort you to your wedding." The guard opened the door wider to reveal another guard in the hallway.

Perhaps after returning, Gunnar thought to change garments and groom himself and was even now doing so. Meeting in the chapel would certainly save some time.

"I need to find Ami." I fidgeted with one of the ribbons in my hair. "She said she would watch Rikissa and Renate so Nanna can come with me."

The guard shook his head. "The master said the affair will be private with only the priest and witnesses."

"Nanna can serve as a witness."

"He has enough witnesses already."

Nanna set aside her ironing. "Gunnar said that?"

The closest guard shrugged his shoulders. "We are following orders. That's all."

Nanna's expression turned more severe. Before she could argue, I smiled, hoping to reassure her. "I'll speak with Gunnar, and we'll send someone to fetch you."

She stared at the guard for another moment, then nodded.

With a final smile at Nanna and the girls, I exited into the passageway, smoothing my hands over my skirt. This was it. I was going to be married.

Over the past hours of waiting, I'd had plenty of time to consider the consequences of marrying Gunnar. While I would certainly be criticized for aspiring after someone far above my station, Gunnar would carry the bulk of the censure.

Our differences meant nothing to him. They never had and never would. I hadn't cared about our differences either, and I couldn't start now. Even so, I didn't want to cause him hardships as a result of marrying me.

The lead guard took my arm and guided me away from the nursery. With each step his grip tightened until it began to feel like a chain upon my arm. When we turned the corner, I realized we weren't going in the direction of the chapel.

"The chapel is the other way."

"You're not getting married in the chapel."

Unease skittered up my backbone. Something wasn't right.

I halted and attempted to jerk my arm free.

The second guard came alongside me and grasped

my other arm.

"Release me." I struggled now against them both.

The lead guard kept going without a waver in his steps. "The earl commanded us to make sure you are locked away until your wedding."

Dread began to pulse through my blood. Yes, something was most definitely amiss. "Why would the earl command such a thing?"

"It's not my place to question the earl."

What was Bernhard up to? Was he trying to prevent me from marrying Gunnar? Or maybe this was his way of exacting revenge upon Gunnar for speaking the truth and standing up to him. Hiding me away, perhaps forcing Gunnar to grovel before handing me over.

As we traversed the passageways, I was tempted to call for help. But I didn't want to bring anyone else into this situation and heap the earl's wrath upon them too. I searched every open door and every corner for a sign of Gunnar, but I didn't catch sight of him or any of his squires.

Maybe Gunnar hadn't yet returned and Bernhard planned to do something to me in his absence.

My mind filled with the image of Lola with weights tied to her ankles as she fell from the cliff and drowned in the fjord below. Maybe Bernhard would do the same to me. What if the earl took me out to the cliff, then pushed me off just as Gunnar came riding up? Such cruelty would be typical of Bernhard and the perfect way for him to show Gunnar never to cross him again.

My stomach churned—not so much at the thought of meeting my death by drowning but because of the pain and blame Gunnar would have to live with.

When the guards halted before a chamber door in a wing of the castle belonging to the more prominent servants, I tried once again to break free. But they swung open the door, shoved me inside, and slammed it shut behind me. The click of a key told me they'd locked me inside. "The earl would like you to wait here for the wedding ceremony. The priest and your husband will be along shortly."

I took in the stark furnishings of the room: a leather satchel hanging from the bedpost, a stack of parchment and a pot and ink upon a writing table, and a long black robe hanging from a peg in the wall, a robe that belonged to one group of people—the wisemen. I didn't need anyone to inform me that I was in the room of the earl's advisor, the Sagacite, Pontus.

What could this possibly mean? Certainly not what I thought it did.

I shrank against the door and groped for the handle. I tugged it, hoping it would open and that I could flee. But even as I wriggled it, I knew I'd never escape. I was locked inside. And the guards were no doubt waiting on the other side for the arrival of the priest. And Pontus.

Bernhard was giving me in marriage to Pontus. It didn't matter that I'd never spoken to the man. It didn't matter that he was old enough to be my father. It didn't matter that he made my skin crawl every time I saw him. Bernhard intended to marry me to the Sagacite. And there was nothing I could do to stop it from happening.

Chapter 29

GUNNAR

I SLID FROM MY MOUNT AND TOOK OFF AT A SPRINT ACROSS THE bailey, not bothering to give instructions to the groom. The high sun overhead indicated that the noon hour was fast approaching, which meant I was hours later than I'd anticipated.

Bernhard's men had chased us for some distance before we'd lost them. Even then, I'd led Sven and my squires deeper into the moorland before finally deciding they would be safe without me. I'd urged them to keep up the punishing pace until reaching Vordinberg and finding sanctuary with the king.

Then we'd parted ways, and I'd circled back around, using an alternate route to return to Romsdal.

Now as I took the steps two at a time and barged into the front entrance hall, my heart pulsed with the need to be with Mikaela, a need that had grown as I'd drawn closer to the castle, so that now she was all I could think about.

Although I wanted to go directly to the nursery and

pull her into my arms, I had to make the arrangements for our wedding first with both the priest as well as Bernhard.

My footsteps pounded hard in the quiet passageway that led to the chapel. My leg wound slowed me only a little now, hardly paining me after the poultice had soaked in and worked its healing. Though a throbbing at the back of my head reminded me I hadn't slept in hours, I pushed myself.

The chapel door was open, and the priest was pacing back and forth in front of the altar, clutching at the cross that hung from a long leather strip around his neck. At the sight of me, he stopped abruptly and heaved a breath.

"I have been praying for your arrival, sire." The priest was new since I'd last visited Likness Castle years ago. Attired in a brown woolen cowl, he bowed his head, which was shaven except for the tonsured ring that circled above his ears. His smooth face was youthful, and he'd struck me as a sincere man of faith in the few interactions I'd had with him thus far.

His prayer request was a strange one, but I didn't have time to think on it now. "Make ready. I will be here with my bride shortly for my wedding."

"Then you have set her free?" His voice held a hopeful note.

My thrumming pulse slowed to a crawl. "Set who free?"

"Mikaela."

Even as he spoke her name, my body tensed with a terrible foreboding, and a dozen scenarios flashed through my mind. "What has Bernhard done?" If he'd harmed her in the least, I would make him pay.

"He is planning to give her in marriage to the Pontus, the wiseman."

"Pontus?" My mind tried to register what the priest was saying, but panic ripped through me with the force of a winter gale. "Has he already . . . ?"

"Not yet. But the earl has ordered me to be ready for the ceremony. And I have been praying he would not summon me until I had the chance to speak with you first and discover if the rumor is true that you intend to marry her for yourself."

"'Tis true." Nothing had ever been truer. How dare Bernhard even think about giving Mikaela away to someone else. It didn't matter that legally she still belonged to him. She was mine in body, soul, and spirit. And I intended to have her.

"That's what I thought, sire. And I've been praying you would return before I was required to perform the ceremony."

Silently, I cursed myself for leaving her here. I should have known I couldn't trust Bernhard and that he would devise a way to torment me now that I'd made a stand against him.

I needed to find her and marry her immediately. "Where is she?"

"She is locked in the advisor's chambers."

I spun on my heels only to find myself face to face with Bernhard. And half a dozen of his guards. Pontus waited several paces back, his plump face pale and his eyes wide. He wrung his hands in front of his protruding belly as though he wanted to run off and hide.

Was he afraid of me? Of what I might do to him now that I knew he was planning to marry Mikaela? Or was he afraid of Bernhard? Either way, he ought to be fearful. I would do anything to keep him from having my bride.

As though sensing the same, Bernhard's lips turned up

into a calculated smile. "You are just in time. We are about to begin the wedding of Mikaela and Pontus."

My fingers twitched with the overwhelming need to squeeze Bernhard's neck and strangle him. "You wouldn't dare try to wed her to another man."

"You are wrong, my dear brother. I have already told you the maiden is mine. I own her. And I shall do with her as I please. It pleases me to bestow her on my faithful advisor, who has expressed a desire for her."

I shot a glare at Pontus, but the man had the presence of mind to duck his head and avoid my wrath.

I worked loose the purse at my belt and tossed it at Bernhard's feet. "That's more than enough to purchase her freedom. And once I return to Vordinberg, I shall earn enough to account for each member of her family."

Bernhard kicked the pouch aside. "I may yet give her to you. But I require something besides money as payment."

"What?" As soon as the question was out, I guessed the answer. He wanted Sven.

Bernhard's grin inched higher. "I see you already know."

"And I also know why you want him. So that you can use him to help in your quest to find the chalice."

"Is that not why you also took him away, so that you could use him in your quest? We are not so different, you and I. We both see his value."

We were very different, as different as two brothers could be. "So you do not deny wanting the chalice?"

Bernhard leaned casually against the door frame. "Why would I deny it? There is no crime in seeking the sacred relic. In fact, I should think you would be grateful I am doing what I can to eliminate the jotunn and make the discovery easier."

Bernhard was an expert at twisting a situation to fit his aspirations. But he needed to learn he could no longer twist me. "I'm not bringing Sven back."

"I do not just require Sven. I require your assistance as well." He kicked at my bag of coins again. "That is the only payment I will accept for the maiden's freedom."

It was suddenly all clear. Bernhard wanted me to exchange my freedom for Mikaela's. He would compel me to bind myself to him and do his bidding. I would become a slave for Bernhard in the same way Sven had been a slave for the jotunn.

For a moment, I waged an inner war. If I gave in to Bernhard's demands I'd gain Mikaela. But if I denied my brother, I would seal my fate as his enemy. And he'd never willingly give me Mikaela. I would have to fight for her.

I eyed the soldiers standing at the ready behind Bernhard. Could I battle them all?

An inner voice cautioned me to do the sure and easy thing—to take Bernhard's bargain. Or at least to pretend I was but then continue to undermine him. Such a strategy had worked well for me for years, hadn't it?

I shook my head. I'd lived in fear of Bernhard for too long. I'd made my decision to stand up to him, to stay strong in living the truth, and I couldn't back down now.

I gauged the positions of my opponents and inched out my knife with one hand and gripped my sword with the other. Then I spoke the truth, even though it would lead to the greatest battle I'd yet to fight. "I will remain loyal to the king and will never work for you or Rasmus."

Bernhard's grin slipped away. He pushed away from the doorframe and straightened, his eyes glittering with warning. "Be careful what you say, brother."

I held his gaze for a moment so that he could see I knew the truth, that he was working in conjunction with Rasmus. "I don't know what Rasmus promised you, but I do know that any alliance with him is treason."

"I have given you the opportunity to cooperate willingly. And now you leave me no choice but to make you see where your loyalty should lie."

I unsheathed my sword. "You will never have my loyalty."

He nodded and his men began to close in around me. Then he spoke over his shoulder to two guards who lingered in the hallway. "Take the maiden to the whipping post."

"No!" I lunged, trying to make my way out of the chapel, but I was already surrounded and would have to fight my way free. As I parried my first blow, panic lent me renewed strength, especially as the two guards in the hallway dashed away to do Bernhard's bidding.

Chapter 30

Mikaela

Was I smelling smoke? Sitting on the floor with my back against the door, I lifted my head from where I'd rested it on my knees.

I'd been waiting in the Sagacite's chamber, my dismay mounting with every passing hour. I'd tried every trick I could think of to get the guards in the passageway to open the door, but nothing had worked.

Now, I could only hope that Gunnar would return before my fate was sealed. Even then, I didn't know how he'd be able to free me. Not with Bernhard taking so much care to have me guarded.

I sniffed, testing the air. The smoke didn't have the usual wood or charcoal scent. Instead, it had the earthiness of burning thatch.

I expelled a breath of frustration. Which roof was on fire this time? If Bernhard would only provide slate for the roofs, the number of fires would diminish. But he'd refused to listen to any advice regarding a less flammable alternative.

The fire that had destroyed the forge's roof was still too recent. Who would suffer today? I just prayed that everyone would work together to put out the fire before it spread.

A bell began to clang in the bailey, calling all available hands to assist. I could hear the guards outside the door arguing with each other, and then their voices faded as they rushed to help put out the fire before the destruction could spread too far.

I leaned my head back. It didn't matter whether they stood guard or not. I couldn't escape. I was stuck for now. Maybe forever.

"Oh, Gunnar," I whispered. "I'm sorry."

We'd tried to break free of the constraints ensnaring us. But somehow, we hadn't been strong enough. Maybe I'd been too idealistic and too naïve to think I could start to bring about changes. Maybe we were all stuck in our way of life and simply needed to accept the lot we'd been given.

At the approach of rapid footsteps down the passageway, I sat forward. Someone else was coming my way. Two sets of steps, one heavier and one lighter. Was it Pontus, the Sagacite, with the priest? Were the guards returning?

As the newcomers paused on the other side of the door, I held my breath. *Please, let it be Gunnar.*

A key rattled in the lock.

I quickly stood. Did I dare attempt to run away?

As the lock clicked and the door swung open, I tensed, ready to spring out.

"Mikaela?" Nanna's worried face peered through.

Relief poured over me, making me sag. "Nanna, what are you doing here?"

She pushed the door wider, revealing the castle steward holding a ring of keys. He lifted a questioning brow at Nanna. "Do you need anything else?"

She shook her head. "Mikaela can do the rest from here."

The steward glanced both ways before continuing down the hallway.

Nanna had my bag and cloak. She thrust them into my arms, then pulled me into the hallway. "Go now while the guards are distracted by the fire. It's not a big one and won't last overlong."

Had Nanna purposefully set a fire? Or asked one of the staff to do so in order to free me? Even if she hadn't, she'd clearly involved the steward in this escape plan. After years of faithful servitude and quiet influence on her charges, why was she putting herself and others at risk with overt rebellion?

"After watching you and Gunnar take a stand for what's right no matter the cost," she whispered, seeing the question in my eyes, "how could I do any less?"

If Bernhard learned of her role in my escape, she would pay dearly for it. I dreaded to think what he would do. How could I let her suffer on my account?

"I've needed to do more." She pressed a hand to my cheek. "Let me do this. Please."

I leaned into her touch. She'd saved me that day long ago when she'd brought me to work in the nursery. And she was doing it again. I owed her everything. Once I was free, I'd find Gunnar and we'd figure out a way to keep her safe and repay her. "Thank you, Nanna."

Tears pooled in her eyes. "I love you, Mikaela-girl. You go, now, and do all the great things God has planned for you to do."

I fought back tears of my own. "I love you too, Nanna."

She pushed me forward. "Find your way out of the castle. Then slip through the side wall door and make your way to your hidden hot spring along the cliff."

How had she known about my hot spring?

"Wait there," she said.

I hesitated. The echo of more footsteps, a loud clomping, came from an adjacent passageway.

"Do it, Mikaela." Her whisper was an urgent plea. "And don't look back."

Clutching my bag and cloak, I ran. And I did as she asked. I didn't look back.

Chapter 31

GUNNAR

I WAS OUTNUMBERED. BUT I FOUGHT LIKE A MADMAN, MY NEED TO protect Mikaela driving me with desperation. I couldn't let the two guards get their hands on her. They'd drag her outside to the post at the center of the bailey, would bare her back, and begin to whip her.

Bernhard was right. I'd have no choice but to submit to him then. I'd never be able to stand by and watch Mikaela suffer.

I ducked and dodged a blow at the same time as I parried another. I regretted we were having this battle in the chapel, but I prayed God would understand that I was fighting for the truth and would show me favor today for my efforts to do what was honorable.

The clanking of weapons rent the air along with grunts and labored breathing. I'd eliminated at least six men and was surrounded by four men, each thrusting at me. I was glad I still wore my chain mail, that I hadn't shed it when I'd returned. But I feared I would only last a short while longer, especially since Bernhard had shouted down the hallway for reinforcements.

"You may as well give up, brother," Bernhard called. "You are too weak and will not win this battle now or in the future."

His words taunted me, reminded me of my faults. It was almost as if in putting me down he made himself look better.

If only he could have loved and encouraged me the way I'd always longed for.

From the corner of my gaze, I glimpsed the sneer, the cold eyes . . . and the trickle of blood dripping from his nose.

I ducked to avoid another swipe directed toward my head. As I rose, one of the guards moved out of the fray and another stopped to stare at Bernhard. I battled the remaining two.

The sound of coughing filled the air, deep coughing that echoed off the walls. It was coming from Bernhard. As he stumbled backward and fell against a bench, the two soldiers I was fighting cast him glances, only to freeze, their eyes rounding with what seemed to be horror.

With labored breathing, I paused in the sword-fighting, determined to use the break to retrieve my knife. But as I moved, my gaze landed upon the splatters of bright crimson at Bernhard's feet.

More blood drizzled from his nose, over his lips, and down his chin. He coughed again, and blood sprayed from his mouth.

My mind thundered with a dozen thoughts, and one boomed louder than the others. Was Bernhard suffering from the bleeding curse?

I shook my head. How could that be? According to

everything Sven and Mikaela had told me, the jotunn had passed the bleeding curse to Sven's firstborn.

Whatever the case, I had to use the moment of distraction to break free and get to Mikaela. By now, the soldiers would have arrived at Pontus's room. Did I still have time to intercept them before they dragged her outside?

I dashed past Bernhard's men, and they made no move to prevent me from going. Either they were too consumed by what was happening to Bernhard, or without his direction, they didn't care what became of me.

I raced along the passageway, trying to remember how to get to the area of the castle where servants like the Sagacite had their rooms. All the while I ran, I prayed I wouldn't be too late.

As I started up one of the stairwells, I bumped into an older servant coming down. Upon steadying the thin frame, I found myself looking into familiar eyes. "Nanna?" Her cheeks were wet with tears that she rapidly brushed away.

"Where's Mikaela?" Was I too late? Was that why Nanna was crying?

"I set her free," she whispered.

"Free?"

"Not more than thirty minutes ago."

My muscles tightened with the need to go after her. "Where to?"

"I told her to wait in your secret hot spring along the cliff. If she made it, that's where she'll be."

I released Nanna and spun, tripping down the steps in my haste. I needed to thank her and wish her well, but I couldn't waste another second. And ultimately, I knew

Nanna wouldn't want me to stop, that she wanted me to chase after Mikaela.

As I bolted out of the castle, the air was filled with thick smoke and the bailey was in chaos, with every available castle staff and guard working to extinguish a fire blazing amongst the thatch above the forge.

Hadn't the forge sustained a fire in the thatch already this spring? How had it caught ablaze again, especially since it was new and not as dry as the older thatch on some of the other structures?

I didn't stop to get answers. Something told me this catastrophe had been created on purpose, that perhaps Nanna had rallied the other bondservants to cause a distraction so that she could free Mikaela and allow us to escape from Bernhard.

Searching for Mikaela, I darted around people and animals and water buckets and made my way to the stable. I found that my horse was still halfway saddled, that the groom had abandoned his task, likely to fight the flames.

I cinched the girth and climbed astride. Then while everyone was still consumed with the fire, I headed through the gatehouse and kicked my horse into a gallop toward Trollveggen Cliff.

I rode low and hard, all the while glancing over my shoulder to make sure no one followed me. By the time I steered my horse out of the open and into the brush, I allowed myself a full breath. As far as I could tell, not a soul was in sight. None of Bernhard's knights had noticed my leaving, or if they had, they were too busy to care.

I slid down from my mount, hoping Mikaela had made it away from the castle undetected too. I hiked along the narrow trail, the rushing of waterfalls and the crashing of the fjords below the only sound.

My mind flashed to the image of Bernhard, the blood flowing from his nose and mouth. What would happen to him? I would never wish death upon him, not even after the way he'd abused me. But maybe the illness would help him see the evilness of his ways and give him a change of heart.

Upon reaching the section of the path that led to the hot spring, I secured my steed in a secluded area and then climbed up as stealthily as I always did. When I reached the top, I crouched low and expelled my relief.

She was there, sitting near the edge, her feet drawn up, her arms circled around her legs and skirt. Her hair hung unfettered, with two thin braids pulled back at her temple and tied with ribbons. She stared through the steam into the clear water. From the tenseness of her expression and the stiffness of her body, I could tell she was worried.

I wanted to say something, but emotion rose swiftly and clogged my throat. I topped the ridge and began my descent toward her.

Upon catching sight of me, she released a small cry and scrambled up. When I reached her, she threw herself against me at the same time that I wrapped my arms around her.

She shuddered and pressed in, as though she hadn't expected to see me again.

"I'm sorry, Mikaela," I whispered against her hair. "I'm sorry you had to go through that. I didn't know until I returned that Bernhard was holding you hostage to manipulate me."

She pulled back, her brows pinching above her beautiful, expressive eyes. "I hope you didn't give in to his demands."

"I was tempted to. But I stayed strong."

"Good."

This wasn't the time to share the details about Bernhard's bleeding. We'd be able to share more in the hours and days to come. For now, I wanted to get her out of Romsdal and as far from Bernhard as I could.

Even with the urgency, I clung to her, needing to assure myself she was here and out of harm's way. "I never should have left you behind."

"You had to help Sven escape."

I breathed her in and let her presence soothe my pounding pulse. "Henceforth, whatever we do, we'll do it together. Can we agree upon that?"

"I can agree."

I didn't realize I was shaking until that moment, when my trembling ceased.

"Gunnar?" Her voice was grave. "I fear you will face overmuch criticism for being with a woman of my low status. If Bernhard refused our union, surely many more will shun you for it."

I shifted so that she could view my face and my sincerity. "My friends will see what I do, that you make me a better and stronger man. And they will heartily welcome you because of that."

She pushed against me lightly. "You're jesting with me."

"'Tis the truth. I've sensed something was missing inside me, but it wasn't until I was with you again that I realized when you're by my side, I'm finally whole, complete."

She studied my face, seeking the truth.

"I need you."

A smile tugged at the corners of her lips. "What

exactly do you need most? My wit? My intelligence? My inner fortitude? My sweetness? My—"

"Your kisses." I bent down and fused my lips with hers. I meant for the kiss to be light and teasing, but as soon as we touched, the heat that always simmered below the surface rose swiftly, flowing through me, turning me on fire, and making me only want to keep on kissing her.

I loved that she met me with as much desire, melding into me and moving as though she would kiss me forever too.

As much as I wanted to revel in this bond between us, we needed to be on our way. For the time being, staying was too dangerous. I would take her away, and we would make our way to Vordinberg and the king, where we would find refuge from Bernhard's schemes and gather reinforcements.

I broke the kiss but rested my forehead against hers. "Never forget. We are meant for each other."

"Are you sure?"

"We always have been and always will be." No matter what would happen in the days to come, I would relish spending the rest of my life showing her just how true that was.

We rode all afternoon, through the night, and well into the next day. Though I kept a fast pace, I didn't want to overtax my horse bearing two riders instead of one. At midday we reached the remote fortress of Lindseth within the Moors of Many Lakes. 'Twas the home where I'd lived and trained during my years as a page and squire. I respected Lord Lindseth and knew I would find an ally in him should Bernhard send his men after me.

As the Lord welcomed me inside, I drew Mikaela into the shelter of my arm and body. The day was cloudy and cold, and though I'd tried to keep her warm, she shivered. She'd slept off and on during the long ride, but I could see the weariness in her features. I was exhausted, too, and couldn't recall the last time I'd slept for any length.

"My home is your home," Lord Lindseth said after I gave him a brief explanation of my current circumstances and the danger I faced from Bernhard. "You will stay here as long as you have need, and my fighting men will keep you safe."

He looked pointedly at the young men in the front entryway. From their dusty tunics and padded gambesons, I guessed they'd been outside training but were now taking their meal in the great hall.

I nodded my thanks to Lord Lindseth. I'd served him well for many years, and he was repaying me for that. It also didn't hurt that I'd earned prestige and prominence as a Knight of Brethren and was a close companion of the king.

"I will have my servants deliver more food to the head table." He motioned to a nearby manservant, who scurried away down a passageway that led to the kitchen.

Before I gave way to refreshment and slumber, there was one thing I needed to do first. "First, if you would allow me the use of your chapel and priest, I would be grateful."

"Certainly." If Lord Lindseth was puzzled by my strange request, he hid it well.

"My brother interfered with my wedding yesterday." I drew Mikaela closer. "I would that we complete our marital vows today, anon, before anything or anyone else can interfere again."

Lord Lindseth's attention shifted to Mikaela. As his keen gaze swept over her, I could feel her stiffen. I knew she was worried about what the nobility would think of me marrying a bondservant. Even though the Norvegian law had changed last year allowing for royalty and nobility to marry commoners, Mikaela, as a slave, fell outside of the new law.

I hoped my buying her freedom changed her status and allowed for the legality of our union. Either way, I intended to marry her and have her for my wife no matter the repercussions.

As Lord Lindseth's gaze returned to my face, I guessed he could see my resolve, for he nodded. "I and my wife shall stand as your witnesses."

Within minutes we found ourselves at the front of the chapel with a priest leading us through our vows.

I faced Mikaela, holding both of her hands. Lord Lindseth, his wife, and several other knights stood nearby and acted as witnesses so that no one—especially Bernhard—could call into question the validity of our union.

"I, Mikaela, take thee, Gunnar, to be my wedded husband, to have and to hold from this day forward, for better, for worse, for richer, for poorer, in sickness and in health, to love, cherish, and to obey, till death us do part, according to God's holy ordinance. Thereto I give thee my troth."

The sincerity in her voice and the love in her eyes made me feel as though I was in a dream from which I never wanted to awaken.

The priest turned to me. "Your turn, Sir Gunnar."

I smiled down at Mikaela, hoping she could see my love for her too. "I, Gunnar, take thee, Mikaela, to be my wedded wife, to have and to hold from this day forward, for better, for worse, for richer, for poorer, in sickness and in health, to love and cherish till death us do part . . ."

I paused, then continued with my own vow. "I promise that nothing else matters to me except that we are together through the joys and trials of life, nevermore to be apart."

Her smile widened and brought solace to my soul.

"According to God's holy ordinance. Thereto I give thee my troth." I bent my head and brushed my lips against hers with a kiss that was only the beginning of forever.

Chapter 32

Mikaela

As I walked down the aisle toward the dais where King Ansgar and Queen Lis sat on their thrones, I wanted to pinch myself to make sure I was awake and not dreaming, but my hands were trembling too much, and I didn't dare remove them from Gunnar's arm. I was thankful now more than ever that Lady Lindseth had offered me one of her gowns to wear at court. The exquisite garment was pale pink with a jeweled bodice and a flowing train.

I wasn't accustomed to such luxury, but Gunnar had assured me that I was beautiful in anything, whether frayed rags or fine linen. And I knew he wasn't merely flattering me, because he looked at me the same—with love and appreciation—no matter what I wore.

Gunnar had dressed in his best too, in wool leggings, a tailored surcote over his shirt, a belt slung low around his waist, and his golden sword pin. Even though he'd groomed his hair earlier, it flopped over his forehead, begging me to comb my fingers through it.

We'd arrived in Vordinberg only an hour ago. Upon our entrance into the royal castle, we'd been greeted by his fellow Knights of Brethren. There had been much back slapping and teasing the Slayer that he'd finally been slain. All the knights were present except for Torvald, who was still at his family estate at Wahlburg Castle.

According to Gunnar, Torvald's father had arranged a marriage for him to help save his family fortune. Torvald hadn't wanted to marry, but he'd returned home out of duty and planned to resume his duties as a Knight of Brethren after his affairs were in order—at least until he completed his mission to find the chalice.

I knew Gunnar also wanted to continue his work as a Knight of Brethren, but I'd learned the that once a Brethren got married, he was expected to retire from his position and go home to live with his wife and family.

Though I worried he might eventually regret marrying me and giving up his place in service to the king, he'd reassured me in a hundred beautiful ways over the past few days since our wedding that I was more important to him than anything else. He was already living out his vow that nothing else mattered except that we were together through the joys and trials of life.

Now, as we approached the king and queen, I could only pray they would have mercy upon Gunnar for marrying a woman like me.

At the moment, the king, a strong and imposing

man, didn't seem to be paying us any heed. Instead, he held his wife's hand, their fingers laced together intimately. He leaned toward her, whispering in her ear, something that made her smile.

The queen lived up to the rumors of her beauty. Even though she wore a golden circlet around her head and sheer veil, nothing could hide the gloriousness of her long, reddish-blond hair. Her face was pale and thin—no doubt from her illness—but her green eyes danced with a spark of life that told me she was every bit as strong and independent as the tales declared.

Behind the king and queen stood another couple, both attired in the black robes belonging to wisemen— and wisewomen. I guessed they were Maxim and Princess Elinor, the advisors to the king and queen. They, like the royal couple, stood hand in hand, clearly a strong force.

Next to the king's right hand was another man, one I hardly recognized. So changed was his appearance that, if not for the scars on his face, I wouldn't have known he was Sven. His gray hair was cut and combed into neat submission, his face was cleanly shaven but for a small beard, and he was attired in tailored garments of bright blue and red and gold.

As we stopped at the bottom step of the dais, Sven nodded at me, his eyes filled with the warmth of a loving grandfather. Somehow his acceptance served to calm the flock of birds trying to take flight in my stomach.

As King Ansgar's attention shifted to us, his expression was guarded. Was he upset at his trusted knight for choosing marriage over duty to king and country?

"Gunnar, welcome back," the king said in the now quiet hall, which was empty of all but the Brethren.

Gunnar bowed, then as he straightened, he smiled down at me. "Your Majesty, I present to you my wife, the love of my life."

I smiled back, drawing strength from his love as I had over the past days. Then I curtsied before the king and queen.

"Welcome, Mikaela." The queen was the first to speak. "We have heard much about your valor from Sven. He speaks highly of you."

I again exchanged a look with Sven. His eyes held deep gratitude.

"If not for you, Sven would still be a prisoner of the jotunn," the king continued. "He indicated that you sacrificed greatly to set him free."

My fingers went to my pocket beneath my skirt, now empty of the beautiful purple shell that had connected me to my twin sister. At first, it had been strange to feel the emptiness where the shell had always been. But I was learning to finally accept the sacrifice she'd made for me, knowing that I could spend my life doing the same for others, that Sven was just the first. As Sven had said, *"One act of courage has the power to clear the path for more."*

I prayed Sven would get to experience much of the life he'd lost, that his last days on earth would be filled with all the good things he'd missed while being a prisoner in the forest.

The queen clutched a handkerchief in one of her hands. Even though it was mostly crumpled, she couldn't hide the blood stains within it. "We have just received news of your brother Bernhard's recent death."

Gunnar startled as I did. After spending two days with Lord Lindseth and then taking our time in riding the final distance through the moorland to Vordinberg, we'd been isolated and alone—which had suited us just fine . . . except that we'd clearly missed the news.

Of course, during our time together, Gunnar had explained Bernhard's sudden onset of bleeding during the fight in the chapel at Likness. We'd puzzled over the turn of events together.

I'd done my best to repeat word for word what the jotunn had spoken: *I pass the curse from Sven to the firstborn sons in his family.* In analyzing the statement, Gunnar and I had concluded the jotunn hadn't specifically cursed Sven's firstborns, since he'd neglected to say the word *direct.* Thus, we could only speculate that the ailment would afflict all firstborn sons in the Likness family, including Gunnar's children someday.

Although we couldn't say for certain, we'd discussed the possibility that the queen's bleeding disease might have been established by a jotunn too, perhaps by the same jotunn who lived in Hardanger Forest, since we knew of no others in Norvegia.

Gunnar had confided in me the tale of the chalice bringing healing to people who drank from it. I understood now why the king sought it so desperately, so that he could bring about healing for the queen.

"I have returned the Earldom of Likness to Sven." The king waved a hand toward the older man as though giving him leave to speak.

Sven bowed his head to the king before clearing his throat. "I have only agreed to resume the earldom until Gunnar is ready to do so—"

"'Tis rightfully yours, my lord," Gunnar interrupted.

"No. I am old, and the people do not know me."

"They will accept you if I tell them to."

"I have already made up my mind." Sven's voice still contained a raspy quality. Perhaps it had been that way since the fire he'd endured as a young man. "I will govern in your stead, receiving your direct guidance for the laws of the land."

Gunnar exchanged a look with me.

I understood what he was silently communicating—that together we would provide guidance to Sven. My heart swelled with the thrill of the possibilities. This was what I'd hoped and prayed for, to have the opportunity to better the lives of all the people of Likness and Romsdal.

"I hope you find the agreement suitable?" The king was watching Gunnar intently. "This will allow you to continue on in my service, knowing Romsdal is in good hands."

Was the king intending to allow Gunnar to remain a Knight of Brethren after all? Was that what this meant?

I almost allowed myself a moment of excitement until I caught sight of the gravity in Gunnar's demeanor. "I have pledged my life in service to you, Your Majesty. And I would serve you as long as I am able. But I cannot be apart from my wife. She is my life blood. She makes me into the man I have always wanted to be but never had the strength for on my own."

The king's eyes seemed to hold hurt. "In all our years together, you never trusted me with the truth of your love for only one woman."

Gunnar held the king's gaze. "I regret that I couldn't share it with you, Ansgar. But I guarded the truth to keep her safe." His informality with the king told me their friendship had once been vitally important.

I squeezed Gunnar's hand to assure him I understood his need to keep his feelings private. After Bernhard nearly married me off to his Sagacite, I couldn't fault Gunnar for anything. He'd only done what he'd thought was best for me.

"I pray you will forgive me, as I am learning to be more truthful to myself." Gunnar bowed his head toward the king again. "And I pray you will accept her as my wife."

"Of course we accept her." The queen rose to her feet, and the king stood by her side in the next instant, his features taut with concern. "She has proven her bravery, loyalty, and kindness in freeing Sven from servitude and the curse."

"In doing so," the king said, "she has given me the greatest gift—hope that we will find the chalice and that we may yet save Lis in time." He bent toward the queen and kissed her cheek.

The love between the king and queen radiated with such strength that tears sprang to my eyes. Suddenly I understood Gunnar's devotion to this couple and his desire to serve them in any way he could.

I was relieved they would accept me as Gunnar's wife, but surely they could also accept Gunnar's wishes. "Your Majesty, you could ask for no better knight than Gunnar. I pray you will find a way to allow him to remain in your service while granting his wish to stay with me. I can assure you that I will only help him and you in any way I can."

"As I said, Your Majesty," Gunnar said again, this time more formally, "she makes me better."

The king cleared his throat. "I have spoken with the rest of the knights this morn after we received word you would be arriving. We all agreed that we want you to remain at the table among the Knights of Brethren, that we will no longer abide by the rule that marriage disqualifies a knight for service. If anything, when we men unite with the right women, we are only more qualified."

The queen nodded. "Rest assured, you need not be apart. You have permission to stay together as much as you're able."

Princess Elinor nodded in agreement. The two sisters stood beside their husbands as equals, serving together. Was it possible Gunnar and I could do the same?

As though sensing my unasked question, Gunnar quirked a brow at me. I could see the happiness in his eyes in knowing he could continue doing what he loved. And I understood then that I'd been given even greater opportunities for making changes than I'd ever believed possible.

"I accept," I said.

"As do I." Gunnar's voice rang true and certain.

The king finally smiled. "Then henceforth, I hereby declare that the Knights of Brethren shall consist of my knights and the brave women who serve by their sides. Together we are stronger."

The knights and the brave women who served by their sides. I liked the sound of that. A lifetime of serving beside Gunnar was all I could ever ask for.

Gunnar leaned in and pressed a kiss against my ear before whispering, "Next time we see Rikissa and Renate, I'll have another tale to tell them."

At the touch of his lips and the warmth against my skin, my body tingled with pleasure. "And what tale is that?"

"The story of how a beautiful and brave woman defeated a jotunn with the aid of her daring knight."

"What about the story of how the woman ensnared the knight with her wit and impertinence?"

"I like that tale even better." He smirked. "But of course, methinks it wouldn't be complete without the part about how the knight equally ensnared the woman with his charm and kisses."

I laughed and stole a sweet kiss, not caring that everyone was looking on.

There was no place I'd rather be than with Gunnar. Ensnared.

Take a peek as the real story of the Holy Grail continues…

Chapter 1

TORVALD

I LOATHED THE SIGHT OF WAHLBURG CASTLE.

I halted my mount in the river bottom, rested my reins on my thigh, and turned a critical eye upon my boyhood home and the estate I would one day inherit.

Perched upon a steep rocky cliff that bordered the Blood River, the fortress was impenetrable on the two sides built against the cliffs. If an enemy attacked, they would have to attempt a takeover by way of the southern and eastern portions, which were fortified with thick double walls that rose higher than any ladder or siege engine could span.

If only my father hadn't allowed the place to fall into such disrepair . . .

The crenellations were crumbling. The arrow slits were collapsing. One of the turrets was tottering. The family banner streaming from a spiral tower roof was in tatters. The emblem of a bear standing with claws extended—representing strength, cunning, and ferocity— was barely recognizable. The once-bright green background—that stood for hope, joy, and loyalty in love—was now faded to a pale olive.

I expelled a bitter breath. Nothing regarding my family crest was true, especially of my father. He had no strength, cunning, or ferocity. And he certainly had no hope or joy. The only trait he maintained was loyalty in love, much to his detriment. He'd remained loyal in love to my mother, even though she'd abandoned him many years ago when she'd run away with another nobleman.

His undying obsession over her had been his downfall, had led to a melancholy so great that he'd ceased living and had instead wallowed in despair. Thereafter, he was as broken and in as much disrepair as the fortress.

At a splatter of a raindrop against my face, I nudged my horse toward the pathway that led up to the gatehouse. Behind me, the clomping of hooves indicated that my squires were following closely.

Our surcoats contained the king's emblem—dragon heads on a background of royal red—designating us as the king's men. As my most trusted squires, they'd been with me throughout the winter and spring during the search for the sacred chalice on behalf of King Ansgar, who was desperate to find the ancient relic with the hope it could bring healing to his wife, Queen Lis, who was perishing from a bleeding disease.

I was grateful for the quiet, steady presence of my squires during this difficult homecoming. Even so, I regretted not accepting Gunnar's offer to come with me. Instead, I'd encouraged my fellow Knight of Brethren to remain in Romsdal and continue looking for the chalice without me. I'd assured him I would return in a fortnight.

Two weeks was sufficient for the task at hand. In fact, it was overlong.

Any amount of time was too lengthy for a wedding I didn't want to a woman I didn't know.

I was tempted to do my duty tonight and leave on the morrow. But I had too much principle and would force myself to remain for a polite duration.

Another raindrop hit my face. At the darkening clouds overhead, I nudged my mount to a faster pace. The April afternoon was almost spent, and I wasn't surprised a spring storm was greeting my arrival home. It was all too fitting.

Dusty and gritty from the past couple of days of hard riding, I drew up the hood of my cloak over my chain mail. With each plodding step up the path, my heart sank lower. By the time we reached the gatehouse, the heaviness inside threatened to hold me back.

Though the portcullis was raised, I reined in. Upon the high plateau of the riverbank, the wind slapped against me, the coldness reminding me of the long winter we'd endured. Now, with the coming of spring, 'twould not be long ere King Canute rallied his army and attacked Norvegia again. The Swainian king had a grandmother who'd been a royal Norwegian princess. Because of his connection to the Oldenberg bloodline, he insisted he was the rightful heir to Norvegia's throne.

Our scouts were keeping an eye on King Canute's movements. And once he launched his initiative, I intended to join in, even though custom dictated that an elite Knight of Brethren who took a wife was to resign from the king's service. I prayed no one would object to my continuing as a Brethren, at least until King Canute was defeated.

While I'd hoped to serve King Ansgar for many more years, I'd been born and bred to be an obedient son. I understood that as the future heir of Wahlburg, I had an obligation to take a wife and have a family. Now that my father had summoned me home to wed, I would do as he had requested, even though it was the last thing I wanted to do.

Peering through the gatehouse past the outer bailey and into the inner courtyard, I could see a group of people congregated outside the central doors of the main building of the keep. Clearly, the guards on lookout had seen us coming for some time and had made the announcement of our approach.

I couldn't hold back a scowl. I didn't want to be greeted by anyone, not household staff and certainly not by strangers—including my future wife and her kin. No doubt this was Ingold's doing. The steward had likely brought our dwindling fortune to my father's attention, suggested I marry someone with a large dowry who could restore our wealth, and then sought the best candidate. In addition, Ingold had probably made all the preparations for the maiden's visit.

All my father did—in addition to wasting our fortune—was nod his permission. Yes, he excelled at wasting things—time, wealth, land, lives... and love over a woman who hadn't deserved it.

I ducked my head to hide my irritation and steered my horse into the fortress, praying for the strength to be patient over the coming days. I knew people talked about my ruthlessness in battle as well as my brooding and severe nature. The rumors weren't false. I was a hard man.

But for today, for a fortnight, I had to temper myself and remain gracious as best I was able. I'd had to do so on other occasions, like the week I participated in Princess

Elinor's courtship last autumn. As one of twelve noblemen chosen to compete for her affection and the position of future king, I'd gone to Vordinberg and done what was expected of me, although I'd had no heart for the challenges or for her.

As I drew nigh the keep, the wind picked up and brought with it more rain.

"Greetings, my lord." Ingold stood at the forefront of the gathering, the wind threatening to blow away his diminutive, lean frame. He clung to his hood, anchoring it in place over his bald head. "Welcome home."

I nodded at the middle-aged steward my father had appointed to run Wahlburg estate many years ago. As a former Sagacite, he was an intelligent man. If only he had the courage to put an end to my father's foolish use of Wahlburg's resources.

Alas, now the burden was upon my shoulders to save my father and our family name from utter ruin by marrying a wealthy noblewoman. What did I have to offer the maiden and her kin in return? What had Ingold bargained?

The question had nagged me throughout the ride back. I not only planned to find out, but I also needed to take time during my stay to investigate the ledgers and put an end to the wastefulness so that we didn't find ourselves in this same financial ruin again one day.

I slid from my horse. Before I had the chance to straighten and take a breath, Ingold was waving his hand at the group behind him, nearly a dozen noblemen and women along with their servants. "I am very pleased to introduce you to Lord Royse, my lord."

A large man with a hefty girth stepped forward. He wore a flat hat over bright red curly hair. His big face was made even bigger by a bushy beard as fiery as his hair. He carried himself with an imposing air, but it was his clothing that made him stand apart. His cloak was thick and finely embroidered. The surcoat underneath was of the richest quality linen, woven with a myriad of colors, including golden thread. His leather belt, calf-length boots, and gloves all appeared new and of excellent quality.

"Lord Torvald." The man spoke reverently and with a bow, almost as if I were royalty. "It is a great honor to meet you. Great honor, indeed. We are familiar with all the tales of your renown and heroic deeds."

I bowed my head in return. I never knew how to respond to the flattery bestowed upon me since becoming a Knight of Brethren. Being singled out made me uncomfortable, so most of the time, I ignored the comments.

"We thank you for inviting us here to Wahlburg and considering the possibility of a union." He slid a glance to the women clustered behind him. "I hope you will find Lady Karina to your liking and will agree to take her as your wife."

So, the deal wasn't solidified? I caught Ingold's gaze. I'd assumed I was all but married to the maiden he'd selected for me. Was I to have some say in the matter after all?

Ingold wasn't paying me heed, was instead beaming at Lord Royse, as if he was the savior come to deliver us from all our woes.

What did it matter if I liked Lord Royse's daughter? Hadn't I told myself many times that whether I liked my wife or not was of no consequence? In fact, I would prefer not to find her attractive and appealing. Then I would have no reason to fear having my heart broken and turning into my father.

It was for the best to have a loveless arranged marriage, to remain unattached and aloof. Besides, I needed to stay focused on the other tasks that required my attention during my brief time home.

Even so, I couldn't keep my gaze from shifting to the women Lord Royse had referenced. Two were standing directly behind him. A petite woman wore a nun's habit, and a wimple surrounded her head, covering her hair. As the wind blew at her, she wrestled with the veil that was blowing over her eyes and across her face, obscuring her from view.

Why had a nun accompanied Lord Royse? Was she a personal attendant to Lady Karina?

With a knot forming in my stomach, one that I could only attribute to nervousness, I forced my gaze to the second woman, Lady Karina. At the sight of her face, the coils inside me unraveled. Her unremarkable brown hair was styled simply. Her brown-green eyes, while kind, did not draw me in. And though another man might consider her features pretty, I found nothing in her face that would make me want to take a second look. She, like her father, was stockier of frame and attired in fine garments, although hers were much simpler and less elegant.

I didn't let my gaze linger over her. I'd seen enough to know I needn't worry about falling for her. She was a perfect candidate for becoming my wife.

Wife. The word pricked me. Even if she wasn't someone I had to worry about losing my heart to, did I really need to get married now? Could I wait a few more years? Was the financial situation so dire that I must marry immediately?

From the outside, the castle was in disrepair. What about the inside?

Lord Royse was talking about their travels south from Finnmark. I listened with one ear while, with a sinking heart, I took in the demise all around. The thatched roofs of the outbuildings needed repairs. The inner bailey wall was crumbling, similar to the battlements. Shutters on the keep were hanging at angles or gone altogether. Even the once-thriving garden and orchard were overgrown and in need of pruning.

I'd noticed the deterioration last autumn when I'd returned home for a short visit after being sent away from court. I'd known the coffers were dwindling. But the truth was that the estate had been declining for years. I'd simply been too preoccupied by other duties to pay heed.

Now, faced with the imminent prospect of having to get married to save my family home, I could no longer overlook the problems and only wished I'd done more sooner to stave off the predicament in which I found myself.

A crack of thunder split the air, and the rain began in earnest. Lord Royse and the others took that as their cue to race up the stone stairs and into the castle. I didn't watch their retreat. Instead, I led my mount toward the stables and extinguished the last flicker of hope I'd allowed myself to harbor—the hope that the need to get married had been a mistake.

However, my father had truly and utterly brought not only himself to ruin, but he'd done so with Wahlburg. Now I was left with no choice but to salvage the wreckage. I would have to get married. There was no way around it.

Author's Note

Hi again, dear readers!

Thanks for coming along with me on this new adventure in the Knights of Brethren tales. I hope you loved getting to know Gunnar a little better. Isn't he a sweetheart?

Initially, as I wrote this story, I planned for Gunnar and Mikaela to go from being enemies to lovers. But as Gunnar came to life on the page, he simply rebelled against my plans. Instead, he let me know that he'd always loved Mikaela and always would.

And you know what? I really liked his version of the story much better than the one I'd planned for him. So I went with it. I hope you like it too!

Obviously, Torvald's love story is next. What will happen to this strong, brooding knight? Will he really have to marry a woman he doesn't know in order to save his family's estate? I hope you'll keep reading the series to find out!

If you want to find out more about the other books in this series, please visit my website at jodyhedlund.com or check out my Facebook Reader Room where I chat with readers and post news about my books.

Until next time . . .

Jody Hedlund is the best-selling author of over thirty historicals for both adults and teens and is the winner of numerous awards including the Christy, Carol, and Christian Book Award. She lives in central Michigan with her husband, busy family, and five spoiled cats. Learn more at JodyHedlund.com.

More Young Adult Fiction from Jody Hedlund
Knights of Brethren

Enamored

Having been raised by her childless aunt and uncle, the king and queen, Princess Elinor finds herself the only heir to the throne of Norvegia. As she comes of age, she must choose a husband to rule beside her, but she struggles to make her selection from among a dozen noblemen during a weeklong courtship.

Entwined

After growing up on a remote farm, Lis learns she is the rightful heir to the throne of Norvegia. Even as she does her part to thwart a dangerous plot against the king, she resists pursuing her new identity and resigns herself to a simple life helping her elderly father with their farm.

Ensnared

Nursemaid to the Earl of Likness's two young daughters, Mikaela despises the earl for his cruelty to his subjects, and she longs for the day when she can make a difference in the lives of her suffering friends and family.

Enriched

Lady Karina lives in a convent and expects to become a nun someday. When her wealthy father asks her to help his textile business become more successful by marrying one of the popular Knights of Brethren, Karina complies, ever the dutiful daughter.

The Fairest Maidens

Beholden

Upon the death of her wealthy father, Lady Gabriella is condemned to work in Warwick's gem mine. As she struggles to survive the dangerous conditions, her kindness and beauty shine as brightly as the jewels the slaves excavate. While laboring, Gabriella plots how to avenge her father's death and stop Queen Margery's cruelty.

Beguiled

Princess Pearl flees for her life after her mother, Queen Margery, tries to have her killed during a hunting expedition. Pearl finds refuge on the Isle of Outcasts among criminals and misfits, disguising her face with a veil so no one recognizes her. She lives for the day when she can return to Warwick and rescue her sister, Ruby, from the queen's clutches.

Besotted

Queen Aurora of Mercia has spent her entire life deep in Inglewood Forest, hiding from Warwick's Queen Margery, who seeks her demise. As the time draws near for Aurora to take the throne, she happens upon a handsome woodcutter. Although friendship with outsiders is forbidden and dangerous, she cannot stay away from the charming stranger.

The Lost Princesses

Always: Prequel Novella

On the verge of dying after giving birth to twins, the queen of Mercia pleads with Lady Felicia to save her infant daughters. With the castle overrun by King Ethelwulf's invading army, Lady Felicia vows to do whatever she can to take the newborn princesses and their three-year-old sister to safety, even though it means sacrificing everything she holds dear, possibly her own life.

Evermore

Raised by a noble family, Lady Adelaide has always known she's an orphan. Little does she realize she's one of the lost princesses and the true heir to Mercia's throne . . . until a visitor arrives at her family estate, reveals her birthright as queen, and thrusts her into a quest for the throne whether she's ready or not.

Foremost

Raised in an isolated abbey, Lady Maribel desires nothing more than to become a nun and continue practicing her healing arts. She's carefree and happy with her life . . . until a visitor comes to the abbey and reveals her true identity as one of the lost princesses.

Hereafter

Forced into marriage, Emmeline has one goal—to escape. But Ethelrex takes his marriage vows seriously, including his promise to love and cherish his wife, and he has no intention of letting Emmeline get away. As the battle for the throne rages, will the prince be able to win the battle for Emmeline's heart?

The Noble Knights

The Vow

Young Rosemarie finds herself drawn to Thomas, the son of the nearby baron. But just as her feelings begin to grow, a man carrying the Plague interrupts their hunting party. While in forced isolation, Rosemarie begins to contemplate her future—could it include Thomas? Could he be the perfect man to one day rule beside her and oversee her parents' lands?

An Uncertain Choice

Due to her parents' promise at her birth, Lady Rosemarie has been prepared to become a nun on the day she turns eighteen. Then, shortly before her birthday, a friend of her father's enters the kingdom and proclaims her parents' will left a second choice—if Rosemarie can marry before the eve of her eighteenth year, she will be exempt from the ancient vow.

A Daring Sacrifice

In a reverse twist on the Robin Hood story, a young medieval maiden stands up for the rights of the mistreated, stealing from the rich to give to the poor. All the while, she fights against her cruel uncle who has taken over the land that is rightfully hers.

For Love & Honor

Lady Sabine is harboring a skin blemish, one that if revealed could cause her to be branded as a witch, put her life in danger, and damage her chances of making a good marriage. After all, what nobleman would want to marry a woman so flawed?

A Loyal Heart

When Lady Olivia's castle is besieged, she and her sister are taken captive and held for ransom by her father's enemy, Lord Pitt. Loyalty to family means everything to Olivia. She'll save her sister at any cost and do whatever her father asks—even if that means obeying his order to steal a sacred relic from her captor.

A Worthy Rebel

While fleeing an arranged betrothal to a heartless lord, Lady Isabelle becomes injured and lost. Rescued by a young peasant man, she hides her identity as a noblewoman for fear of reprisal from the peasants who are bitter and angry toward the nobility.

A complete list of my novels can be found at jodyhedlund.com.

Would you like to know when my next book is available? You can sign up for my newsletter, become my friend on Goodreads, like me on Facebook, or follow me on Twitter.

Newsletter: jodyhedlund.com
Goodreads:
goodreads.com/author/show/3358829.Jody_Hedlund
Facebook: facebook.com/AuthorJodyHedlund
Twitter: @JodyHedlund

The more reviews a book has, the more likely other readers are to find it. If you have a minute, please leave a rating or review. I appreciate all reviews, whether positive or negative.